"AND OF COURSE, CAPTAIN GOLD IS HERE NOW."

Were Christa Duffy not still holding her arm, Gomez might have stumbled. *That bastard is* here? *How dare he show his face in this house?*

"He brought the Federation Medal of Honor they gave Kieran, and— Oh, but where are my manners? Come in, please. Let me show you the house."

Christa tried to lead her in, but Gomez started to move backward. "Maybe it's best if I—"

Then the captain himself appeared behind Christa in the doorway. "Gomez. Good to see you. I was starting to get worried."

Just standing there, like nothing happened. "I don't have anything to say to you," she said coldly.

Gold flinched, as if he'd been slapped. *Good*, Gomez thought.

Christa looked back and forth between the two of them. "Am I missing something?"

"If you are, Ms. Duffy, so'm I. Gomez, what's the—"

"It's all your fault! You killed him, you son of a bitch, and then you have the *gall* to show your face here!"

"Gomez—"

"You *murdered* him! He wanted to marry me, and you killed him, and you wouldn't even *tell* me!"

STAR TREK®
S.C.E.

BOOK 7
BREAKDOWNS

Scott Ciencin, Keith R.A. DeCandido,
Kevin Dilmore, Heather Jarman, and Dayton Ward

Based upon *Star Trek*® and
Star Trek: The Next Generation®
created by Gene Roddenberry,
and *Star Trek: Deep Space Nine*®
created by Rick Berman & Michael Piller

POCKET BOOKS
New York London Toronto Sydney Nasat

POCKET BOOKS, a division of Simon & Schuster, Inc.
1230 Avenue of the Americas, New York, NY 10020

This book is a work of fiction. Names, characters, places and incidents are products of the authors' imaginations or are used fictitiously. Any resemblance to actual events or locales or persons, living or dead, is entirely coincidental.

This book is published by Pocket Books, a division of Simon & Schuster, Inc., under exclusive license from Paramount Pictures.

ISBN: 1-4165-0326-9

First Pocket Books paperback edition May 2005

10 9 8 7 6 5 4 3 2 1

Cover design by Zucca Design

Manufactured in the United States of America

These titles were previously published individually in eBook format by Pocket Books.

CONTENTS

HOME FIRES

Dayton Ward
& Kevin Dilmore

ACKNOWLEDGMENTS

We would like to thank Allyn Gibson, Jim McCain, and Alex Rosenzweig, members of the group who so diligently maintain Pocket Books' Official *Star Trek* Novel Timeline, for their assistance. They helped us to pin down the best place to set the flashback portion of *Home Fires* and provided interesting historical tidbits for us to reference, thus preventing yet another couple of bumbling writers from destroying the very fabric of *Star Trek* continuity as we know it. Be sure to check out the latest edition of their Timeline (as of this writing, at least) in the conclusion to the *Star Trek: Gateways* saga, *What Lay Beyond*.

CHAPTER 1

Stardate 53704.8, Earth Year 2376

Domenica Corsi hated landings.

How many times had a rough approach or a bad set-down offered reasons for her never to set foot on the deck of a spacecraft again? Corsi had lost count, though she recalled a few instances with clarity. The entry into the steel-gray atmosphere of Svoboda II, a buffeted drop through a storm of howling wind and dangerous coatings of ice, almost ended her first command of a security detail before it even started.

Getting that beat-up two-seater settled on Pemberton's Point all those years ago had been a chore, too; a landing she would have aborted had it not been for Dar's insistence. Then there was the time that her father allowed her to pilot and land that transport, and a rented transport at that. Her attempts to dazzle him on touchdown almost cost them the vessel as well as its shipment of Bolian spice nectar, a cargo precious enough that its spoilage would have ruined the family business.

Despite the animosity she held for those experiences, separately or together, they and many others had failed to shake her resolve for duty and responsibility to her family, friends, and career. Time after time, the security officer picked herself up from the deck, brushed off the front of her Starfleet uniform, and leapt back aboard whatever passage she needed to press onward.

That was the way it had always been, at least until Galvan VI.

Corsi's memories of that roiling gas giant were more vivid than they had any right to be for her. Visions of being tossed and bobbled within the planet's turbulent and electrically charged clouds of liquid-metal hydrogen should not be putting her so ill at ease. She should not be able to recall most of it. At her ship's time of greatest need, a time when nearly two dozen of her friends and crewmates were sacrificing their lives aboard the *U.S.S. da Vinci*, the ship's security chief was down for the count.

I was unconscious, comatose, useless to the people who depended on me, she thought as her right hand clenched the armrest of her seat. *I didn't go through the hell they did, not really. So why is this even an issue? Damn, for as many times as I've done this and walked, you'd think . . .*

"Whoa!"

The shuttle pitched as it altered course, and Corsi felt her stomach lurch and the blood drain from her face. She pinched her eyes shut, trying to turn away mental flashes of white-hot lightning against boiling gas. Relaxing and letting her eyelids open, she turned to look out the port window with the hope that its view might calm her a bit. As expected, her destination lay below, and she studied the rooflines and landscaping of the well-maintained residence that appealed to her as oddly familiar even though she had never set foot within it.

Corsi felt the touch of a hand on her left forearm, followed by a voice. "You okay?"

"Don't hover over me," she snapped, not even turning

from the window. The pressure on her arm disappeared and she missed it immediately, more so than she would have dared admit just a few days ago. Turning to face Fabian Stevens, the shuttle's only other occupant, she saw him offer a slight smile that seemed to work better at calming her stomach than did her view of the ground. "Sorry." She managed a weak smile of her own in return but knew it had to appear forced, especially to someone with whom she had shared so much.

Including, well, my bed.

"Corsi, you're as white as a ghost," Stevens said with concern in his voice. "Are you sure you're all right?"

"Fine," she replied as she returned her gaze out the window. Corsi chided herself for appearing vulnerable in front of a shipmate, particularly the one most likely to crack wise about it in front of others back on the *da Vinci*.

Well, she admitted to herself, *maybe that's not giving Fabian enough credit. Things have changed between us. They're changing every day*.

In a soft tone, Stevens's voice broke through her ruminations. "We're almost there. Nothing to worry about."

She would have preferred to beam down from the transport ship, but that had not been an option. Many of the settlements on Fahleena III, including the one where her parents had chosen to make their home, possessed rules permitting only minimized use of many forms of technology found on just about any other Federation world. Among the restrictions the settlers chose to live with was on the use of transporters, limiting their employment to emergencies. Otherwise, more traditional forms of land, sea, and air travel were the norm.

Probably just as well, Corsi thought. *It's not like I'm in a rush to get down there*.

The house and the patch of land surrounding it were growing in the viewport as the shuttle continued its descent. She could not help the smirk as she caught her first look at the property. Its greenish hue, adobe-like finish, and Vulcanesque architectural lines came as no surprise to her; such aspects only fit into the pattern she had seen throughout her life.

She heard the hydraulic whine of the shuttle's landing pads lock into place for touchdown, then felt herself settle into her upholstered seat as the craft softly landed several meters from the entrance to the property.

"Ta-daa! See? Safe and sound," Stevens said as he rose from his seat and reached for the keypad on the bulkhead that controlled the shuttle's hatch. "Ready?"

She said nothing as she got up and grabbed the carrying strap of her Starfleet-issue duffel bag, slinging it over her shoulder. She passed Stevens a hard-shelled travel case, then retrieved from under her seat a rectangular wooden case with a clear top. Tucking the case under her arm, the two stepped from the shuttle. Corsi keyed a command into a panel on the shuttle's exterior and stepped back as the hatch closed. Once they were clear of the craft, she lingered to watch as it rose from the ground and disappeared into the sky.

"Welcome home, Commander."

Corsi cast a look at Stevens. "Yeah, well, this is the first time I've been here. I'm not sure how homey it all feels just yet."

"I don't care how it feels so much as how it smells. Do you suppose your mom baked that Yigrish cream pie she promised?"

She deliberately left Stevens's question to hang unanswered as the two started up the footpath leading to the house. As they walked, she felt her free hand move almost of its own will to smooth some of the wrinkles from the front of her knit blouse. Civilian fashions were hardly her strong suit, she admitted, but the weight and weave of the fabric was well suited to the climate for the time and duration of their stay. She would have preferred to travel in her Starfleet uniform and save the civilian clothes for later, but she knew better.

The last thing that Dad wants to see is me in uniform.

Corsi turned to notice Stevens visibly shudder. A crisp breeze cut the dry air, rippling through Stevens's lightweight, short-sleeved shirt and tousling his hair. She could tell he was gritting his teeth, probably to keep them from chattering.

"I told you to dress differently," she said, allowing herself to have some fun at his expense. "This part of Fahleena III is nothing like the resort cities that get listed in the travel databases."

"What? Oh, I'm okay," Stevens said, belying what his body communicated through gooseflesh and quivers. "Hey, we have to dress the part. We're on vacation, after all."

Once more Corsi shook her head at Stevens's behavior. Since their trip began, the tactical specialist had put out this attitude of leaving the *da Vinci* for a fun getaway, and it was this distinction that had acted as a gulf between them these past days. She could see that it was an act on his part, but one he was determined to carry on despite the anguish and sense of loss Corsi knew he had to be feeling. There had been a few occasions where his façade had slipped, but for the most part Stevens had managed to keep up the appearance of having not a care in the world.

Like now, for instance. There he was, wearing that foolish shirt, acting as if he were heading to summer camp. This was not the time for some sort of pleasure trip, and he of all people should know that.

It was all so wrong.

Our ship is crippled. Our people are hurt. And Duffy . . .

This is no vacation. We're running away from a situation rather than facing it. That's not the way to serve anybody.

As they walked, Corsi felt herself begin to seethe all

over again, just as she had when she had learned how Stevens had set them on this unavoidable collision course with her parents. She bristled once more at the idea of his intercepting that subspace call from her mother and answering her questions about Galvan VI once word got out via the Federation News Service of the disastrous mission. Stevens was the one who told her mother about her getting hurt onboard the *U.S.S. Orion* when he should have known it would just cause needless worry. And once that story made it back to her father . . .

And then to top it all off, the guy introduces himself as my boyfriend. He even uses that stupid word. Boyfriend. That's so like him, and damned if Mom didn't take that tidbit of information and run with it. I can't believe she even invited him to come home with me. I'm not sure I'm ready for how all this is going to turn out.

Stevens had called in his marker, however, just as Corsi had known he would one day.

Upon learning of his conversation with her mother, she had unleashed herself on Stevens, yelling about his having no business talking to her parents about her missions. She spat through a rant about his having no claim at all to her private affairs, and how he likely had an overinflated perception of their relationship, and that her reaching out and showing him some compassion on the death of his best friend was turning into a big mistake.

Then he brought up that night. The one that seemed like ages ago. The one that helped me forget Dar . . .

She remembered his words. *"You said you needed me that night, no questions asked. And I've never asked a one. Not one! Now it's my turn. Captain Gold wants us to take a break and we're taking one. You're going home and I'm going with you. Fair enough?"*

It was nothing if not fair, so here they were.

As they stepped onto the house's front porch, Corsi

reached toward an illuminated button on the door frame to signal their arrival. As she did, Stevens stayed her hand. "Wait a second, Domenica." She snapped her hand back, maybe a bit too sharply, and glared at him. He recoiled a bit, as he always did when he steeled himself for one of her outbursts. "Before we go inside, I just wanted to thank you for this. I know this wasn't your idea, but it means a lot to me." Despite her scowl, he offered a kind smile.

Okay, how is it that his dumb looks can calm me down?

Corsi sighed, releasing the steam that she had let herself build up during the walk up here. "Fabian, this will all work out. We'll be fine." She had hoped her words would sound more convincing than they did as she rang the doorbell.

Moments later the door before them slid open to reveal a woman who Corsi admitted to herself was, if not for two decades of time, her mirror image. The woman's face broke into a beaming smile as her eyes darted back and forth in her attempt to absorb instantly as much as she could about each of them.

"Oh, Dommie! I still don't believe it." The woman stepped forward and embraced Corsi, wrapping arms around her in the kind of hug that hardly differed in its intensity from when she was half her present size and stature. Corsi rested her chin on the woman's shoulder, releasing the gulp of air she had known to take before the hug. As she looked over to Stevens, he quietly formed a word on his lips in an exaggerated enough of a fashion that she could read it easily.

"Dommie?" he whispered, his eyebrows arching in delight, and Corsi skewered him with a look that she hoped would communicate that his next usage of the nickname would be his last.

"Hi, Mom," she said as the two released each other. "It's good to be here."

"Dommie, are you okay? I mean, are you still hurt? Can you walk all right?"

She nodded, not surprised that the questions had started right away. "I'm great, Mom. It was a spinal cord bruise and neurological shock, and that's all." She looked over at her travel companion and did not mask disdain from her voice. "You probably got a much more dramatic description, I'll bet."

The elder Corsi frowned at her daughter. "Oh, hush. He was just as worried as we were, Dommie." She extended a hand to Stevens. "Welcome to our home, Fabian."

Stevens smiled at her mother, but in a way that Corsi had not seen before. It was a gentler look for Fabian, she thought. Something . . . authentic.

"Thanks, Ms. Corsi. I'm glad to be here." Stevens took the woman's hand in a gentle grasp, then paused, tipping his face up toward the open door and sniffing the air. "Is that . . . ?"

The woman laughed. "Yigrish cream pie. Just as I promised."

"I don't believe it!" Stevens strode into the house right past the Corsi women, his next words echoing out to the porch. "Only you and my Nana have made that pie for me."

"Call me Ulrika, please," the woman said around a laugh. "And let me cut that for you." Then she followed him into the house, leaving Corsi on the porch alone.

With the luggage.

Corsi sighed and whispered, "Uh, thanks for the assist there," as she hefted the duffel and the suitcase from the porch and set them inside the door. She then lifted the wooden case and took a moment to look in on its contents. Inside, the antique wooden-handled fire-fighter's ax rested unscathed. She sighed in relief as her eyes moved over the ax's rubberized handle to its broad, spike-backed head. After nearly four hundred years and uncounted disasters, the ax persevered and stayed in the hands of the Corsi family.

This last brush with disaster was too close, she thought as she surveyed the centuries-old tool of safety and survival. *You're coming home to stay.*

As Corsi walked inside, she heard the door slide shut behind her. She followed the sound of voices and laughter through a pair of rooms into the kitchen, where she saw a sight all too common to her during her tour of duty on the *da Vinci*: Stevens talking with his mouth full.

"I'm telling you, Ulrika, this is incredible," he said, wiping a glop of purple cream from his chin. "Dommie, you gotta have a bite of this." He grinned at her, knowing that the nickname was not his to use, but thankfully kept his lips pressed tight as he swallowed. Still, she admitted, it was good to see him smile and acting happier than he had been in days.

And all because of her mother, whose smile mirrored Stevens's.

Oh yes, this is just going to be one hell of a week.

CHAPTER 2

"Mom! What are you doing?"

Ulrika Corsi turned with a start from an open dresser drawer, clutching a drab-colored sweater knit from Yridian yak wool. "Just helping you get settled. You can't live out of a duffel bag for a week, after all."

"I've only been here for an hour, Mom," Corsi said. "You don't need to cater to me like this." Stepping farther into the room, she studied the arrangement of furniture and knickknacks that was all too familiar. On the uppermost shelf of a painted wooden bookcase rested the same trio of swim-meet trophies that her mother surely had been dusting for more than a decade. She glanced along a wall to find the same framed family portrait, a sepia-toned photograph of herself on Galor IV with her brother and parents, that had hung in similar proximity to the bookcase in probably half a dozen houses on half a dozen planets since it was taken. On the dresser near her mother, a large candle burned, wafting the scent of pine needles into the air.

Although Corsi had never set foot in this room, there was no mistaking this place as *her* room.

"I just want you to feel at home, Dommie," Ulrika

said as she folded the sweater in her hands. "Allow a mother that simple pleasure at least."

"But some of those things are, well, mine."

Ulrika laughed. "I assumed that all of these things were yours or else you wouldn't be carrying them."

Corsi huffed as she moved toward her duffel bag, which sat on the floor next to the bed. "You know what I meant. There are some things in there that I'd like to put away myself."

"You mean like that?" Ulrika nodded to the edge of the dresser and Corsi followed the gesture with her gaze to see her phaser resting next to a satin-covered jewelry box.

"Yes, like that." With a speed that even Corsi did not anticipate, her hand darted to the dresser and snatched up her sidearm. She slipped the phaser into the pocket of her slacks, where it bulged noticeably. "I'm sorry about bringing it into the house. I know the township rules about weapons, but I just don't feel comfortable without it anymore."

The elder woman said nothing in response as she shook out the sweater in her hands, refolding the garment into a more compact bundle. Corsi saw her mother force a smile, a sure signal that a change in topic was coming. "I'm surprised to see this old thing in your bag. Didn't Roberto give you this for your birthday one year?"

Corsi found it was her turn to smile. "Yeah, he did. And I told him that it looked like the yak had thrown up on it."

Ulrika laughed softly as she placed the sweater in an open drawer. "You always have such a lovely way with words for your brother. That's your father talking in you, you know."

I know.

Corsi silently watched her mother reach into the open duffel bag and pull out a few more pieces of clothing, putting each into a drawer. Then she saw the elder woman pause as she drew out a Starfleet uniform tunic. "Mom? Maybe that ought to stay in the bag."

Ulrika looked up and met her daughter's eyes in the mirror above the dresser. As she studied the reflection of her mother's face, Corsi enjoyed the reminder that the woman before her seemed scarcely to have aged in comparison to the mental images she had carried during her years away from home. It was somehow comforting to believe that her mother seemed as unaffected by time as the objects within the room.

"You probably won't need it anyway," Ulrika said as she turned, grabbing the duffel bag from the dresser's varnished top and passing it to Corsi. "You're on leave for a while yet, right?"

"A few weeks," Corsi said. "But some of that will be travel time back to the *da Vinci*. It's not as if Starfleet runs a shuttle service to come pick us up."

"Stay as long as you like, Dommie," Ulrika said as she stepped around her daughter and moved to the bed. She smoothed out a spot on the bedspread and sat down, her light frame not making much of an impression on the mattress. "I left the other thing inside the bag. It looked like a picture frame?"

Corsi felt her throat tighten a bit at that as she nodded in reply.

"I didn't look at it."

"You never were one to drop a subtle hint, were you, Mom?" She saw Ulrika smile, and then Corsi knew that she had been roped into a show-and-tell session with the same signature deftness that her mother wielded with each member of the family. The Corsis as a rule never were ones to open up with conversation around the family dinner table, so typically it fell to Ulrika to pepper their talk with loaded questions or open-ended statements that no one dared avoid.

Mom could teach the Cardassians a thing or two about

interrogation techniques, Corsi thought as she fished in her bag and brought out a flat black-framed photograph about twice the size of a data padd. "This is for Fabian. He doesn't know I have it."

She passed the photograph to Ulrika and smiled a bit as she saw her mother analyze it with her trademark scrutiny. "That's your Fabian on the right, isn't it?"

"He's not *my* Fabian, Mother. He's not my anything."

Ulrika looked up with a smirk as Corsi sat down on the bed beside her. Indicating the picture with the fingers of her right hand, she said, "That's the bridge of the *Defiant*, an old Starfleet ship we rescued . . . well, it seems like ages ago, now. Captain Gold is sitting in the command chair, there, and . . ." Her hand froze as it moved from the image of her captain to the next figure in the photograph. "And that's Commander Duffy on the left."

Ulrika's smile dimmed. "That's your friend who died, isn't it? He's the one who meant so much to Fabian."

"Yeah, Mom." Corsi could not help staring at Kieran Duffy's broad smile, captured in midsentence as Captain Gold and Fabian looked to be laughing along with whatever story he must have been unreeling at the time. It illustrated best what she knew she would miss most about Duffy: his love for telling a story, particularly an embarrassing one, to whoever would lend an ear.

The photograph's mere existence startled Corsi when she first saw it in the hands of Bart Faulwell, who had plucked the image from optical data scans made to record the *Defiant*' s condition on its journey back from Tholian space. He slipped the framed shot into her hands moments before she was scheduled to leave the *da Vinci* with Stevens. When he did so, she noticed several additional frames under his arm; memorial gifts headed to other members of the crew, no doubt.

"I'm waiting for the right time to give it to him, I guess," Corsi said to break their silence. "We don't have much time on duty to take pictures, you know. He'll be pretty surprised."

"Well, this is sure to mean a lot to him, Dommie," Ulrika said. "You mean a lot to him, too, you know. He went on and on to me while you were in showering. He said . . ."

"Mom, I don't want to hear it." Corsi's desire for her mother to get past the notion that Stevens and she were some sort of romantic item brought an edge of frustration to her voice. "I did not bring him here to 'meet the parents,' okay? Fabian is a shipmate. No, I mean . . . well, okay . . . he's a friend, but it stops there. So, let's drop this talk, please, especially before he overhears it."

"Then you'd better tell him soon because he's certainly sweet on you. I think he was just as worried about your getting hurt as we were."

Great. This is what I get for trying to help the guy.

"Mom, he's clinging to me because I owed him a favor," Corsi said, swinging her body away from her mother. "He's got plenty of other friends on board. I'm not really sure why he's here."

Reaching over, Ulrika placed a hand on Corsi's shoulder. "He could have reached out to anyone, but he chose you. It sounds like he needs you."

Plenty of other people needed me, too. And what good was I?

Ulrika continued, enough pressure in her touch that Corsi turned back to face her despite the burning desire for this line of discussion to cease. "You have the words he needs to hear, even if you don't yet realize it. You'll find them, probably when you least expect it. And he may have a few words for you, too, Dommie. Open yourself to listening." She paused, then added with a smile, "I know that's not the Corsi way, but still . . ."

Motion at the doorway prompted the women to look up with a start and see Stevens's head and shoulders peering from around the door frame. "Hey, am I interrupting?"

Corsi's shouted "Yes!" mixed in the air with her mother's spoken "No," bringing a laugh from Stevens. She fumbled a bit to speak to her shipmate before her mother could open her mouth again. "I guess not, then. We were just talking, Fab . . ."

The photograph! He'll see it!

Corsi snatched the frame from her mother's grasp and flipped it facedown onto her duffel bag, which still sat on the floor between their feet.

Stevens stepped into the room, his eyebrows furrowing mischievously. "Baby pictures, Dommie?"

"Not your business, Fabian," Corsi said with her best security-officer tone. "Just move along."

"Well, I guess I can wander back to the kitchen and wait for your father, then. He just pulled up. That's what I came to tell you."

Corsi felt her stomach flutter as the news sunk in.

I guess it was too much to hope for his running into an ion storm or something.

Standing, she brushed some of the ripples from her blouse, and with them, she hoped, some of the emotional trappings she had allowed to latch onto her the longer she sat in this facsimile of her childhood bedroom. Though she was not bracing for some sort of showdown with her father on his arrival, Corsi knew that just seeing him for the first time in years would surely fuel her internal fires if she let it. Sighing in resignation, she walked past Stevens and turned toward the kitchen, knowing that her father would come in through the back door and head straight for the food cooler.

Some things never change.

Walking just behind her, Stevens said, "You really haven't seen him since you finished at the Academy?"

She swallowed hard. "A few times, but it wasn't for

long. He made it pretty clear at graduation that Starfleet officers weren't welcome in his home."

"Well, good thing I'm a noncom, then," Stevens said with a sly grin. "Want me to run interference? Maybe he'll forget you're here."

"What I would like you to do is stop talking about me to my mother." The curtness of her response was a surprise even to her. "And I definitely don't want you to start sidling up to my father the way you have with her. I don't need that kind of pressure."

"Or maybe that kind of competition?"

Corsi felt heat rise in her neck as she glared back at Stevens, and turned to respond accordingly, when the sound of the front door opening interrupted them.

Aldo Corsi stood in the doorway, his eyes widening a bit on Corsi while the doorknob rested in his meaty hand. He drew a breath, making his barrel chest puff out even farther, and narrowed his eyes again as he stepped forward and pushed the door shut behind him.

"You're home."

"Hi, Dad." Corsi could not help judging her father's appearance against her memories, just as she had minutes earlier with her mother. He had not fared as well against the passage of time. She let her eyes dwell on his salt-and-pepper hair, the frown lines that creased his face, the slight stoop in his posture. The hint of immortality loaned to Corsi by her mother was stripped away when her father's eyes met hers.

The imposing man nodded quietly, then turned his attention to Stevens and offered his hand. "Aldo Corsi."

Stevens returned the handshake as Corsi noted his hand being almost swallowed up by her father's grip. "Fabian Stevens, sir. I've been looking forward to meeting you."

"I heard you were coming," Aldo said. Corsi knew that was about as committal as her father would get at showing any return interest in their arrival on Fahleena

III, at least until he wound down a bit from his latest cargo run.

Stevens must not have picked up on that signal, however, as he kept talking even after Aldo had turned from the pair and moved to open a brushed metal door set into a kitchen wall. "Domenica has told me some about your transport service. I'd like hearing about it and maybe seeing a few of your freighters. My parents run shuttles in the Rigel Colonies. Ever make it out that way?"

Aldo reached into the cooler and took out a bottled beverage, most likely some blend of fruit juice, Corsi thought, and screwed off the top while the cooler door slowly swung shut. Before taking a swig, Aldo leveled a questioning glare at his daughter. "Rough ride you took. I suppose you lost the ax."

Well, that certainly didn't take long.

Corsi knew that talk of her family's most prized heirloom would surface sometime during her visit, though she had not imagined it as the opening volley upon seeing her father. Still, she figured that he would at least ask about its condition, or even ask for its return to a safer haven than a starship. She would not dare tell him that the centuries-old Corsi ax might have been reduced to a mere memory had it not been for the kind actions of Carol Abramowitz, who scooped it up during a hasty raid of the *da Vinci* for medical supplies on Galvan VI. Not long after its retrieval, her ship's quarters would be flooded and its contents eradicated by a rush of liquid-metal hydrogen vomited forth from the gas planet.

"It's fine," Corsi said, gritting her teeth. "I brought it home, for good this time."

The man drew another deep breath, then looked past Corsi to Ulrika, who had stepped into the kitchen behind them all. To her he said, "The Thelkan traders are arriving a week early. I'll be leaving in an hour for the rendezvous."

Corsi turned to look at her mother as she tried to keep a pained expression out of her father's view. The fallen features on her mother's face, Corsi imagined, rivaled her own. "Aldo, that's a four-day round trip."

He tipped the beverage bottle to his lips and swallowed a long draw. "I can't be late. Not with this shipment." Aldo stepped past Corsi without so much as a glance and walked into the living room and down a connecting hall.

"Pretty convenient," Corsi said. "I guess that's one way to avoid an argument."

Stevens frowned. "He didn't seem antagonistic, Dom. Just tired. Give him a few . . ."

"Not antagonistic? What did *you* make of the ax remark? Maybe he's wanting it reappraised?"

Stevens did not waver despite Corsi's small hope that he might step back from her. "All right, I don't know what to make of it. Actually, you never told me the whole story about the ax and the family connection. I just know it's important."

Spite tinged Corsi's humorless laugh. "Important enough that he made sure it was unharmed before he asked about me."

As if deciding that a recess was in order, Stevens nodded quietly before turning to follow Aldo. Corsi shook her head as she watched him leave the room.

I really don't need this.

"You're not being fair, Domenica," Ulrika said, her tone the one Corsi knew her mother reserved for making a point above the din of heated talk amongst the family. "Don't underestimate your father and his love for you. You are not here to see him sit in your bedroom, sometimes for hours. Your communications don't come as often as ours go out. If you'd like to raise a point about shows of concern, you ought to choose your words with care."

Corsi started to reply, but stopped as her mother

stepped closer. Ulrika leaned in and kissed her daughter on the cheek. "Take a tip from the Thelkans, Dommie. Meet your father halfway."

Then Ulrika left the kitchen, leaving Corsi alone and feeling as though she were frozen in place. She hovered on an edge of emotion that she might have cultivated were she in uniform and on shift as a Starfleet security officer. A good helping of anger would have been welcome, or perhaps a tinge of embarrassment or even an undercurrent of ache for a connection to her father. None of those, she realized, were realistic goals for this trip, if ever. Instead, she felt herself giving in to fatigue and resignation.

Pulling out one of the wooden chairs situated around the kitchen table, Corsi sat down. She propped two elbows on the table and cradled her chin in her hands. Closing her eyes, she began to enjoy the silence, thinking that a few days of rest without the tension of interacting with her father might be just what the doctor ordered.

No sooner had she started to relax, however, than Corsi heard footsteps approaching the kitchen. She opened her eyes to see Stevens wearing a knowing grin on his face. "So, did your mom put away your entire duffel?"

Corsi shook her head a bit to focus. "Yeah. Yeah, she did."

"Better repack on the double," he said, the grin giving way to a full smile. "I made us some new plans. We're shipping out with your dad."

CHAPTER 3

What I wouldn't give for a Starfleet-issue inertial damper right about now.

After just a few hours at warp four aboard her father's freighter, Domenica Corsi got a big reminder that her space legs just were not what they used to be. The steady humming of the *Pharaon*'s deck plates, a vibrating sensation that seasoned space travelers equated with being cradled in their mothers' arms, was exaggerated on this older craft and consequently wreaking havoc on her equilibrium and her nerves. Even more so than during her travels since leaving the *da Vinci* less than a week ago, the usually stalwart security chief found herself once again walking wobbly and feeling queasy as the ship sped toward its meeting with Thelkan traders.

"Oh, Miss Dee, you're still lookin' pretty green around your gills, there. Lemme take one more crack at fine-tuning the fields for ya."

Corsi smiled toward the voice despite her urge to curl up in a ball on the deck. "Please don't bother with that again, Mr. Wilson," she said to the white-haired man standing near the mess hall table where she sat alone in the dim lighting. "It's not the ship. It's me. I'm not myself these days."

Wilson returned her smile as he stepped into a pool of brighter illumination. The man looked to be nearing a hundred years of age, Corsi thought, and had looked that way since joining her father's business when she was a child. The unusual dialect he employed when speaking was one of the things she liked most about him. It was a product of his having been born and raised in the New Paris colonies, one of the first human settlements established in the early twenty-second century.

His wiry frame showed muscle tone he had acquired over years of loading and unloading freight, running from place to place aboard her father's various ships, and fixing problems and breakdowns on the spur of the moment. It occurred to her that, in a way, Wilson was her father's personal one-person S.C.E. troubleshooter. She had long admired the man's technical skills, which he managed to put to use without the litany of indecipherable mumbo-jumbo that most Starfleet engineers employed. That, along with the man's genuine warmth and ever-pleasant personality, might very well have had something to do with her own ability to appreciate engineers while at the same time understanding little about whatever it was that they did.

"Never a bother, Miss Dee," said Wilson, using the name he had given Corsi from their first meeting when she was but ten years of age. "I'm headed back that way to give that cranky intermix chamber a kick in the antimatter pods." He started to head for the door but instead turned back to her. "Hey, ya need something cold to drink? Maybe some *Q'babi* juice? Ya know, your daddy still stocks bottles of the stuff for when we're on long hauls. I remember ya used to drink us dry back in the day."

They shared a laugh at the joint memory. "Thanks, but I'll pass, Mr. Wilson. I probably haven't had *Q'babi* juice in ages, and I don't think it would set well with my stomach just now."

"Bah!" the elder man replied. "That stuff is perfect for settling a queasy gut. Tell ya what. I'll go check on the intermixer and I'll bring ya some juice when I come forward. Why don't ya go look in on your daddy and that Mr. Stevens ya brung. They're in the cockpit."

Corsi groaned at what such a meeting might bring. "I knew Stevens would jump on a chance to prod Dad with all sorts of questions," she said as she rose from her seat. "He's probably ready for a break."

"He seems to be kinda enjoying it," Wilson said. "After all these years, he and I are about talked out. It's a change for us, having warm bodies aboard, that's a fact."

As Wilson headed toward the freighter's engine room, Corsi silently agreed that it must have been a change for the pair to bring someone on board the decades-old ship, which her father had named the *Pharaon* after a ship featured in a centuries-old novel he had loved since childhood. The ship's two guest cabins had not been tended in what looked like years, states of condition she and Stevens noted as soon as they laid eyes on where they would be bunking for the next few days.

Freighters had come and gone from her father's ownership, but Aldo had held on to this particular vessel, the first that his father had entrusted to him when he had come of age and earned the position of shipmaster in the family business, well beyond its prime operational life. Rarely assigning it to his hired pilots, he ran the ship with only Wilson, knowing full well that its size and operational requirements meant enough routine work to keep six people busy. Her father's theory, however, was that ship work was the best thing to occupy the hands and energize the mind when in space on long hauls.

As she made her way forward, Corsi heard Stevens's voice filtering back to her above the hums and beeps of the ship's various systems.

". . . and so while she's away from the table, Duffy tells the waiter to add some Jimbalian fire fruit to Domenica's dessert bowl. I couldn't believe it, but that's just what happened. The stuff looked like it belonged there." Stevens obviously was enjoying this tale at her expense. "So we all dig in, and I don't know what happened next because I was too afraid to look, frankly, but Dom leaps up and just spits the fire fruit out all over Duffy!"

"She never was one for spicy foods, Mr. Stevens," said Aldo with a hint of good humor in his voice.

"I'm surprised she didn't force the stuff down his throat," Stevens said, chuckling. "But we all were laughing and I think she knew it was in fun. She has a bit of a temper, you know."

Is that . . . Is Dad laughing?

"Oh, I know," Aldo replied. "Allow a father to admit that she comes by it honestly."

As the two men continued to talk, Corsi shook her head in amazement. It had been a long time since she had heard her father laugh, about anything, and it was a welcome sound. The same with Stevens, whom she had not heard expressing that level of joviality in . . . well, in far too long. It did not even bother her that she was serving as the source of their amusement.

"She'd probably phaser me if she knew I told you this," Stevens said, catching her attention once again, "but some of the crew call her 'Core-Breach' Corsi."

"Not to her face, I'd bet."

Stevens laughed again. "Not after the time Duffy rerigged a security alert Klaxon to shout out . . ."

Okay, that's enough sharing, Corsi decided as her eyes widened in recognition of the tale Stevens was about to recount. Stepping around the corner and into the cockpit, she announced, "Hello, gentlemen. Having a good time, are we?"

The two snapped around in their respective seats at the *Pharaon*'s controls. "Hi, Dom," Stevens said. "I was dusting off some stories for your dad."

"Nice," she said, adding some chill to her voice, "but

something tells me you're probably not in a rush to tell him the one about you and the Tellarites on Syrinx III?"

Stevens's smile dimmed. "That one's not so funny."

Though Aldo still maintained his good humor, Corsi noticed that he had returned to the distant, professional demeanor that he normally adopted when interacting with his shipping clients.

And her.

His features once again schooled in the manner she knew all too well, her father said, "It sounds as though you have had many adventures since you joined Starfleet, Domenica."

"You could look at it that way, I suppose," she replied. "Fabian has quite a gift for making things sound more interesting or exciting than they were at the time."

Stevens said, "But I never embellish. I only add perspective."

"So you say," Corsi replied. "I don't want to interrupt. Maybe I ought to hit my bunk for a while."

"There are four seats, Dom." Stevens indicated one of the cockpit's empty chairs. "Why don't you sit? I won't even interrupt you if you want to set the record straight on anything I say." He paused as they made eye contact, and Corsi wondered whether he could read her face and sense what she really wanted. "Or maybe I could go back and get us all something to eat?" he added a moment later.

"No," she said, almost too quickly. "The last thing I need is . . ."

The ship lurched a bit and slowed dramatically, noises from its systems whining down and fading away. A red light began flashing on the console before Aldo as the view on the forward screen shifted from a pattern of diverging streaks to still points of light.

"We've dropped out of warp," Stevens said. "What happened?"

Aldo grumbled and pulled himself from his seat. "Damn. I thought he took care of this." He pushed past Corsi and stormed toward the engine room as she and Stevens followed closely behind him.

The threesome entered the *Pharaon*'s sizeable but cramped engine room and Corsi saw Wilson, the bottom half of him, at least, protruding from an access hatch in the room's far wall.

"I know, I said it was fixed," he shouted, his voice echoing from inside the access. "I see the problem, at least."

"Is it the antimatter injector again?" Aldo asked, his hands on his hips. "You did warn me against getting the refurbished one."

Wilson wriggled his lean body back out of the access hatch and stood up, wiping his sweaty brow with a sleeve. "Nope, but the articulation frame for the dilithium crystals is shot." He held up a metal-alloy piece of the ship's warp drive for them to see. "I should have known to check it when I made the other repairs."

Corsi was puzzled. "Just because I fly around with a bunch of engineers doesn't make me one of them. What's the problem?"

Stevens spoke up. "This is no big deal. The articulation frame holds the crystals firm in the matter and antimatter streams. I can rig up a . . ."

"If it's all the same, Mr. Stevens," Aldo said, cutting him off, "I'd rather you let Wilson handle it. He's been keeping this ship at warp since before you even looked at a warp core."

"I'd bet that's not true, Captain," Stevens countered. "When I was young, my parents let me crawl all over their transports back on Rigel. I was passing tools and playing assistant to our engineers from the get-go."

Corsi spoke up. "And he's been trained by Starfleet, Dad."

"Exactly," Aldo said. A pause hung in the air before

he spoke again. "Just keep your hands to yourself, son. If Wilson needs help, he'll ask for it, I'm sure. Now if you'll excuse me, I need to alert the Thelkans that we'll be delayed."

Corsi's gaze followed her father's path back to the cockpit, then she turned to Stevens. "Did you really help your parents with warp engines, Fabian?"

"No way," he said, smiling. "I'm a tactical guy, not an engine guy. But hey, the S.C.E.'s reputation with your father is on the line here. This looks like a minor deal."

Scowling, Corsi replied, "Yeah, and I know how 'minor deals' go back on the *da Vinci*. Straight into the waste extraction center."

"Just think of all that time I spent watching Duff crack these engine problems," Stevens said. "Some of it had to have rubbed off, right? Just keep your dad out of our way back here."

Corsi looked to Wilson, who was watching their exchange. The elder engineer smiled approvingly. "I'll put your young man to work, Miss Dee. We'll get this old girl up and running again in nothing flat. Go tend to your daddy. Take him a *Q'babi* juice."

"You guys have *Q'babi* juice?" Stevens asked, his eyebrows climbing for his hairline. "I love that stuff."

Corsi rolled her eyes as she spun on a heel and headed to the cockpit. "Just don't drink it all, Fabian," she called back. "Dad hates it when someone drinks it all."

She stopped at a wall cooler in the freighter's mess area and grabbed a bottle of fruit juice for her father, paused, and then grabbed one for herself. As she stepped into the ship's cockpit, her father was concluding his subspace radio transmission to the Thelkan traders.

"This is an unexpected delay, Sebarb, but I assure you that our repairs will not take long. Please know that we have your full shipment and will be back at warp as soon as possible."

The cockpit's speakers crackled a bit with the Thelkan's response. *"We have patience, Mr. Corsi, but we have deadlines as well. This might make a difference on our entering into future contracts with your firm should your delay prevent us keeping up our end of other bargains."*

Aldo hung his head a bit. "Understood." He toggled a switch on the console to terminate the transmission before turning to face Corsi, who offered him one of the juice bottles. He grunted in thanks and took the bottle, twisting off its cap in one of his large hands. "I can't be late with this shipment. Of course, they seem to have forgotten that it was their idea to move the ship date up an entire week."

She watched him drink from the bottle as she sat down and twisted the cap from her own beverage. "Fabian said it's a quick fix, Dad. Things should be fine."

Aldo scoffed at the assessment. "Sure, it's no problem at all. We have a Starfleet officer on board to make all our troubles go away."

Corsi felt the sting of his words, but resisted the cue to take up the same old argument that had ebbed and flowed between them for years. "Yes, we do, Dad, but it's not Fabian. He's a technical advisor. I'm the officer."

Her father leveled a withering gaze at her and she met it, their eyes locking, neither father nor daughter looking away. She searched his face for anything that might reveal the feelings he was harboring, but his weathered features revealed nothing, at least at first. Then, for the first time in her life, she saw him wince before breaking the contact. He opened his mouth as if to say something but almost as quickly clamped his jaw tight again. It was as if he was struggling to find the right words.

I don't think he wants a fight any more than I do.

"Dad, you took a dig at Fabian just because he's in Starfleet, and I'll bet he's as capable a technician as anyone who works for you," she said. "Well, except Mr. Wilson. So why not give him some room to help?"

"I don't need Starfleet's help," he said. "Once is enough for me."

Once?

"What, did you get a tow or something from a Starfleet vessel? I've never heard anything about this."

Aldo's voice lowered. "Let's just drop it."

Corsi stood her ground, hoping that she might get some insight to her father that she had sought for years. "Let's not. I've never heard you talk about working with Starfleet before. I can't imagine your wanting anything to do with Starfleet."

"I didn't!" His outburst made Corsi recoil, sinking deeper into her chair. "And I wouldn't have . . . but your Uncle Gi, well, his vision was different from mine."

Uncle Gi? We haven't talked about him in so long. She held vague memories of Giancarlo Corsi, Aldo's younger brother, who at one time had also contributed to the family business when the family was living on Madellin Prime. He had died when she was young, and when the subject had come up in subsequent years, much against her father's wishes, Aldo's sullen and cryptic response was that his brother had died in an accident during a freight run. Corsi's occasional efforts to inquire further had always met with resistance, and out of respect for her father, she had restrained from pursuing the matter.

Was she hearing him right, however? Had Starfleet somehow been involved in her uncle's death?

What hasn't he told me?

Remembering her mother's advice, Corsi decided that now was a time to meet halfway. She sat up a bit straighter in her chair and looked at her father, who had turned away from her to stare through the cockpit viewport.

"Dad, tell me," she said. "Tell me about Uncle Gi and Starfleet."

Drawing a breath as if in resignation, Aldo nodded. "It was supposed to be just a simple cargo run. . . ."

CHAPTER 4

Stardate 32318.5, Earth Year 2355

Aldo Corsi had never harbored much use for uniforms. To him they implied a willful adherence to rules and regulations and subordination to a larger entity that the individual had no part in creating or controlling, regardless of whether those directives were ethical, legal, or even sane. He viewed them as the embodiment of a sense of order and rigid discipline that, while admittedly necessary to a degree in his own line of work, was at odds more often than not with the lifestyle he had chosen to pursue.

Therefore, as he sat behind his cluttered desk amidst the disaster area that was the kindest way to describe his office, Aldo Corsi regarded the man who now stood before him wearing a Starfleet uniform with an expression of unmitigated contempt.

The man looked as though he could have stepped straight out of a recruiting advertisement. His dark hair was short-cropped, and the black-and-gold uniform, which Aldo thought was unforgivably formfitting, hugged his broad chest and wide shoulders. Three pips along the right side of the neckline, two gold and one black, and a Starfleet symbol on the man's left breast, which Aldo knew also doubled for a communicator device, were all that adorned the uniform. The boots he wore reflected the office lighting better than the dirty mirror hanging next to the door.

Where his uniform personified the cold, rigid world of which Aldo wanted no part, the man's cobalt blue eyes and seemingly genuine yet still reserved smile appeared to offer warmth and friendship, even as Aldo snorted in derision and offered two simple words.

"Absolutely not."

As Aldo expected, though, Lieutenant Commander William Ross did not waver one iota from the composed, relaxed persona he had presented since entering the office. Instead, the man nodded slowly once, twice, and finally a third time before responding.

"I understand your reluctance, Mr. Corsi, and believe me when I tell you that Starfleet would not be making this request if there was another way that offered the same or greater chance of success."

Rolling his eyes, Aldo turned and cast an irritated look in his brother's direction. Giancarlo Corsi sat behind a desk that complemented his own right down to a matching clutter of padds and other such detritus as was wont to accumulate in the manager's office of a busy interstellar freight transport service. Like him, Giancarlo was a man of imposing size and physique, with muscled arms and a barrel chest. The thick mop of unruly black hair and the square jaw were near mirrors of Aldo's own, and more than one person had made the mistaken conclusion that the brothers must be twins.

"What?" Aldo asked, noticing his brother's look of disapproval.

Giancarlo leaned forward in his chair, the springs of which squeaked in protest beneath his muscular frame. "Try to be reasonable, Aldo. The man's come a long way to ask our help. Shouldn't we at least hear him out?"

As always, Aldo realized, his younger brother was trying to be the voice of reason, acting as a counterbalance to his own tendency to react first and consider the consequences of his actions later. It was one of only a few ways in which their personalities differed. Both men, just two years apart in age, had been inseparable in their youth and had carried their relationship into adulthood, and though Aldo was unlikely to admit as much in public, Giancarlo's cooler head was one of the qualities he valued most about his brother.

That did not mean that his younger sibling could not frustrate the hell out of him at times. Now, for instance.

"We leave for Juhraya in less than two days, Gi, and we're behind schedule as it is. Have you seen the size of the shipment? We'll have to use the shuttlebay to fit it all aboard." Turning back to Ross, he added, "We're freight haulers, Commander, not soldiers. Let the military handle that sort of silliness." With that, he grabbed one of the padds from his desk and rose from his chair. "I'll be in Cargo Bay 4," he said, not even bothering to give Ross another look as he moved past the Starfleet officer toward the doorway.

The hallway outside the office, like all of the corridors on *Ulrika's Hope*, was narrow and utilitarian. Metal grating clanked beneath the soles of his boots as he walked. Similar plates covered most of the ship's corridors and overhead maintenance conduits, offering easy access to the networks of pipes and optical cabling running throughout the ship.

Outside the soundproofed walls of his office, the thrum of the *Hope*'s engines was palpable even though they had been cycled down to minimal power as the ship orbited Madellin Prime. All of the metal surfaces vibrated in concert with the faint droning sound that had long ago become a comforting friend to him. So attuned was Aldo to the tone of his ship's beating heart that he could perceive even the slightest variation in the engines' operation by hearing alone. Having witnessed this for himself on many occasions, the vessel's chief engineer had told him many times that Aldo had missed his calling and had wasted his life as a shipmaster.

Sorry, Colv, Aldo mused as he thought of the Tellarite overseeing the engines two decks below as though he were an overworked mother hen, *you're on your own there, my friend.*

Reviewing the details of their latest shipment on the padd's display screen, Aldo did not even look up as he walked. The layout of the *Hope* had long ago been burned into his memory, so much so that he could walk from the bow of the ship to its stern with his eyes closed. He diverted his attention from the padd only to exchange greetings with one of the seven other men and women who served aboard ship not as a member of his crew but rather as a part of the extended Corsi family.

"Still on for tomorrow night, Aldo?" asked Gret, the ship's Bolian navigator, as he walked past.

Aldo smiled as he nodded in response. "Nineteen-thirty hours. Don't be late or you'll go hungry." He too was already looking forward to the following evening when he and the crew would beam down to the Corsi home for his wife's traditional predeparture supper. The festivities would be repeated on the first night after they returned from their trip.

It would be bad luck to leave without some of Ulrika's Kaferian apple strudel, after all, he mused with a small private smile. *Even the gods would not tempt Fate so.*

As he continued to walk, Aldo heard the measured footsteps of Commander Ross keeping pace behind him.

"Mr. Corsi," the Starfleet officer said, "I can appreciate that you're a busy man, and I assure you that I have no desire to disrupt your schedule, but sending one of our ships near the Topin system will almost certainly attract the Cardassians' attention. You, however, travel through that sector often enough that they're comfortable with your presence there."

Stopping in his tracks, Aldo turned to face the officer, for the first time deciding to use his larger and more muscular frame to his advantage. Leaning closer to Ross, he spoke in a low yet forceful voice. "We have been able to travel freely in that part of space, Commander, because we do not bother anyone. In fact, we've even traveled in Cardassian space on occasion, and always with their blessing, precisely because of the trust we have earned from them. The Cardassians have larger concerns than a single small freighter, and I prefer to keep it that way."

"Aldo," Giancarlo began, his tone one of caution. "Please."

If Ross was intimidated by Aldo's proximity, he did not show it. Instead, he responded with an equally stern tone. "Mr. Corsi, though Madellin Prime and the bulk of the area covered by your regular routes might not concern the Cardassians today, you can be sure that won't last forever. Our intelligence reports show that they're working to expand their territory, including into the Juhrayan system. It's critical for us to know how far they've progressed if we're to have any chance of defending against any action they might be planning."

"We'd be helping to possibly protect our families and friends, Aldo," Giancarlo added. "That seems worth a little inconvenience, don't you think?"

Aldo regarded his brother with disappointment and shook his head. For whatever reason, Giancarlo Corsi had always been enamored of Starfleet. Though attending the Academy and serving on a starship in deep space had been a dream of his since childhood, Gi had not passed the entrance examinations. Still, that had not deterred his admiration for the service and his support for other family members who had chosen Starfleet as a way of life.

He had also noticed in recent months that his brother's infatuation was beginning to rub off on his daughter, Domenica. More than once she had mentioned wanting to join Starfleet when she grew up. At first it was easy to dismiss such statements as those of a precocious child who knew nothing of what she might want five minutes from now, much less fifteen years hence. Like her mother, however, Domenica was very much aware of the world and indeed the universe around her. Aldo suspected that this topic would be revisited often as his daughter grew older, especially if Gi continued to be an influence in her life.

Once this trip is over, he decided, *I'll have to make my feelings on this known once and for all.*

However, Aldo found himself thinking with no small amount of reluctance that Gi, damn him, had a valid point. So did Ross, for that matter. The Federation and the Cardassian Union had been at odds for years. Conflicts between the two powers were frequent, and it was not a question of if, he knew, but of when and where such a skirmish occurred in this part of space. When that happened, people like him, his brother, and the thousands of other merchants who traveled this area of space undoubtedly would be placed in harm's way.

He could not help the sigh of exasperation that escaped his lips. "How would this work?"

"My people will install the sensor equipment," Ross said, "and I and a small team will travel with you on the run. The plan is to conduct a brief series of covert scans of the Topin system as we pass nearby on our way to Juhraya. We'll have the equipment calibrated so that it will function without a change to your established route through the area. You won't have to deviate a bit from your normal routine."

"The Cardassians don't look too kindly on spies," Aldo countered. "They'll make no distinctions between Starfleet and simple freight haulers if we're caught."

"Come on, Aldo," Gi said. "They wouldn't be asking us to do this if they thought there'd be any real danger, would they?" He looked to Ross for confirmation, but the commander shrugged as a small frown creased his features.

"I'd be lying to you if I said that there was no risk," Ross said, "but we feel that it's minimal. The whole idea is to get the scans as fast as possible, and when we pass out of range, that's it. No stops, no hanging around the area. We want it to be just another run as far as you and the Cardassians are concerned. In addition, Starfleet will underwrite the cost to you for the entire trip."

At any other time, Aldo might have accepted such an offer. This far out from the Federation's center of influence, the time-honored practice of buying and selling goods and services was still the driving mode of economics, especially when dealing with merchants and customers who were not aligned with the Federation. Maintaining the *Hope* in good working order, keeping it stocked with supplies, to say nothing of paying the crew enough to carry on with their own lives was all done through buying, selling, or trading as appropriate. Gold-pressed latinum, for example, would be most useful when dealing with his Ferengi clients.

There was every reason to believe that this would be a low-risk undertaking, just as Ross and Giancarlo were asserting. It was rare for the *Hope* to be stopped by patrol ships even when the freighter traveled in Cardassian space, let alone boarded. This run would take them near Cardassian territory, though they would not actually cross the border.

Why, then, was his gut warning him that getting involved with this Starfleet officer was a huge mistake?

CHAPTER 5

As he studied his surroundings, Ensign Tobias Donovan had to ask himself, and not for the first time during the past three days, where precisely he had gone wrong.

"This is definitely not what I had in mind when Starfleet Intelligence came looking for me."

Looking up from a compact control console that mirrored the one Donovan was operating, Lieutenant Hu'Ghrovlatrei regarded her companion with an amused expression. "Feeling a bit misled, are we?"

Donovan indicated the interior of their makeshift operations center. "You have to admit that this isn't the most exciting way to spend our day. Sitting around hunched over computer consoles, waiting for something interesting to come along? This isn't what I joined Starfleet for, you know."

An Efrosian, Ghrovlatrei had a long mane of bright white hair that seemed to glow in the tiny room's reduced lighting, contrasting sharply with her dull orange-hued skin and the muted gray of the standard one-piece jumpsuit she wore, identical to those favored by many of the *Hope*'s crew. Her piercing cobalt blue eyes, however, twinkled in the dim illumination cast off from the status monitors arrayed before both officers.

"Part of the adventure of serving in Starfleet is waiting for the unexpected to occur. It is also part of the frustration. Patience, my young friend. Everything cannot always be exciting, even in our line of work."

"Now, there's an understatement if I've ever heard one," Donovan replied, though he knew his friend was right. That did not make it any easier to accept the fact that, for the moment at least, he was bored out of his skull.

A third-generation Starfleet officer, Donovan had grown up listening to the stories told to him by his father, mother, and grandmother of their experiences serving aboard starships and exploring far-off worlds. While his mother had commanded both a science vessel and a patrol ship monitoring the Neutral Zone near Romulan space before retiring, both his father and grandmother had served in the Starfleet Security Division. He had not inherited his taste for adventure from his mother, and it was almost a given from an early age that Tobias Donovan would follow in his father's footsteps.

One afternoon during his final year at the Academy, however, a woman with three pips on the collar of her Starfleet uniform came to visit him. She told Donovan how she had reviewed his record and about how impressed she was with the test scores he had accumulated during his years of study.

"You have a bright future," she had said. The natural talents he appeared to possess, if properly cultivated and allowed to mature with the appropriate level of supervision and mentoring, could become powerful assets to Starfleet.

Must have been a standard recruiting lecture, Donovan decided.

It was impressive, however, as was the additional training he had received following graduation from the Academy and receiving his commission. Uncounted hours of classroom and field instruction in intelligence gathering and covert operations had been only the tip of the iceberg, with the promise of even more excitement waiting for him as soon as he undertook his first mission.

What he had not expected was for that assignment to stuff him inside a packing crate.

Along with Commander Ross, he and Ghrovlatrei had installed their sensor equipment inside a large Type XII storage module, a model often used by colonists when first establishing a presence on a new world. Once emptied of its contents, the interior of the Type XIIs could be converted into a temporary shelter until more permanent dwellings were built. *Ulrika's Hope* was already carrying five such containers in the bowels of this mammoth cargo bay, making it that much easier for theirs to blend in. Should the module be scanned, a masking field projected from within would show the cargo container to be filled with agricultural equipment as described in the ship's manifest.

"I think you will agree," Ghrovlatrei said as she turned back to her sensor console, "that this is one assignment where a lack of activity is not necessarily a bad thing. Besides, it seems that the less Mr. Corsi has to hear from us, the happier he will be."

Donovan chuckled at the remark. While the *Hope*'s master had not been the most cordial of people when the Starfleet officers had first boarded, his brother had been very welcoming. A few of the freighter's crew also were Starfleet veterans and had been enthusiastic about being able to serve once more, even if only in a small capacity. Aldo Corsi, however, had made it clear to Commander Ross that he would tolerate nothing that might distract the crew from their jobs during the run.

"So far it's a safe bet that he'll never see us," he replied. "For a region of space that's supposed to be heavily patrolled by the Cardassians, they certainly don't show themselves very much." In fact, they had encountered only one patrol ship since leaving Madellin Prime, and it had been an uneventful meeting to say the least. The Cardassians had not even bothered to board the ship, and Donovan had detected only a passive sensor sweep as he and Ghrovlatrei secreted themselves inside the modified cargo module and waited to see whether or not their ruse would survive its first test. It had, with the patrol ship leaving the *Hope* to continue on its way; just another freighter on its scheduled run. The rapport Corsi and his crew had formed with the ships in this sector had worked in their favor, at least on that occasion.

Sighing as he leaned back in his chair, Donovan looked to the ceiling and was just noticing that it had not changed much in the three minutes since he had last looked at it, when a telltale beep sang out from behind him. Turning in his seat, he bent forward to examine the sensor control console, ensuring as he did so that the unit's recording functions had been activated. Given the need for the team to maintain absolute stealth, data obtained by the sensors would be retained in the unit's computer memory storage until it could be transmitted to Starfleet Intelligence. Attempting contact while the *Hope* was still so close to Cardassian territory had been deemed too risky by Commander Ross.

Designed for use by ground troops in rugged environments and enhanced for the specific uses of intelligence gathering by field agents, the compact array of display monitors and computer interfaces was housed within a portable container that was only slightly smaller than a standard Mark V photon torpedo tube. One person armed with an antigravity carrier could move the equipment in its case with little effort. Despite its size, however, the sensor control unit possessed functionality nearly equal to that found on the bridges of most Federation starships, and right now that functionality was calling out to Donovan.

"What is it?" Ghrovlatrei asked as she leaned toward his console.

Donovan shook his head. "Automatic alert signal. We're within scanning range of the Saltok system." He knew from the briefing that Ross had provided prior to the *Hope*'s departure that the ship's route to Juhraya would take them past this solar system. Even as he made the statement, however, he knew that something was not right. The alarm should not have sounded simply because they were nearing the system.

As if reading his thoughts, Ghrovlatrei consulted the array of status displays until she found what she was looking for and pointed to it. "Sensors are picking up ship activity."

"Yeah, but just barely," Donovan replied. "Looks like either a small vessel or a larger one running on minimal power. Judging by these readings, I'd bet the *Hope*'s own sensors aren't strong enough to pick it up from this distance." Even set for low-power passive scanning, the Starfleet equipment they had installed in the cargo module was several times more effective than even the freighter's primary navigational sensors.

Frowning, Donovan reached for his padd and scrolled through the information he had downloaded to it in preparation for the mission until he found what he wanted. "According to our files, this system's uninhabited." He reached to the console and adjusted several controls, watching as two of the status monitors shifted their displays in response to his commands. "That ship has a Cardassian power signature." That was surprising, as the Saltok system was outside Cardassian territorial boundaries.

So what are they doing there?

"Look," Ghrovlatrei said as the Efrosian indicated another display where three more readings were registering. "Just like the first. Perhaps they're escape pods." She shook her head after only a moment, though. "No, if that were the case then we would be picking up a distress signal. Besides, I don't see any signs of wreckage or anything that might be a disabled ship."

"I'm starting to get a bad feeling about this," Donovan said as he tapped one screen with a finger. "All of the readings are pretty close to the moon orbiting the fifth planet."

Consulting her own padd, Ghrovlatrei said, "The moon is Class-D according to our information, possessing few useful natural resources, especially for the Cardassians."

"Well, something about it's got their attention," Donovan countered. Of course, their current situation prevented him from really getting a detailed look at the moon or the ships. It would be so easy to bring the vague readings into sharp focus, but that would require increasing the power to the sensors and abandoning the passive scanning mode in favor of more invasive procedures, something they were forbidden from doing, at least for the moment. Donovan was sure, however, that Commander Ross would want to be informed about this.

His hand froze midway to his communicator badge, though, as the sensor console told him that none of their caution mattered any longer.

Aldo was bringing the first bite of his dinner to his mouth, when from across the table he shared with Giancarlo and Commander Ross he heard the sound of the Starfleet officer's communicator badge saying, *"Donovan to Ross."*

Removing the communicator from a pocket of the gray coveralls he wore, Ross tapped it and said, "Ross here. What is it, Ensign?"

"Our sensors have detected four ships in proximity to the moon orbiting Saltok V. They're on an intercept course and they appear to be Cardassian, but there's no way to be sure from this distance without increasing power to the sensors."

The agitation in the young man's voice was obvious,

Aldo thought as he shot a troubled look at both Ross and Giancarlo. Much to Aldo's relief, however, Ross shook his head at the ensign's suggestion. "Negative, maintain passive scanning mode. How much time until they get here?"

"Less than three minutes, sir."

Aldo did not bother listening to the rest of the exchange. He was up from his seat and heading for the *Hope*'s bridge even before Ross finished giving orders to prepare for possible boarding. Ross had explained to him how that would work, with his people sealing up the cargo module containing their sensor equipment and blending in with the rest of the crew. The Starfleet officers had exchanged their uniforms for the gray jumpsuits his own people wore aboard ship, and Ross and Donovan had taken the extra step of trimming their regulation sideburns in an attempt to look more like civilian freight haulers.

As he raced into the corridor with Giancarlo and Ross following close behind him, he cast an accusatory look at the Starfleet officer. "What's happened?"

"Apparently somebody's interested in the solar system we're passing," Ross replied.

"Did they detect your sensor scans?" Giancarlo asked.

Ross shook his head. "I don't see how. If Donovan and Ghrovlatrei are right, those are short-range Cardassian patrol ships. They don't have the kind of equipment to detect our gear operating in minimal power mode."

Snorting in derision, Aldo saw no reason to continue the conversation. They would know soon enough just who and what it was that had taken such a sudden interest in his ship.

It took only moments to reach the bridge, and the first thing Aldo noticed was the harried expressions on the faces of his two crewmates there. The look on the face of his helmsman, Michael Dillone, spoke volumes.

"A squadron of fast-attack ships, Boss. Two-seaters, all engine. No way we're going to outrun them." Aldo noted how his friend had reverted into the clipped tones that belied his normally laid-back nature. The former Starfleet security officer had slipped back into combat mode, already steeling himself for the confrontation he felt certain was coming.

Leaning over the shoulder of the ship's navigator, Gret, Aldo studied the status displays beneath the Bolian's hands and updated himself on their current position. "We're still three days away from where you wanted to take your sensor readings, Commander," he said to Ross. "I've never heard of Cardassian ships in the Saltok system before."

"That's because they're not supposed to be there," Ross replied. "Have the Cardassians ever intercepted your ship and demanded an inspection when you weren't traveling through their space?"

Aldo shook his head. "No, never."

"Then it looks like things have changed in the Saltok system." Looking over at Dillone, Ross asked, "Are their weapons systems charged?"

The question was answered as the ship lurched violently to starboard, pushing Ross into the bulkhead even as Aldo grabbed on to the back of Gret's chair for support. In the corner of his eye Aldo saw Giancarlo and the others flailing about in desperate attempts to keep from being thrown about the bridge.

"I'm guessing they are," Gret said, his voice dripping with sarcasm as he held on to his console to retain his balance. To Aldo he said, "They're moving to surround us."

Another impact rocked the ship and Aldo felt the deck buck beneath his feet. He steadied himself against the navigation console as inertial dampers struggled to compensate for the disruption to the ship's flight path.

As well constructed as he knew the *Hope* to be, Aldo held no illusions that the freighter stood any chance of survival if the Cardassians continued their assault. Gripping the edge of the console, he braced himself and waited silently for the next strike.

Only when it did not come after nearly a minute did Aldo realize he was holding his breath. "Now what?"

A beeping sound erupted from the forward bridge console at which Giancarlo had seated himself. Swiveling around in his chair to check it out, he looked up in Aldo's direction. "We're being hailed."

Aldo allowed himself to relax, but only slightly. If the Cardassians had not blown them to space dust already, then chances were good that they might not do so at all, provided any questions or concerns could be addressed to their satisfaction. Would he know whoever it was who was hailing them, either by face or reputation? How much of the rapport that he and his crew had formed with other Cardassian patrol ships over the past few years of running freight through this sector would he be able to draw on?

There's only one way to find out, isn't there?

Pausing only long enough to cast another irritated look at Ross, Aldo nodded to his brother. "On screen."

The image on the viewer shifted from the patrol ship that had taken up station off the *Hope*'s bow to that of a Cardassian military officer. His dark penetrating eyes seemed to bore straight through Aldo, adding to the alien's already sinister expression. Still, Aldo was at least pleased to see that it was a face that he knew well.

"Gul Mogad," he said to the commander of Cardassian ships in this sector, "why are you firing at us?" While Aldo would never consider himself and Mogad to be friends, they had formed a mutually respectful association in the years that *Ulrika's Hope* had operated in this area. It was a relationship Aldo had used to every advantage in order to keep his deliveries on schedule and with the fewest possible disruptions.

None of that familiarity seemed to be present now, however, as the Cardassian responded with a formal nod and leaned so close to his own visual pickup that his face nearly filled the viewer.

"Bring your ship to a full stop, human," Mogad said, *"and prepare to be boarded. If you do not comply, I will destroy you here and now."*

CHAPTER 6

Watching Mogad stalk around the small open area in the forward section of the shuttlebay, Aldo realized that in all the years he had known him, this was the first time the Cardassian officer had actually set foot aboard the *Hope*. Even on those occasions when the freighter had passed through Cardassian space and Mogad's had been the patrol vessel to intercept them and request an inspection of the freighter's cargo holds, the gul himself had remained aboard his own ship.

That he was here now only served to underscore, at least to Aldo, just how seriously Mogad viewed the current situation.

With his arms clasped loosely behind his back as he paced back and forth, his eyes moved past the stacks of cargo containers that had been staged here. He appeared to be ignoring Aldo and the rest of the *Hope*'s crew, all of whom had been assembled here at the Cardassian's orders and who were currently under guard by five of Mogad's subordinates. Aldo noted once again the hard expression on the gul's face, which had not changed since the moment the quartet of Cardassian fast-patrol ships entered the *Hope*'s cramped landing bay. They had been forced to dock, given their ships' lack of transporters, and the hassle was compounded by the fact that the landing bay was already being used for extra cargo storage space. All four ships had been able to land, but it was a tight fit.

"We detected sensor scans emanating from your ship, Aldo," Mogad said, the corners of his mouth turning upward slightly to create more of a sneer than a smile. "These sensor scans were more powerful than would be considered normal for a vessel of this type. Perhaps you might explain that anomaly for me."

Aldo had prepared for the question with the help of both Ross and Colv, the *Hope*'s engineer. "We've had some upgrades to our sensor equipment, among other things." He hoped that his answer sounded more natural and truthful to the Cardassian's ears than his own.

"These were not the scans of a freighter's navigational sensors," Mogad countered, "nor were they simply searching for potential hazards. Our own sensor logs show that these were aimed specifically at the Saltok system. Why does that area interest you?"

Shrugging, Aldo replied with another coached answer from Ross. "My sensor officer detected what he thought were lifepods. When he realized that they were ships operating under their own power he informed the bridge to continue on our course."

Mogad appeared to consider this for a moment, directing his gaze as he did so toward the other members of the crew. His eyes moved from face to face until they settled on Ross. Aldo saw the Cardassian's brow furrow in suspicion as he regarded the Starfleet officer, who along with Ensign Donovan had blended in with the rest of the crew. "I don't recognize you, human. What is your name?"

Clearing his throat as if nervous, Ross replied, "Uh, Barry, sir. I'm the assistant helmsman."

"I just hired him on last month," Giancarlo added from where he stood to Aldo's right. "Dillone and Gret were begging me for extra help during the longer trips. You know how Bolians can get if you don't give them what they want." It was a hasty fabrication, one Giancarlo and Aldo had contrived, as well as a feeble attempt to play on the familiarity that the Corsis and Mogad shared, but it was better than letting Ross talk too much.

Mogad's attention lingered on the commander a moment longer before he resumed his slow pacing. "There is much here that troubles me, Aldo, and my concern is compounded by the fact that we have known one another for a long time. I do not want to believe that you have engaged in any activities that might harm our relationship, but circumstances being what they are, I am not allowed the luxury of taking anything for granted." Walking until he stood directly in front of Aldo, his smile widened as he added, "So I hope you will understand my insistence on an inspection of your vessel in order to assuage my doubts."

The "request" was more polite formality than anything else, Aldo knew, just as he knew that members of the gul's crew were already sweeping the *Hope* from bow to stern in search of anything that could implicate him or his crew. Ross had assured him that the sensor equipment would not be detected with the special masking field in place, but that did little to ease Aldo's discomfort.

"What doubts?" Aldo asked. "Come on, Mogad, what is it you believe us to have done?"

Leveling a scathing glare at Aldo, the gul replied, "Quite simply, I believe that you were spying, human, and the only reason I have not ordered your ship destroyed already is because of the respect you have earned from me in the past. However, if I find that trust has been violated, you will wish I had simply blown you out of space."

Lieutenant Hu'Ghrovlatrei had to fight the urge to fidget as the Cardassians walked through the hold, gradually making their way toward the grouping of Type XII cargo modules.

The unit holding the Starfleet team's equipment had been sealed and the sensor masking field activated, and other cargo had been situated around it to give the appearance that no one could easily enter the larger model. With just their tricorders to aid them, there should be no way for the Cardassians to know that any of the containers were anything but what they appeared to be.

So why am I so nervous?

Of course she knew the reason, and it had everything to do with being alone in a cargo hold with two Cardassians, a result of Gul Mogad's directing Aldo to supply a crew member who could guide the search party through the labyrinthine storage bays. It was just such an opportunity that Commander Ross had been hoping for, instructing Aldo in advance to offer Ghrovlatrei for the task if and when Mogad gave the order. The Starfleet officers had so far been accepted as members of the ship's company, and her assignment to the detail had raised no suspicions as she led the way through the cargo areas, standing where she was told to stand or opening doors or moving the odd container when directed. Otherwise the Cardassians ignored her, intent as they were on their mission.

The scans she and Donovan had conducted, despite the low power setting and the noninvasive nature of their sensors, had obviously been detected by the Cardassians. Whatever equipment had accomplished the feat had to be more powerful than that installed aboard the patrol ships presently surrounding the *Hope*. That would imply some sort of sensor installation in this vicinity, she knew. Was it located on the moon? If so, that would certainly go a long ways toward explaining the Cardassians' reaction.

It's too bad we didn't get a chance to take a closer look, she mused, trying unsuccessfully to avoid dwelling on the idea that not getting decent sensor readings was really the least of their problems now.

Given the current situation between the Cardassian

Union and the Federation, Starfleet Intelligence was expending massive resources trying to keep track of ship and troop movements throughout Cardassian territory. Encounters between the two sides had been anything but peaceful. There were still other attacks on Starfleet ships that were yet to be explained. One such incident had occurred just recently in the Maxia Zeta system, with the crew of the *U.S.S. Stargazer* forced to evacuate their ship after its near destruction at the hands of an unidentified vessel. Though that confrontation had taken place several light-years from here, it was close enough that Intelligence was not ruling out the possibility of Cardassian involvement.

Watching the Cardassians go about their inspection, Ghrovlatrei could see that the soldiers were getting bored, their behavior in sharp contrast to the manner in which they had begun the assignment. It was obvious in the casual way they examined the cargo modules they passed and in the almost dismissive manner in which they studied their tricorder readings. Still, she found herself holding her breath as one of the Cardassians waved his scanner in front of the module containing the sensor equipment.

From her vantage point, it was difficult to see the tricorder's miniaturized display, but Ghrovlatrei could still make out the scan results, which depicted the false image of the container's supposed contents. As far as she could tell, there was nothing in the readings that should raise suspicion.

"There's nothing here," the Cardassian said to his companion as he returned his tricorder to a clip on the belt of his uniform. "Whatever they are using, it must be installed someplace other than the cargo bays."

The other Cardassian nodded as he took a final look at his own scanner, and Ghrovlatrei was about to allow herself a guarded sigh of relief when the soldier froze in place, a frown creasing his pale features. Facing the cargo module, the heavy brow ridges over his eyes furrowed as he studied his tricorder again.

"Wait," he said after several seconds. "Something isn't right."

The other Cardassian moved closer. "What do you mean?"

Indicating the module with his tricorder, his comrade replied, "The readings show that this contains farming equipment, all packed neatly." He pointed to another of the Type XIIs. "As opposed to the others, the contents of which have been thrown into disarray. That was almost certainly caused by our earlier attack. So why not this one?"

Ghrovlatrei watched as the Cardassian considered the situation before him, her hopes already sinking as she realized what a simple, idiotic mistake she and Donovan had made. Then the Cardassian turned to face her, his expression having grown cold.

"Open it."

It required an almost physical effort for the Efrosian to maintain her composure as she nodded to the Cardassian and stepped to the module. How had she failed to consider that the contents of the other modules would have shifted, violently in some cases, under the brunt of the weapons fire the freighter had suffered and adjusted the masking field's projection accordingly?

What was she supposed to do now? The entire mission was about to be exposed, and there was no telling what Gul Mogad might do once he found out about the Starfleet equipment. The safety of the ship's entire crew was in danger.

There really was only one course of action.

With her right hand blocked as she moved one of the smaller containers that she and Donovan had placed in front of the module's door, Ghrovlatrei was able to reach into the cargo pocket on the right leg of her jumpsuit and retrieve the small Type I phaser she had secreted there.

CHAPTER 7

"Gul Mogad! We need—"

Donovan tensed at the words that erupted from Mogad's communicator, turning as he did so to make eye contact with Ross. The commander exchanged a quick glance with him that spoke volumes: *Don't move.*

Static had replaced the voice coming from the Cardassian's communicator and Mogad tapped the device furiously. "Traket, are you there? Traket?" Pivoting on his heel he whirled to face Aldo. "What have you done? What are you hiding here?" Forgetting the now useless communicator, he instead pointed to one of his subordinates. "Cover the entrance." To the others he said, "If any of them moves, kill them all."

Donovan could see nervousness working against Aldo, his body struggling to remain still as Mogad's anger mounted. "I don't know what's going on," he said. It was not a lie, at least not completely. Aldo could not know what was happening belowdecks. Donovan was not even sure himself. The only thing that made sense was that the Cardassians searching the cargo holds had discovered the hidden Starfleet equipment and that Lieutenant Ghrovlatrei had taken some kind of action. Had she also managed to find a way to jam the Cardassian's communications?

Mogad's frustration was evident as he failed to make contact with his two soldiers down in the cargo holds.

"Why, after all these years, have you seen fit to violate my trust?" he asked as he stepped closer to Aldo. "Do you realize that espionage against the Cardassian Union is an offense punishable by death? Is that what you wish for your crew?"

Mogad was towering over him now, standing so close to him that Donovan imagined Aldo feeling the Cardassian's breath on his face, nearly as hot as the palpable anger radiating from the gul's muscled body.

Shaking his head, Aldo replied, "No, of course not."

"Then your only hope for their safety is to be honest with me, here and now." Mogad somehow managed to step even closer to the freighter captain, his voice now low and menacing. "I am being generous with you, Aldo, because of the measure of trust you've earned from me, but I will make this offer only once."

Donovan saw the no-win situation for what it was. No matter how Aldo answered, he was probably forfeiting his own life. Perhaps Mogad would show leniency toward the rest of the crew, but what about him and Ross and Ghrovlatrei? If their true identities were exposed, the Cardassian would waste no time taking them into custody. Would he even bother to have them transported to an appropriate military installation for trial, or would he simply carry out summary judgment and execute the three officers right here in this very room?

No way.

He kept the movement subtle, his hand sliding with excruciating slowness to the small pocket on his right thigh and the palm-sized phaser there. His fingertips brushed the smooth finish of the weapon as he grasped the diminutive, contoured device. By touch, he verified that the phaser was set to stun. He would have only one chance at this. Was Ross thinking along the same lines? Donovan had to believe that the seasoned Starfleet officer had already considered and discarded a dozen courses of action.

"Mogad," Aldo said, "I really don't know what you're talking about."

With what Donovan interpreted as a sigh of resignation, Mogad regarded the freighter captain, pursing his lips as if in thought. After several seconds, he finally nodded, appearing to have reached a decision.

His eyes never left Aldo's as he said, "Kill them."

The other Cardassians stepped forward at Mogad's command, their phase-disruptor rifles taking aim on the assembled group of cargo haulers. Donovan watched as one of the weapons swung in his direction, its muzzle tracking toward his chest. There was no way he would ever be able to bring his phaser up before the Cardassian fired.

You're going to die.

The whine of a phaser echoed in the shuttlebay, interrupting the soldier's movements as a bright orange beam of energy lanced out to strike the Cardassian in the chest. Another volley shot across the room, narrowly missing Mogad as he dove for cover.

Donovan detected movement to his right and turned to see another of the Cardassians aiming a weapon in his direction. He aimed his phaser and fired as he dropped to a knee. The howl of a disruptor bolt screamed past his ear as his own phaser beam missed the shooter, striking the bulkhead just over the Cardassian's left shoulder.

Then the entire room erupted into chaos.

Bodies scattered in all directions as the *Hope*'s crew scrambled for storage bins, cargo containers, or equipment lockers, anything that might provide protection. Two of the freight haulers teamed up to subdue another Cardassian, their combined weight and strength toppling the soldier to the deck. Donovan recognized one of the attackers as the ship's pilot, Dillone, who retrieved the fallen alien's weapon before scampering for cover.

All this happened as the remaining Cardassians opened fire on anything that moved. Donovan could only stand helpless as one of the *Hope*'s crew members, he did not know the man's name, fell victim to a barrage of disruptor energy. The weapon tore through his body, leaving a gaping smoking wound as the man collapsed in a lifeless heap.

As he sought concealment of his own among the stacks of cargo modules, Donovan envisioned the interior of the shuttlebay in his mind. Most of the *Hope*'s crew had found refuge among the cargo containers arrayed around the room's perimeter, while a few had been forced to resort to whatever protection they could find closer to the center of the room. The Cardassians who were still mobile had sought similar refuge.

Donovan examined his surroundings. There appeared to be no way to escape from the shuttlebay without drawing enemy fire. A quick survey of the room showed him no alternative means of exit. The situation had devolved into a standoff, with the shooting now all but stopped. Holding his breath, Donovan listened for voices or signs of movement from any of the Cardassians while scanning the gaps between cargo containers for threats.

Nothing.

The whine of Ross's phaser nearly scared him out of his skin as the bright amber beam passed directly in front of him from left to right. He pivoted away from the shot and saw the intended target, a Cardassian who had been sneaking up on him. The blast struck the soldier and sent him collapsing to the deck.

Donovan scrambled around the other side of his own module even as he felt a hand on his shoulder. He jerked at the touch and looked up to see Ross. The commander's eyes were not looking down at him but rather tracking along with the phaser in his hand. He fired again as he helped the ensign to his feet.

"Move!" Ross hissed, pulling Donovan back the way he had come. The two men darted between cargo containers until they met up with Aldo Corsi and two of the freighter's crew huddled together behind one of the larger storage modules.

"Where's everybody else?" he asked Aldo.

Anger clouded the freighter captain's face as he shook his head. "Scattered. Colv and Walters went down when the shooting started." He pointed an accusatory finger at Ross. "This is your fault. You promised that nothing like this would happen."

"We don't have time for this," Ross countered, though he never made eye contact with Aldo as he continued to search for threats. "If Mogad gets to his ships, we're all dead." Turning to Aldo, he said, "But we need to get your people to better cover. They're sitting ducks out here."

He pointed to the Cardassian near the doorway, and Donovan saw that the soldier was partially concealed behind a single storage locker staged near the hatch, his muscular frame much larger than the bin itself. It was enough, however, to prevent anyone from getting a shot without being exposed to return fire.

"Donovan and I will secure the door," Ross said to Aldo, "and on my signal you run and you don't stop running until you get behind those modules next to the hatch. Once we regroup, we'll figure out what to do next."

It was a risky plan, but Donovan understood it for what it was, an off-the-cuff attempt to capitalize on the meager advantage Ross had fashioned from the situation. Regardless of the risk, it was still better than staying where they were and waiting for Mogad's men to defeat them with their superior firepower.

"Go!" Ross hissed as he pushed away from the cargo module, firing his phaser without truly aiming the weapon as he moved. Donovan mimicked the commander's actions, firing at movement beside one of the storage lockers positioned along one nearby bulkhead. Cloaked in shadow there, the Cardassian fired in retaliation but it was a shot that went wide as Donovan fired again, sending the soldier into retreat.

As he and Ross crossed the open area toward the door, firing as they went, the hatch itself opened without warning to reveal Hu'Ghrovlatrei. The Cardassian near the door swung in the direction of the new threat but he was too slow to stop Ghrovlatrei, who leveled a Cardassian disruptor at him and fired. Energy washed over the soldier's body and he crashed unconscious to the deck.

"Good timing," Donovan said as Ghrovlatrei joined him behind a larger cargo container.

The Efrosian nodded. "I though you might need some help." She shifted to her left to make room for Ross as the commander situated himself behind the storage module. On his signal, the three Starfleet officers aimed their phasers back into the shuttlebay, their lines of sight crossing over one another to create overlapping fields of fire.

"Let's go, Aldo!" Ross called out, and Donovan saw the freighter captain and members of his crew begin to head in their direction.

From his vantage point, Donovan saw Giancarlo Corsi hunkered down behind a lone storage module near where he had been standing when the fighting broke out. He was watching his friends heading for cover, and Donovan could see from the look in Giancarlo's eyes that he was sizing up the situation and the energy bolts flying around the room, watching for his own opportunity to dash to safety.

"Come on, Gi!" Aldo yelled as he ran toward the door.

Giancarlo shook his head. "Get everybody else!" he yelled back, keeping himself protected behind the cargo container.

Using the disruptor he had recovered to protect his friend's retreat, Dillone remained in the hiding place he had found for himself and laid down a ferocious blanket of covering fire. Ross and Donovan added their own weapons to the mix, and the chamber echoed with the fierce storm of the continuous energy discharges as, one by one, those members of the *Hope*'s crew who had not fallen during the firefight worked their way toward the rest of the group.

The Cardassians in the room were answering the heavy weapons fire with their own. Energy bolts slammed into the bulkhead near the door, and Ross and Donovan both ducked down to present as small a target as possible.

Aldo was the last of the crew to get across the danger area, turning back to his brother once he had reached the protection of the cargo modules. "Gi!"

Seeing that his friends were safe, Giancarlo turned to run toward them. Weapons fire exploded from two different points in the room, and Ross and Donovan renewed their efforts to provide cover as he dashed across the dangerous open area separating him from the rest of the group. One disruptor bolt hit the deck near Giancarlo's left foot and he dodged to the right to avoid it. The move sent him off balance and he stumbled into another cargo module.

He hesitated only an instant before starting to run again, but even that was too long. The first disruptor blast caught Giancarlo in the side, driving him into another of the storage containers. His forward movement now completely arrested, he was an easy target as a second shot hit him in the back.

"No!" Aldo shouted above the din, but it was too late.

The others could only stand and watch as multiple weapon strikes trapped Giancarlo Corsi in a vicious crossfire, and Donovan felt his jaw go slack in horror as the man fell lifeless to the floor of the shuttlebay.

CHAPTER 8

"Gi!"

Donovan grabbed Aldo Corsi by the arm to keep the freighter captain from plunging headlong to where Giancarlo had fallen. It would have been a laughable attempt, except that Aldo was forced to stop as a new hell storm of disruptor fire tore through the air around him. Powerless to help his brother, Aldo instead retreated to the protection of the cargo module, sagging to the deck as he buried his head in his hands.

His features clouded with sympathy, Ross regarded the man for several seconds before directing his attention back to the situation at hand.

Ghrovlatrei's own features were clouded by anguish as she glanced toward Aldo. "I must accept responsibility for all that has happened, Commander." She held up the pair of disruptor rifles she had captured. "The two Cardassians sent to inspect the lower cargo decks were about to discover our equipment. I felt that I had no choice but to disable them."

"You had no choice?" Aldo asked, the question laced with anger and pain. "My brother is dead! Your choice killed him. His death is on your hands!"

Ghrovlatrei's mouth fell open in muted shock at the

verbal assault, and Donovan even took a step backward in response to the man's raw emotion.

"Mr. Corsi," Ross said while somehow maintaining his own composure, "no one is more upset than I am for the loss of your brother and the other people, but right now we have to think about the rest of your crew. Mogad was going to kill all of us, and if he gets off this ship, he'll blow us all to hell. Our only chance is to keep him here, at least until we can figure out what to do next."

Aldo drew several deep breaths in an attempt to bring himself under control. Though the man's grief and fury were still palpable, Donovan could see that the commander's words were having an effect on him.

He watched as Aldo turned and regarded the faces of the four other *Hope* crew members who had survived the firefight. Huddling behind a row of cargo modules stacked two meters high, none of them said anything, the stress of the past few minutes almost certainly still weighing on them. Just like their captain, they too were hurting over the loss of Giancarlo and the others, but Donovan thought he recognized anger and perhaps even determination in their eyes.

Finally, Aldo returned his gaze to Ross. "What do you have in mind?"

By way of reply, Ross looked to Ghrovlatrei. "What's our status?"

"I was able to use the sensor equipment to jam their communications," the Efrosian replied. "Ours are affected as well, however. We cannot signal for assistance so long as the jamming field is activated."

As he absorbed Ghrovlatrei's report Ross said, "Pass out those disruptors." To Aldo he asked, "I don't suppose you've got any other weapons in here somewhere?"

"No," Aldo replied, shaking his head. "We never needed them before today."

One of the *Hope* crew members, a human whose

name Donovan did not know, stepped forward. "We'll use clubs if we have to. Those bastards killed our friends, and they're not getting past us without a fight." The man's words invoked a chorus of fierce agreement from the rest of the crew.

Ross looked to Ghrovlatrei and pointed to the tricorder sticking from the top pocket of her coveralls. "Lieutenant, can you tell me where Mogad is?"

Consulting the device, Ghrovlatrei shook her head. "There are three Cardassians scattered throughout this room that are still conscious. One of them is maintaining his position among the cargo containers near the closest of the patrol ships, but the other two are moving, perhaps to join their companion. I cannot determine which one is Mogad."

From his vantage point, Donovan could see the quartet of patrol ships, their cockpit hatches visible along the top edges of their wedge-shaped hulls. There was no way the Cardassians would be able to approach the ships without being seen.

Small favors, he mused.

With a grunt of frustration, Ross shook his head at the report before looking to Ghrovlatrei again. "Cover this hatch. Make sure none of the Cardassians get past you. Donovan, you come with me."

Her brow creasing in uncertainty, Ghrovlatrei asked, "What do you have in mind, Commander?"

Ghrovlatrei was right, Donovan chided himself. *This assignment was better when it was boring.*

Moving in a crouch, Donovan scurried between the stacks of cargo containers, his ears straining to detect any signs of the three Cardassians who were still hiding somewhere in the shuttlebay. For the third time in as many minutes, he swallowed the lump that had formed in his throat. He cursed himself for not having the presence of mind to have carried a tricorder of his own. The device would have proven invaluable to him right about now.

Of course, you had no idea Commander Ross was going to suggest something this crazy, did you?

Their time and options fading, Ross had decided on a bold course of action. With Ghrovlatrei and Dillone providing covering fire if needed, the two Starfleet officers had set out in search of Mogad. Donovan was circling along the perimeter of the room to the left of their defensive position near the exit hatch, while Ross searched somewhere among the cargo modules to the right. With no tricorders to scan for the locations of the Cardassians, both humans were forced to rely on their own senses to discern any telltale clues of their enemy's presence. So far, Donovan had seen and heard nothing to indicate he was not alone here, despite what his pounding heart and rapid breathing told him.

His thoughts were broken as a voice called out across the shuttlebay. "Mogad!" Donovan froze in place, even holding his breath as the voice, Aldo Corsi's and full of anger, echoed in the room. "Mogad," he repeated, "we have to talk. We have to put a stop to this before it gets completely out of control."

What was he doing? Why was he drawing attention to himself? Surely, Mogad or one of his subordinates would try to home in on his voice. He was placing himself and his crew in danger.

"Mogad, we can't allow this to go any further. Too many people have died or been hurt already, even though you could have prevented it. Are you ready to sacrifice more lives by failing to act?"

Or was he?

Of course.

Donovan smiled to himself, nodding in appreciation for Aldo's savvy. He was trying to get the Cardassian to speak and reveal his location. After years of dealing with Mogad, the freighter captain probably knew the gul as well as anyone outside his own family. But would he know enough to be able to provoke the Cardassian? It was a simple ploy, attacking Mogad's ego and pride.

Simple, yet effective.

"Let us not forget that it was you who chose to engage in espionage, Corsi," Mogad said, his voice crisp as always, though Donovan was more concerned with the fact that it was also close. Very close.

Somewhere to the right, he decided, though the voice was muted somewhat by the cargo containers blocking much of his view of the shuttlebay. He took a tentative step forward, the hairs on the back of his neck standing straight up.

"You have my sympathies for the loss of your brother," Mogad continued, "but his death could have been avoided if you had been honest with me from the beginning."

"You bastard! I'll—"

Donovan heard the words choke off, and his stomach heaved at the Cardassian's unmitigated gall. That, and the fact that he, along with Ross, was more than likely responsible for the death of Giancarlo Corsi as well as the other *Hope* crew members.

Assuming they survived, the official reports submitted by the three Starfleet officers at the conclusion of this mission would likely exonerate them from blame with regard to the tragedy that had already unfolded here. Such thoughts did not make it any easier for Donovan to cope with what had happened, however.

You don't have time for this, he scolded himself. *Focus*.

Aldo was not talking anymore. Had Mogad's words wounded him that much? Donovan imagined how the freighter captain must have reacted. Gret had more than likely been forced to restrain the man from yielding to blind rage and storming into the line of fire.

There was movement to his left and he whirled to see

a Cardassian, not Mogad, crouched down between two large storage modules. His body and his disruptor were facing away from Donovan, and it was this unfortunate choice that bought the ensign the precious second he needed to fire his own weapon.

Even as the Cardassian succumbed to the stun beam, Donovan heard footsteps behind him. He pivoted toward the sound but he was too slow. Mogad loomed in his vision. Donovan tried to bring his phaser around but Mogad seized his wrist and parried the move, twisting the weapon away from him until it fell from Donovan's hand. The ensign's efforts to resist were useless against Mogad's superior strength and in short order he stood mere centimeters in front of the Cardassian. Then he felt the gul's massive left hand gripping his throat.

"A Starfleet phaser," Mogad said, eyeing the fallen weapon. "I knew this ship carried spies." Sadness seemed to wash over the gul's expression and he actually shook his head as he added, "Aldo was lying to me after all."

The Cardassian's fingers were digging into Donovan's throat, and he could feel his breathing already becoming labored. Light reflected off something metallic and he saw Mogad's right arm coming up, the muzzle of the disruptor pistol in the Cardassian's hand a yawning black maw as it drew closer.

"Hold it right there," a voice called out, and Donovan shifted his eyes to see Ross emerging from behind a cargo module. The commander pushed forward with incredible speed and agility until he was standing right next to Mogad, pinning the Cardassian's weapon arm against his own body and pressing his phaser into the gul's right cheek.

"Let him go," Ross hissed, menace enveloping each word as it left his mouth.

"Lower your weapon or I'll kill him," Mogad replied.

His breath coming in shallow gasps now, Donovan

heard more movement behind him and then another voice that made his heart sink. "Drop your weapon, human."

Ross dropped behind Mogad, using the Cardassian for a shield as he pressed his phaser even harder into the gul's face. To the other Cardassian he said, "Drop it or your boss dies." Looking back to Mogad he added, "Make him back off and let my man go."

Smiling as his fingers dug even deeper into Donovan's throat, Mogad said, "It appears that we've reached an impasse."

Stars were swimming before Donovan's eyes and color was beginning to wash out of everything in his vision, when another voice joined the fray.

"Wait!"

CHAPTER 9

Aldo held his hands out and away from his body to show that he was unarmed as he beheld the surreal scene before him. Mogad held Donovan by the throat, while Ross held a phaser to the gul's head and another Cardassian trained his weapon on the commander. Ghrovlatrei had maneuvered to cover the scene with the disruptor she had confiscated from the Cardassians she had subdued.

Aldo's shout made Mogad look up in alarm, his distraction enough for Ross to act. The commander pulled his phaser from the gul's face as his right arm lashed out, sweeping downward to strike the arm Mogad was using to hold on to Donovan. The Cardassian's grip was broken and Donovan fell to the deck. All of this happened as Ghrovlatrei fired on the other soldier who had been aiming his weapon at Ross, catching the Cardassian by surprise and stunning him where he stood.

Stepping to his left to avoid another attack by Ross, Mogad raised the disruptor pistol he still carried in his hand. Ross was faster, however, striking out with his right foot and kicking the weapon from the gul's hand. The pistol clattered to the deck as Ross aimed his phaser at Mogad once more and the Cardassian froze, though he seemed to be considering his next attack despite the weapon pointed at his face.

"Wait, Mogad," Aldo repeated. "It doesn't have to be like this!"

Standing his ground, Mogad regarded the freighter captain with an incredulous expression. "You are guilty of espionage, Corsi. At the very least, you've been aiding this spy. That crime cannot be allowed to go unpunished."

"This isn't Cardassian space," Ross said, punctuating his words with another jab of his phaser into Mogad's cheek. "You have no authority here. Why are you so worried about what we find in the Saltok system? There has to be some kind of high-power surveillance equipment on that moon if you detected our sensors, so what's going on there?"

Mogad sneered at the commander. "Do I look like a fool to you? Are you really expecting me to answer that question?"

"All I care about," Ross countered, "is that you've attacked a Federation vessel in Federation space, apparently to cover up whatever you're doing in a star system outside your territorial boundaries." Leaning closer, he added, "Even that backward justice system of yours will see you don't have a case, not to mention how the Federation Council and Starfleet will regard what's happened here today. I've got enough sensor data to prompt a full-scale investigation into whatever it is you're hiding out there. It could be interpreted as an act of aggression against us."

Mogad shook his head. "None of that will matter when I make it known that I was protecting our interests in this sector, and you will stand trial for crimes against the Cardassian people."

"Trial?" Ross countered. "Crimes? Do you really think the Federation will allow that to happen?"

"Shut up, both of you!"

Aldo regarded the human and Cardassian who were now looking at him, the ferocity with which he had bellowed the command muting them in identical shock. In fact, he had the attention of everyone in the room. Even Donovan, the young ensign whom Mogad had nearly choked to death, was staring at him. All of them stood in stunned silence. That was good. He wanted them quiet. He wanted them all to listen, but most especially the two idiots he was looking at right now.

Glaring at Mogad, he said, "You come aboard my ship and murder my brother in defense of your illegal encroachment into an area of space that does not belong to you. Are you planning to enslave another culture like all of the others you've crushed beneath your boots? Is Giancarlo but the latest victim in your endless thirst for conquest?"

Rather than the defiant response he had expected from Mogad, Aldo instead thought he saw remorse and perhaps even guilt in the Cardassian's eyes. "The deaths of your brother and the others are regrettable, Corsi. I did not want any of your people to be hurt, but I have my duty. Soon my people will send ships to see what has happened here, and when they arrive, I will have no choice but to take you into custody."

"What makes you believe you'll be alive when they get here?" Ross asked, his phaser still trained on Mogad.

The gul hesitated before answering, and when he did Aldo thought he detected a sliver of uncertainty in his voice. "Perhaps I won't be, but that changes nothing. You will still be prisoners of the Cardassian Union, and you will be executed for espionage."

Something in the way Mogad spoke, Aldo decided, was wrong. Struck by sudden inspiration, he turned on the Cardassian. "Somehow I doubt they'll cross into Federation space without your authorization. After all, you're not even supposed to be in this region of space, are you?"

He stepped closer until he stood almost nose to nose with Mogad. "I'd bet that your superiors would even disavow any knowledge of your activities in this sector if you were found to be involved in an incident taking place in Federation space." He knew he had struck a chord when he saw Mogad's once assured demeanor begin to dissolve. The gul tried to school his features but he was not fast enough, and Aldo smiled in triumph.

"Looks like you'll be staying with us for a while, Mogad," Donovan said, his own expression one of barely restrained glee as he pulled himself to his feet.

"No," Aldo said. "We're letting him go." To Mogad he said, "Take your people and get off my ship."

Neither Mogad nor Ross made any effort to hide the surprise on their faces, though the Cardassian was the first to react. "What makes you think I won't destroy your ship the moment after I've launched?"

"Because I'm going to give you the sensor logs from the Starfleet equipment that was used to detect your presence in the Saltok system."

Though he was expecting a negative reaction from Ross, Aldo was surprised when the commander said nothing. Instead, it was Lieutenant Ghrovlatrei who responded.

"Mr. Corsi, that sensor equipment is sensitive Starfleet technology. The data it has recorded is classified. We cannot allow . . ."

"Enough!" Aldo roared, cutting the Efrosian off as he directed renewed fury at Ross. "I allowed you to install that equipment aboard my ship with the assurance that nothing would happen. The security of the Federation, you said. No one would ever know what we had done, you said. Yet here we are. Those three deaths are on your head as surely if you had pulled the trigger yourself." The commander's jaw slackened in astonishment as he weathered Aldo's scathing verbal assault.

He looked to Mogad once more. "I want it off my

ship. Take it all. It will prove that we saw none of whatever it is that you have there. All I ask in return is that you allow us to go on our way."

The Cardassian stood in silence for several moments, his eyes studying the deck at his feet as if considering the offer. Finally, he looked at Aldo and nodded slowly. "I accept your offer, Corsi. You have my word that no harm will come to your ship once I leave." He paused, drawing a deep breath before adding, "I owe you that much, I think."

"Aldo," Ross began, "please. You can't do this."

"I can, and I will," Aldo replied, venom lacing his words. "That equipment is the reason my brother is dead. If you don't approve, you're free to get out and walk home."

"What am I supposed to tell Starfleet?" Ross asked.

Turning away from the group, Aldo stalked across the shuttlebay deck toward the exit, ignoring the compassionate faces of his remaining crew. As he walked, he cast a final answer over his shoulder. "I don't give a damn what you tell them."

Aldo had more urgent things to worry about. How would he explain to Domenica that the organization entrusted to keep the peace with the Federation's enemies, the same group that Giancarlo had idolized and that his young daughter hoped to one day join, had killed her cherished uncle? How would he do so while sparing her the rage and pain that weighed on him? He did not know if such an act was even possible.

He did not know if it would *ever* be possible.

CHAPTER 10

Stardate 53709.2, Earth Year 2376

Silence blanketed the cockpit of the *Pharaon*, broken only by the periodic beeps and clicks of control consoles and computer displays. It was a silence born of death and despair, of pain buried for far too long beneath a veneer of anger and detachment. Domenica Corsi found it stifling as she regarded her father through eyes blurred by tears, as he sat across from her in the cramped cockpit.

She watched him take a final drink of his juice, then sigh and begin to fidget with the now-empty bottle. Remembering her own beverage, Corsi looked down at the juice in her hand. Though her throat was parched, the thought of drinking the juice made her stomach lurch.

Instead, she returned her attention to her father and saw that his expression was one of misery and fatigue after unburdening himself of the secret he had carried all these years. Corsi thought she saw a hint of relief in her father's eyes, however, as if the confession might somehow have begun the process of cleansing the anguish from his soul.

"I've never told anyone what really happened that day," he said after several moments. "Not even your mother knows. After we got home, I swore the crew to secrecy. I didn't want one of them saying something around you or your mother."

Nodding, Corsi replied, "Thanks for telling me, Dad. It's good to know the truth, about anything." She paused before asking her next question, unsure of the reaction she would receive. "You've always said Uncle Gi died in an accident. Why did you lie about it?"

"It was no lie," Aldo said. "He did die in an accident; a horrible accident caused by Starfleet officers who were incapable of doing their own jobs."

"Dad," Corsi said, her tone one of gentle caution, "Starfleet didn't kill Uncle Gi. The Cardassians did."

It was not the first time her father had endured discussion of this topic, she realized as she watched his features harden. The line of his jaw tightened beneath the weathered skin of his face and his nostrils flared in the way they always did as his temper rose toward its boiling point. The index finger of his right hand leveled at her, his hand still gripping the empty juice bottle, and his eyes were wide with anger.

"Did you even listen to me? Are you so schooled by your superiors that you believe everything they do is right? Is your loyalty to Starfleet stronger than your family blood?"

Corsi felt her own ire mounting at the words, the same ones her father had used against her before on those rare occasions that they actually had spoken to one another. He knew just which buttons to push to set her off, playing her family loyalty against her sense of duty and service, those aspects of her character that made her just like him.

And just like her uncle, as well.

He's not driving me away. This time, I'm meeting him halfway.

"Dad, I listened," she began slowly. "I can't defend what Starfleet asked you to do, but it was a different time then. They were all but at war with the Cardassians and they asked for your help, but you knew what you were getting into. It's not as if you were commandeered."

"I might as well have been," Aldo replied. "As soon as that Ross started talking, he had to have seen the fire in Gi's eyes. Ross knew he was excited about helping, and he played us for suckers."

"Uncle Gi was no sucker," Corsi countered, "and he knew what he was doing just like you did." She remembered the tales of Giancarlo Corsi's life that her parents had shared with her in the years after his death. His enthusiasm and level-headedness in the face of adversity and even crisis were recalled often at the family dinner table, and accounts of his trust and loyalty were cited among them as unmatched, even by Corsi family standards. Her impression of the man was almost larger than life, she knew, a hero to be admired and even emulated. With all of that, it was no surprise that he would jump at the chance to help Starfleet, the organization he had admired but could not join.

Uncle Gi wanted to shine in Starfleet's eyes. He wanted to make a difference.

"But his death wasn't enough for them," Aldo said, his face reddening in seething rage. "Oh, no. Starfleet wanted revenge for my giving up their precious sensors and secret data. They destroyed my business. They restricted access to my shipping routes, and that cut me out of contracts for shipments I had been running regularly for years. I had to sell every ship I owned but this one, Domenica. I rebuilt the business from the bottom up, but I didn't have Gi to help me this time. I worked like hell so you kids wouldn't know the difference."

Corsi's own jaw clenched in anger at the remarks. "Starfleet did no such damn thing, Dad, and you know it. Ours wasn't the only family shaken up by the war, either. Much of the territory you and other freighters traveled fell under Cardassian rule, and Starfleet had no choice but to restrict travel in certain sectors. They did everything possible to make the quadrant safe for everyone."

"Not everyone," he corrected. "Not Gi."

Sighing, Corsi shook her head. "It's hard to explain, Dad. It's different for Starfleet officers than it is for other people. It was different for Uncle Gi, too, at least if I'm to believe all those stories you told me about him. He understood the risks, but he was on a mission, not just standing by."

"Your uncle was not a Starfleet officer, Domenica."

"He was in his heart!"

It exploded from her lips, startling both of them into momentary silence. Aldo recoiled at the force of his daughter's words, and Corsi herself had to pause to consider how she had reacted before continuing. How could she explain with mere words what drove her to put on her uniform each day?

"Dad, it's like what I feel for you and for Mom, and for the family, but different. I feel completely responsible for the security officers on my detail, for my captain, my ship and its crew, for, well, the Federation and everyone in it. I've been called to serve, Dad. I have duties to perform, and people depend on me. It makes me feel alive to serve them. Uncle Gi felt the same way, and you do, too. Who do you think gave that to me?"

Corsi watched as moisture gathered in the corners of her father's eyes. After several moments, he nodded slowly. "I know. I've known for a long time. Your mother has talked of it for years, and I didn't want to admit it, but I see it now."

"What, Dad?"

"In your eyes," he said, "and when you talk like that. I see Gi. All that time you two spent together when you were little, all of the games you would play, all of the dreams he shared with you when you were too small to really remember, Dommie. They really are there, inside you. I see it now."

New tears welled up in Corsi's eyes, and she reached over and placed her hand over her father's. "If that's really true, then maybe Uncle Gi realized just what he was getting into that day. I bet he was willing to give up everything for what Starfleet was trying to accomplish. That was his chance to live his dream."

"Your mother said the same thing about him once," Aldo said. "It took me years to accept that I'd lost him to that dream, just as it's hard to cope with the idea that I might lose my only daughter to that dream, too."

The words caught Corsi off guard and she found herself unable to respond to them. She had felt confident while explaining why she served in Starfleet, but during those fleeting moments she had forgotten the price for that service, as paid by half of the *da Vinci*'s crew.

Now, her father had thrust her backward in time, back to the boiling, deadly clouds of liquid-metal hydrogen that made up Galvan VI. He had plunged her back to the point of the ship's near-destruction, to her own near-fatal electrocution, and the deaths of so many friends and shipmates.

Maybe I should be dead, too.

"As strange as it sounds, though," Aldo said, "I think I understand better now. I'm not saying I'm comfortable with it, but this is good for me, and for both of us." Looking up from the deck, his eyes locked with hers once more. "And I want you to know, Dommie, that I'm proud of you. If you do have anything of your uncle in you, then you probably feel like you've failed your friends and your captain, but you didn't. You showed them how to fight until you couldn't fight anymore, and then you showed them how to get up and fight again. That's what Corsis do."

Corsi smiled, letting the pride she had sought from her father for so many years wash over her. "Dad, you know I'll be in danger again. Maybe not as bad as on Galvan VI, but it's sure to happen," she said. "You can't keep worrying about me."

"Oh, I'll worry, but not as much as I might," Aldo replied, "because you'll have the ax with you."

It took a moment for that to register, and when it did Corsi caught herself gasping in shock. "I . . . Dad, I don't understand."

"When I think back to that day," her father said, "I wonder if things might have been different had the ax been aboard. But it belongs with you now, Domenica. You earned the right to carry it, and you honor the family when you do."

The tears came freely now, as Corsi absorbed her father's words. For centuries, the ax had been a cherished family memento, its history rife with both triumph and tragedy. Passed down through the generations, it had grown to be more than a simple heirloom, taking on the role of good luck talisman and even, perhaps, that of guardian angel. Her father had begrudgingly entrusted it to her once, his concern for the upholding of family custom that the ax travel with a member sworn to the service of others winning out over his disdain for his daughter's commitment to Starfleet.

Now, however, he was giving it to her with his blessing and the assurance that she too had done her part to sustain her family's tradition.

Rising from her seat to go to her father, Corsi realized he had met her halfway when she felt his muscled arms wrap around her. She sank into the comforting embrace, a welcome act after so many years. Though they were a long way from closing the rift that had separated them for so long, she knew that the healing had begun, even in a small way, today.

As they stood there, the deck shuddered beneath

their feet and Corsi heard a humming from somewhere below them that she recognized as the *Pharaon*'s main warp drive coming back online.

"I guess Wilson and Stevens are finished," she said, wiping new tears from her eyes.

Pulling away from their embrace, albeit reluctantly, Aldo sighed in relief at the soothing drone of the ship's engines. "Wonderful! I think we're back on the road." They heard footsteps bouncing along the metal deck plates of the corridor outside the cockpit and turned to see Stevens appear in the hatch opening, a smile on his face.

"We're good to go," he said. "Wilson's checking a few readings but I think the replacement articulation frame will hold just fine. We found a couple of pieces in storage that did the trick. I only had to dig into the . . ."

He paused, the realization of what had just been said now evident on his face. Looking to Aldo, he stammered through the remainder of the sentence. "Uh . . . dig, into the storage hold and look for spare parts. Wilson did all the work, Mr. Corsi. I didn't touch a thing without his being right next to me."

Waving the explanation away, Aldo smiled. "Domenica spoke well of your abilities, Mr. Stevens. Forgive me for doubting them. I trust all went well?"

Stevens smiled and gave a thumbs-up. "Yes, sir. Now if you would excuse me, I'd like to wash up and get something to eat. Can I get anything for you two?"

Aldo shook his head. "I need to get us under way and contact the Thelkans to let them know we'll be a bit late."

"I'll catch up in a bit, Fabian." Corsi watched Stevens nod and return down the corridor. Behind her, Aldo had retaken his seat and started tapping commands into the control console. She waited in silence for the several minutes it took him to contact the Thelkan shipmaster and to make his preparations to get the *Pharaon* under way again before saying anything. "Dad?"

"Yes, Dommie?"

"This trip . . . this talk . . . meant a lot to me," she said. "I hope it's not our last."

Aldo smiled. "It won't be. Now go catch up to your friend. He's a good man, Dommie, from what I can tell. It's plain that he likes you a lot."

"Yeah," Corsi said. "And that's part of the problem."

As she headed in the direction of Stevens's quarters, Corsi realized her pace was quickening the farther she walked. She wanted to tell him about the conversation with her father. For the first time in years, she felt reconnected to her family and completely proud of her chosen career in Starfleet, and she could not wait to share her newfound good feelings with *him*.

Tapping the keypad next to the door to Stevens's room, she stepped inside as the hatch slid aside. "Fabian? Are you in here?"

Then she stopped short as she looked into the room's small bathroom and saw Stevens standing at the sink, naked but for a towel around his waist.

"Uh, I'll come back," she said, turning to head back through the door.

"Hey, it's okay," Stevens replied as he turned from the sink, rivulets of water in his hair as he wiped his hands with another towel. "Come on in."

Nodding, she made a concerted effort to avoid looking toward the bathroom as she stepped into the room and took a seat on the unmade bunk. "You guys made pretty quick work of the warp drive. I think Dad was impressed."

"Wilson did all the real work," Stevens admitted as he put away a washcloth and soap. "But play up the S.C.E. angle for your father. Maybe he'll start coming around on his Starfleet issues."

Corsi smiled at that. "He might be already. While you were working, we talked like we've never talked before.

He may be starting to understand why I've stayed in Starfleet all this time."

"That's great, Dom." As he moved from the bathroom, it seemed to be Stevens's turn to avoid eye contact as he went through the motions of tidying up the small sleeping quarters. "Maybe you can explain it to me later, if you want."

Something in the way he said the words caused her brow to crease in puzzlement. "What's that supposed to mean?"

Stevens turned from a storage compartment to meet her gaze. "I'm getting out," he said. "I've decided to leave Starfleet."

"What?" Corsi shuddered at the thought, a chill reaching from her belly into her throat with his words, and questions rang in her mind. *Fabian is leaving the ship? For good? Where had this come from?* "When did you decide this?"

"I've been thinking about it the whole trip," he said, "since before we left the *da Vinci*, really. Seeing you at home with your family, though, that really set the hook in me. I can do what I do for the S.C.E. in plenty of places and not get myself killed." He shrugged. "Maybe I'll head back to Rigel, or maybe your dad can hire me on for one of his freighters. It doesn't really matter. I just think it's time for me to move on."

"The hell it is."

For the second time that day, Corsi found herself surprised by her tone of voice and the conviction of her words, this time directed toward an unsuspecting and now dumbstruck Fabian Stevens. Once more, Corsi's thoughts turned to her mother, who was convinced that she would have the strength to find the words that would help Stevens when he needed it most.

If only I could feel so confident.

"Don't just look stupid at me," she said, her voice hardening with each word. "You know you're not leaving. It sounds great, running away when the going gets tough, but that's not how we handle things on the *da Vinci*."

"So that's how it is," Stevens said, regarding her with his own look of determination. "You put on your 'Core-Breach' mask and charge your way through another situation. That may work for you, Dom, but not for me. I left too much behind on Galvan VI."

The rage Corsi had been holding in check, first with her father and now with Stevens, erupted to the surface. "*You* did? I lost seven members of my security detail. Seven! Half the crew was killed! Do you know that for over a week I had to keep a highlighted list of the ship's complement next to my bed, so that when I woke up from my nightmares I could check to see who was still alive?"

Stevens's mouth fell open in shock, but he said nothing. Corsi did not give him a chance, either, rising from the bunk and pointing one long finger at him.

"This is not just your burden, Fabian," she said, her pitch and volume continuing to climb. "We *all* are hurting, and we'll hurt even more when we start seeing all the new people assigned to the ship when we get back, but we have our duty."

"Duty!" Stevens shouted in response, the word echoing off the walls of the small room. It was his turn to vent anger, and she had never seen him do so with such force. "It wasn't Duff's damn duty to jump out of the ship for that warhead! Now he's gone! It wasn't his job but he took it, and now he's dead!"

In barely a whisper, Corsi spoke. "It was my job."

Stevens stopped in the midst of drawing breath for his next outburst, her response undercutting him. "What?"

"Fabian, it was *my* damn job!" She gritted her teeth and turned away from him, not wanting him to see the pain in her face and the tears in her eyes. "I was supposed to disarm the Wildfire device, but I got hurt! I was useless, and a damned engineer did my job! Do you think I don't know that Duffy died because of me?"

Corsi threw away any restraint she had left and slumped back on Stevens's bunk. The sobs racked her body with the sorrow, frustration, and anger that she had held within her since the moment she had learned of Duffy's death.

Sitting down beside her, Stevens put an arm around her shoulders. "Dom. Duff did what he did for all of us. He saved the ship, and he would have done it a hundred times over if he could have. It's not your fault."

Meeting his eyes with tears running down her cheeks. Corsi asked, "If I can remember that and keep going, do you think that maybe you can, too?"

Stevens said nothing for a moment as Corsi tried to regain her composure, offering her one end of the towel slung over his shoulder. She dabbed at her eyes and blew her nose, drawing a disgusted look from Stevens before he handed her the rest of the towel.

"Keep it."

She could not help the laugh that escaped her lips, and she had to wipe her eyes again as more tears flowed forth. "Damn you," she whispered, a small smile forming on her face.

Drawing a deep breath, Stevens said, "You know, back during the Dominion War, when Duff and I hadn't known each other very long, he dragged me out of a Breen firefight and saved my life. He said we were phaser-proof, and even bragged about it at this bar where we . . . well, that's not important. What is important is that for some silly reason, I believed him. There were times I thought we were invincible, Dom." He shook his head. "I don't think I can go back to the *da Vinci* knowing that Duff won't be there."

Corsi paused, then offered her hand to Stevens. As he took it she said, "I'll be there, Fabian, just like you were there for me when I needed you. No questions asked, you can lean on me as much as you need to." Squeezing his hand, she added, "We'll get through this together."

"I could use a friend, you know," he said after a moment, "especially one who knows her way around a good bar brawl."

"What, you planning on talking to some more Tellarites, Fabe?"

He chuckled at that as he excused himself to the bathroom to finish getting cleaned up. There was a hint of the old Fabian Stevens in the smile he wore as the door closed behind him, one she was grateful to see. The door closed behind him, leaving her alone in the room with only her thoughts for company.

In just a few hours two men, whose importance to her she was only just now beginning to realize, had taken a few steps toward healing and understanding, both with her help. Corsi steeled herself for the journey ahead, both with Fabian Stevens and with her father, keeping mindful of her duties as a daughter, a friend, and a Starfleet officer. She was ready for anything.

After all, she was a Corsi, and that's what Corsis did.

AGE OF UNREASON

Scott Ciencin

To Denise.
With thanks to Keith DeCandido.
—S.C.

CHAPTER 1

The world was coming to an end.

Again.

Farhan Tanek struggled to keep his hands from closing on the neck of the oily little man quavering before him. Tanek knew that as spiritual leader of the Varden faith, he had certain traditions to uphold, and cold-blooded murder performed without a ceremonial blade and before the first hour of dawn would be a break with ceremony, and thus looked upon unfavorably by his people. If only he could say honestly that the killing would be an act of passion, a manifestation of ultimate rage, such matters would have no bearing. But such forward thinking nullified that possibility. No, this killing would be a testament to annoyance, and for that, there were protocols.

Tanek's gaze drifted from his advisor to the open window of his private chamber, wondering *where* he had put his knife and *when* the sea of stars in the night sky would be replaced by the blood-red hues of dawn.

Not soon enough, he decided, sighing inwardly and again fixing his attention on his advisor, Ezno Clyvans. The two men were alone in Tanek's chamber, a handful of guards posted outside the heavy door. Tanek was tall and brawny, two meters in height, with a thick mane of wild auburn hair, a beard so long it had been braided into two strands tossed behind his back and tied midway down his spine, brutish features, and a plethora of rippling muscles reflecting the amber glow of hastily lit candles in each corner of the room. He wore only a strip of dark cloth hastily tied about his waist that reached to just above his knees. Even so, Tanek held himself with power and pride, his spine ramrod straight, his chin raised imperiously. In a more superstitious age, he might, quite reasonably, have been considered a god.

Clyvans, on the other hand, might have been mistaken for a goat. Though he wore the many-colored robes of their order over his flabby form and carried the Scepter of Truth, he slouched and was constantly arranging his ill-kept, inky-black hair with pudgy, trembling fingers, trying and failing to the point of distraction to keep it from covering his forehead and obscuring his third eye.

The third eye was simply a genetic anomaly serving no practical purpose, yet those rare beings (often only one in a generation) bearing the mutation were invariably elevated to the role of advisor as per the prophecies of the Ancients.

Tanek had wanted, for quite some time, to see the sacred scrolls revised to eliminate that particular bit of business. Right at the moment, he was tempted to take care of the matter himself.

And why not? If what Tanek suspected was true, the war between the followers of the One True Faith and the heathen Nasnan was about to come to pass, and with it would come global annihilation.

If am I going to die, if we are all *going to die, should it not be with every fantasy fulfilled, every heartfelt desire sated?*

He could practically *taste* his advisor's blood. . . .

"Stop your blathering," Tanek said firmly, bringing

an immediate halt to his advisor's incessant chatter. "Let me see if I understand you correctly. After all, I am not highborn, I am simply a barbarian who seized his position by force of arms. I have none of your breeding, education, or culture. My mind is minuscule and unable to grasp greater concepts and greater truths, and I have all the sense of a rutting animal. Yet here I am, standing tall, while you are on your knees before me. Fate mocks us, yes?"

Tanek took cruel satisfaction in placing Clyvans in the impossible position of coming up with a response that would not entitle his superior to beat him to within an inch of his life. In point of fact, everything Tanek had said was true, or was, at least, the popularly, if silently held position of the highborn. Yet Tanek was brilliant, and knew more about his people, their needs, and the intricate inner workings of every facet of their society better than any other member of the Varden.

Clyvans stammered yes, no, and maybe in quick succession, then fell silent and closed his eyes, waiting for the blows to fall.

Smiling, Tanek instead retired to a chair beside his bed. "As I was saying, *if* I understand you correctly, the plans for the device that might have rid us of the Nasnan once and for all have been stolen. The only person who could replicate these plans lies dead in a chamber three stories below us in this keep, his throat cut ear to ear. All evidence points to a single suspect who has fled the keep. It seems to me our course is clear."

Clyvans nervously tapped his scepter, giving Tanek no choice, by the will of his people, but to listen. "Not *all* evidence points to a lone suspect. There are no witnesses. What this man might stand to gain is unclear. And he, ah . . . he seemed nice."

Tanek waited, crossing his huge arms over his barrel chest.

"Oh!" Clyvans cried, then tapped his scepter again.

"In any case," Tanek said, "we have one killer, who is also a thief, and, by all reports, a collaborator. Our course seems simple enough. Find the bastard before he can meet with Tirza Sirajaldin. Either take the plans from him or torture him into revealing where they've been hidden, then give him to me that I may amuse myself with his long, lingering death . . . an event I will choreograph with amazing creativity."

"Our best trackers have already been dispatched. The Elite will find him."

"Then *why* are you here, precisely?"

"I, ah . . . interpreted your likely response to this crisis."

Tanek rubbed his temple. His head was beginning to throb. *God's teeth, for just a ray of sunshine through that damnable window.*

"Anticipated," Tanek said. "You mean to say that you 'anticipated' my likely response."

"Exactly so. This man is an offworlder. Our people are interested in offworlders. To treat him as you might a member of the enlightened Varden who has fallen from grace or even a heathen Nasnan would not be advisable."

"Offworlders know the risks in coming here. Our planet may be beautiful and *interesting* to them as our culture is not like theirs, but once they step foot on the ground that is mine to hold sway over, once their vessels penetrate the atmosphere of our planet . . . there is no turning back for them."

"But we are talking about a Federation citizen, my liege. And, as I may remind you, the Federation recently extended an invitation—"

"A Federation . . . *citizen* . . ." Tanek whispered, his expression unchanging. "And that means what, exactly?"

"Well," Clyvans began, unaware at first that he was not being asked for his opinion and expertise. Tanek leaned forward and froze the smaller man with his powerful and vengeful gaze before the advisor could say another word.

"I just wonder," Tanek said with terrifying softness, "does his status as a Federation citizen make him a superior physical specimen of some kind?"

Still unsure of how to respond, or even whether or not he should, Clyvans panted, "Um, ah, that *alone,* no, I wouldn't think it—"

"Able, for example, to withstand multiple knife wounds without flinching? Amputations with an only slightly sharp surgical saw? A beheading, even, without it being a particular bother or inconvenience?"

"I would think not," Clyvans said, quivering at the images Tanek had ruthlessly placed in his own head. "No. But the political and social ramifications must be considered."

"Done and done," Tanek said coldly. "Now find this soon-to-be-screaming bag of flesh and *bring him to me!*"

Tanek watched with no little pleasure as Clyvans rose, spun, and practically tripped over his robes fleeing the chamber. In moments he was gone, and Tanek went to the window, surveying the city he made his home in these warm summer months. Though it was still the hours before dawn, the city was abuzz with activity. Merchants swarmed about the jagged spires in airships to deliver their wares, workers hurried through the winding streets to be at their jobs on time, lovers met with breathless anticipation or parted with sorrow and regret. Somewhere, at least one duel to the death was taking place over a matter of honor, perhaps because a show of anticipation was mistaken for anxiety and neither party would take responsibility. And elsewhere, a child was being born. The city, and thousands more like it upon this precious world, teemed with life.

If his people failed, if the Elite did not do their duty well and retrieve the plans, all life that did not serve the Nasnan would be eliminated. The buildings would remain, but the people, his people, would all be dead.

He'd lived through such crises before. He'd brought about resolution through peaceful negotiation or through relentless battle. Yet this time felt different. There was change in the air, and he could sense it.

It was the end of the world.

Again.

Perhaps this time, there would be no reprieves.

Ezno Clyvans scurried from the keep of his lord just as the first rays of sunlight burst upon the horizon. He carried two things with him. One was in his flowing robes, and he had to reach an elevated point, a clear field, to make it work. The other was in his head. It was knowledge, and that meant power, pain, and responsibility.

Ezno had hoped things would go better with Tanek. The man was *brilliant,* no question of that, but he was also very proud, and his righteous fury, once engaged, was almost impossible to disarm.

Thus, technically at the very least, Ezno was about to commit treason. In his heart he was true to the Varden faith, the order that also ran all government upon the planet Vrinda. Yet he was certain that Tanek would be the death of them all. He had to take extreme measures.

Twenty minutes later, Ezno stood atop the mound housing the Shrine to Unreason. He stole up through the spiral staircase, ten stories, twenty, his unique status having provided him sole and unlimited access to the tower. The sun was now peeking from between the clouds, the sky a furious meld of crimson and ochre.

He reached the rooftop only seconds before an airship cruised within firing distance and came to a stop, hovering menacingly.

"Advisor Clyvans!" roared a synthesized voice from the airship. *"Your duplicity has been uncovered. Recordings have been found of you speaking with the criminal* after *Menzala Trivere's killing. Keep your hands at your*

sides, turn, and proceed to the base of the tower, where you will be arrested."

Fear ripped through Ezno as the chilling realization came that he would die atop this shrine if he did not absolutely and immediately comply. Yet, his life, one life, compared to so many others . . .

His hands slid into the pockets of his robe.

"Advisor, please, do not force us to damage the shrine!"

Ezno almost smiled at that. *He* would be cut in half, but it was the shrine these soldiers worried about. Good—that was as it should be. There was hope for his people yet.

Hauling out the small device the offworlder had given him, Ezno raised it high, and struck the button to engage its transmission signal. He never heard or felt the bolt of blue-white lightning that took his life and seared a hole in that tower, causing its upper two levels to collapse.

Then all was silent . . . but for a receiving beacon in deep space that captured the transmitted signal and instantly forwarded it to Starfleet Headquarters.

CHAPTER 2

Carol Abramowitz stared out the viewport into the endless reaches of space, startled to hear the mad, shuddering clinking of ice cubes coming from the drink in her hand, an actual Napoleon Brandy. A few months ago—a lifetime ago—a Ferengi lieutenant named Nog had promised her this bottle in exchange for one of her recordings of Sinnravian *drad* music. Nog had come through a few weeks later, and Carol had put the bottle away, saving it for the right occasion. She was lucky to have been able to rescue it from the slag heap that her quarters had become in the turbulent atmosphere of the gas giant Galvan VI—the planet that had become the grave site for twenty-three of her crewmates.

Shifting her gaze from the flowing array of stars and suns, she focused on her hand and saw that it was shaking. There was no turbulence from the transport *Lionarti,* the only means of travel available to her at this late date. The ship was an old, ill-conditioned Belgarian freighter, true enough, but there were no external forces preying upon her, all the critical stresses she was experiencing were coming from somewhere deep within.

"Nice view, wouldn't you say?"

Carol whirled, the glass falling to the floor, shattering, the centuries-old alcoholic beverage splattering across the deck. A breathtakingly handsome raven-haired man stood before her. She drew in a sharp breath, momentarily backing away from her bout of nerves, now compounded by embarrassment. Looking closer at his angular face, she could see minor flaws, a slight asymmetry to his features, little scars, and eyes that were a shade lighter than perhaps they should have been.

"I'm sorry I startled you," he said, crouching quickly at the same moment as Carol, the two of them snagging old rags shoved against the interior bulkhead and gingerly picking up the broken pieces of glass.

"It wasn't you," Carol said, eyeing a nearby airlock and wishing she could just pop it open and let herself be blown into space rather than face any further humiliation. Her companion was well dressed and well groomed, a man who looked every bit as out of place on this junker as Carol herself. His tunic's design reminded her of something she had seen for sale on one of the pleasure planets whose brochures she went through before charting her current course, and she said as much.

He smiled, glancing down at the soft dark fabric of his tunic, his strong hand unconsciously tracing the thin white detailing. "You're right, that's exactly where I found this."

"Been to many of them?"

"No, that was my first. It was . . . interesting. But the lack of spontaneity surprised me. There was very little truth in it, if that makes any sense at all."

"It does." Carol felt herself flushing, and the heat rising within her now had very little to do with embarrassment. Soon they were on their feet, her unknown gentleman leading her from this overstuffed storage area to what the crew had laughingly called "the lounge." The only difference between the two areas was that this one lacked a viewport and the crates had been arranged in a semblance of furniture in an ancient living room: three for a couch, two for a love seat, a smaller one for a coffee table, and so on. The crew themselves were clustered in the aft deck, working on some repair or gambling, or perhaps even both. Carol had come to see that every moment she spent in space was a gamble, but where else might she feel at home?

The man smiled. "Ian," he said.

"Oh. Carol."

Sitting together on the couch, they shook hands, the contact electric and immediate, lingering far longer than necessary.

For the simple fact alone that he hadn't asked what was troubling her, she thought she could hug this man. How could you talk about the death of friends, the immediacy of grief, and the terrible dawning of one's own true mortality with someone you've only just met? That left her only the option of lying, a thing she despised.

Then again, maybe an old quote she had once read was indeed true, that confessing to strangers was easier somehow.

"Critical stresses," Carol said, biting her lip.

"Pardon?"

"That's what I was thinking about."

Ian surveyed their surroundings. "This ship may be old, but it's a war horse. No worries of it tearing itself apart."

I wasn't talking about the ship, she thought. And in that moment, something changed in his eyes. He seemed to get it without her having to speak a single word.

Sighing, Ian shook his head. "There is no order to the universe, only chaos."

"Pardon?"

"Well, if a beautiful and clearly extraordinary woman

like yourself can be so stressed, so burdened by hardships, how can this be anything but an age of unreason?"

She grinned at the play on words. They chatted for several hours, Carol revealing her position with the S.C.E. and recounting a few of their less harrowing recent adventures—avoiding Galvan VI altogether—while Ian said very little, his attention fixed solely on her. She did learn that he was a "quality inspector" for a major ten-world corporation, and that after she was dropped off on Caliph IX, he would continue on to a client meeting on Pacifica, some ten days off.

"So, a conference," Ian said.

"I know. What could be more boring than a hundred cultural specialists sitting around talking, giving lectures, handing out awards . . ."

Ian's brow furrowed. "Why do you do that? This is something you're excited about, isn't it?"

"Well, yes."

"Then why run it down like that? Why assume that someone who's interested in you would *not* be interested in what's important to you?"

Carol shrugged. "I guess I've just been in what a friend of mine would call 'negative space.'"

"I understand."

"To be honest, it's been *years* since I've been to one of these," Carol said, feeling herself perking up.

"Really? Why so long? Has work interfered?"

"No, not really. It's just . . . it's going to sound stupid."

"Carol."

"But it is." She hesitated. "There was a man. Martin Mansur. I thought he was a friend. It turned out he was a thief. He took my ideas and built a presentation around it that won him the highest honor possible among our professional association. Since then, he's bilked it to become famous on a thousand worlds."

"I always thought that guy looked like a fake."

"You know who I'm talking about?"

He nodded. "I've seen his holos. I wasn't impressed."

Ian leaned closer, his hand almost, but not quite, touching Carol's leg. "As I said, what impresses me is truth."

Carol slowly eased her leg upward, edging herself toward his hand. Would it be so terrible of her to simply indulge herself for once? To lose herself in a momentary fling, a bit of passion, just to have some time to forget all that had happened aboard the *U.S.S. da Vinci,* the fate of Duffy, McAllan, Barnak, and a score of others, the sorrow of the surviving crew . . . in point of fact, getting away from it all while the ship was being repaired was the entire point of booking this journey. That, and finally being able to attend a conference where Martin-the-thief wouldn't be around. He'd canceled at the last minute, leaving the way clear for Carol to take his place.

A figure appeared in the doorway. A scruffy young man with dull, tired eyes. One of the crew. "Carol Abramowitz? There's an urgent communication for you from a Montgomery Scott, I believe—"

Scotty, Carol thought. *Good lord. What happened now?*

"Why don't we pick this up later?" Ian suggested as Carol rose.

She hesitated. "I don't think there's going to be a later. Not for this."

And she was right.

CHAPTER 3

Before the day was out, the *Lionarti* had been met by a Federation runabout, and Carol was back on active duty, winging her way to the planet Vrinda, Bart Faulwell at her side. With the exception of a few polite words here and there, Carol had been silent for the entire trip. It wasn't until the runabout was approaching Vrinda's atmosphere that Bart spoke up.

"You're pouting," he said.

"I don't *pout*. It's not in my nature."

Bart smiled. "Concurrent sentences. I'm relieved that's actually possible."

Carol looked away. "I've been reading the mission briefing."

"No, you've been staring at a screen. And you've been pouting." Bart hesitated. Then, "Look, I was supposed to go to Starbase 92 to see Anthony. But, like Captain Gold says, when you wear the funny-looking A on your chest, you dance where they tell you, even if you'd rather be wallowing in grief. Heck, even Soloman's not quite himself over this. He's meeting us planetside, by the way."

"I'm fine," Carol insisted. "You know me. I've never been one to give in to my emotions. You know how uncomfortable I am around all that business."

Bart looked at her strangely.

"What?"

"The mission briefing," he said. "I think you should look at it again. And this time, you might consider actually reading it."

Carol was about to protest, but Bart was right, she *hadn't* really read it. So her gaze fell back to the screen, and this time, she read what was there.

"Oh," she said, growing a little pale.

"That's one way of putting it." Bart followed a series of automated commands from planetside and guided the runabout into the planet's atmosphere.

It was midnight when the runabout set down on a docking pad atop Farhan Tanek's keep. They were greeted by a dozen men, and half as many women, all wearing heavily padded leather armor with steel trim. Weapons that looked somewhat like ancient crossbows but pulsed with alternating green and amber energy were held at the ready. Each guard carried an identical and very recent scar, a single gash from forehead to chin, beginning above the right eye and ripping downward across the mouth.

A particularly brutish guard stepped forward and greeted them. "There is no joy, no sorrow, no pain so great that the heart cannot tolerate."

"I . . . grieve for fallen friends," Carol admitted, hesitantly.

"As do I," Bart said grimly.

The guard grunted. "The last off-worlder who followed our traditions so well revealed himself as a betrayer, a thief, and a murderer. He was of your *sect.*"

"A member of the Federation, you mean," Bart said softly.

"Blood calls for blood," the guard said gruffly. "I am Alhouan."

Carol and Bart introduced themselves and were told that Soloman was in a different quarter of the city, reviewing technical specifications for the job at hand. Alhouan led them down two stories and through the ancient stone keep. Seemingly incongruous bits of technology were scattered about: viewscreens, replicators, and more.

I feel like I'm in King Arthur's court, Carol mused, *if he'd been visited by aliens who liked to spread their tech around. . . .*

"We have not forgotten the souls of our ancestors," Alhouan said, gesturing down a darkened hall at the thick set of heavy wooden doors. "The traditions and beliefs of five thousand years are as healthy for us today as they were in times long ago. However, advances in science and new discoveries of the fabric of time and space are inevitable, and we are not above the use of a few conveniences. Does it anger you that we *primitives* have toys that are so advanced?"

Carol would not rise to the bait. According to the mission briefing, the entire Varden society was highly ritualized and based primarily on the myriad colors of emotion. It was for this reason she and Bart had been forced to reveal an emotional truth when greeting Alhouan.

"I see only splendor," Carol said without emotion. "A harkening back to what our people would consider a simpler time . . . only with a handful of improvements. I assume you have running water?"

Alhouan laughed and clasped Carol's shoulder. "Indeed. And you must try not to find yourself accidentally drowned in it." He pointed to the end of the corridor. "Identify yourselves to the guards before Lord Tanek's door. They will grant you access."

The guard, whose grip would leave a bruise, released the shaken Carol and stalked off in the opposite direction. Carol looked to Bart.

"I feel like we've been dropped into a lunatic asylum," he whispered.

"You don't hear me arguing the point."

Upon giving their names, they were led into Farhan Tanek's private chamber, a surprisingly sparse affair that also doubled as his bedchamber. Tanek wore armor similar to that of his guard, only his muscular arms were exposed and his vest offered a glimpse of his equally muscular chest, covered in ringlets of auburn hair. The man stood near a throne set beside an open window, moonlight bathing his regal, but very tired-looking form.

Tanek looked to the newcomers and dismissed his guards with a gesture. The door was closed and locked, sealing the off-worlders in with the burly man, whose eyes seemed to capture the moonlight and hold the power of the stars.

Carol raised her chin imperiously. It wasn't in her nature to be intimidated by the physical presence of another being. The sensation annoyed her terribly.

"You were the best they could send?" Tanek said darkly as he looked her up and down.

"I am eminently qualified," Carol said, flushing with anger despite her predilection for avoiding strong emotions. "I was under the impression the listing of my accomplishments had been forwarded to you. I have been told that you are without a permanent advisor. I wonder if the file wasn't simply misplaced or not read—"

"I *meant* that if these are the end days, as I believe they are, it might have done to have had a prettier face than yours to look upon."

Carol was stopped for a moment, unsure of how to respond. Was Tanek simply testing her? From the look in his eyes, she felt reasonably sure he was not, or, at least, that placing her in a crucible was not his primary objective, but instead, perhaps, an act that was second nature for him with any unknown quantity.

"You're not my type, either," Carol said flatly.

At this, Tanek returned his gaze to his visitor. He almost looked amused. "I think we may get along after all." He gestured to Bart. "And this one? Your slave? Your concubine—or would it be 'consort' in your culture?"

Always trying to get a rise, Carol noted. "Not hardly. As I'm sure you know, Bart is a top linguist. We have been assured his skills were necessary."

"'Necessity' may be too strong a word," Tanek offered. "To me, it suggests the possibility of success in your current endeavor. This is a notion I find dubious at best."

Carol shrugged. Tanek looked like a barbarian, all right, but his tongue was sharp, his mind agile and ever seeking openings for verbal onslaught or retaliation.

"We are here to help," Bart said. "Perhaps if you could tell us, in your words, what this is all about?"

Laughing, Tanek settled in his throne. "The seditionist did not explain all in the message he sent?"

Carol shook her head.

Tossing his head back, Tanek laughed a full five minutes, practically until he was hoarse, or on the brink of hysterics, tears forming in the corners of his eyes. Carol and Bart stood frozen, transfixed by the disturbing display.

"Then let me show you the problem. Much has changed for our people in a very short period of time," Tanek said, holding up his arm and displaying an ornate wristlet sparkling with jewels. "For example . . ."

Carol started as someone tapped her on the shoulder from behind. *That's impossible, we're alone in this chamber—*

The sight that greeted her as she spun was even more impossible. The figure behind her was Tanek. She looked back to the throne and saw that the ruler hadn't moved an inch. She looked back and forth several times. This was impossible. He was in two places at once!

"All right," Carol said. "Some kind of holo-technology—"

"Much more than that," Tanek said from his throne. "You, Faulwell. Come here and take my hand."

Bart did so.

"Real, yes? Flesh and blood?"

"Indeed."

Tanek did not release Bart's hand as he instructed Carol to try to touch his duplicate, who stood behind her. She reached out to the figure—and her hand passed through the second Tanek, as if he were a wraith.

"I don't—" she began, then "oofed" as the wraith suddenly became corporeal and shoved her back a few feet.

"Total control," Tanek said. "To touch, but not be touched."

Bart wrested his hand from Tanek's grip. "What are we looking at here?"

"This is a working prototype made from the plans your man stole from us, which we retrieved, but not quickly enough," Tanek said. "The technology in question has many possible uses. Some are benign. Others . . . quite deadly."

Carol gasped as Tanek's duplicate drew a knife and charged at her with a bloodcurdling war cry, vanishing an instant before his blade could cleave her heart.

"The mystics call it astral travel," Tanek explained. "The ability to send your soul or consciousness out of your body so that it might instantly travel to any place imaginable. Though many have claimed such a thing was possible, it was never quantified. Not until recently."

"So . . . this began as a way of spying on others," Carol said, still catching her breath.

"*Yesss,*" Tanek hissed, regret mixing with anger in his tone. "Then its uses as a means of assassination, even extermination, became evident."

"You can travel to any point of reference with this?" Bart asked, gesturing at the wristlet.

"Anywhere on this planet," Tanek said. "I won't tell you how this is possible. It has to do with the interconnectedness of all things, the manifestation of a being's force of will. What's important is that the astral self has always been viewed as an ethereal entity, unseen by others, unable to impact the physical world. This is better. With this, problems of every kind can be solved."

"You mean . . . mass killings. Penetrating any walls of defense—" Bart began.

"Problems of every kind, yes," Tanek replied curtly.

Carol crossed her arms over her chest. "I don't understand. I thought this was about forging an alliance between your faction and your enemies."

Tanek settled back and turned his gaze to the window. "Because of the interference of your Starfleet compatriot, the schematics for this device reached the hands of heretics at exactly the same moment they were returned to us. Our scientists, and theirs, have built working prototypes. There is a balance of power, which is not what I wanted when I commissioned research on this device. I wanted the Nasnan wiped out. Now . . . it seems I must find a way to reach an accord with them. This device could bring an end to all our people, and even if this technology can be nullified, and we have good reason to believe it can, we have seen that where one device of mass destruction can be created, so can another. Annihilation will come if things do not change; it is only a matter of time."

Suddenly, a figure appeared before Tanek. There were no telltale effects of a transporter beam, no warping of the physical world to allow the intrusion. The figure, who wore a shimmering, light-refracting garment from head to toe, lunged forward, plunging a ten-inch blade into the heart of Farhan Tanek.

CHAPTER 4

Carol and Bart had not been relieved of their phasers. Each had their weapons out and was calling for the guards as the assassin looked down at Farhan Tanek and drew back.

The blade had passed through Tanek and buried itself in the wooden backing of his throne.

"Fare you well, little wraith," Tanek said, touching his wristlet. The assassin screamed, and it was a man's voice, clearly, as his body was pulled this way and that, finally shattering like a mirror before dissolving away into the unseen world.

The guards who burst into the room leveled their weapons at Carol and Bart, but were quickly dismissed by Tanek. "A test of your alertness, nothing more," he told them. Shaken, the guards withdrew, once again sealing Bart and Carol into . . . an empty room?

"What is real, and what is illusion, have, by necessity, been placed on a need-to-know basis," Tanek said.

"Multiple projections. More than one doppelgänger," Bart said. "You're not real."

"Define reality." Tanek struck his chest, the blow created a resounding thud. "The flesh and blood from which I was first willed into reality is *elsewhere,* yes. But even in this form, I could cripple or kill either of you if you were to incur my rage. As to willing into existence more than one version of oneself, that is an accomplishment that only I, so far as I'm aware, have had the strength and discipline to accomplish."

"How did you get rid of the assassin?" Carol asked.

Tanek only smiled. "A short-range burst of the energies needed to nullify the weapon's power. This is how I know a planetwide null field is possible."

"This technology," Bart said, "it could bring about an age unlike any your world has ever seen."

Tanek rose and paced. "Ah, the less deadly uses, yes. It has been considered. Imagine a child is hurt in an accident, and only one physician in the world could save her. But he is occupied saving the life of another. With this technology, he could be in two places at once, performing two tasks at one time. The child would not die."

Carol was surprised to hear anything other than talk of blood and death from the man.

"Or imagine an end to acts of passion," Tanek said, his volume rising, the timbre of his voice becoming even more passionate, "murders which are, of course, perfectly legitimate and sanctioned provided the emotional state of all parties is properly aligned and the scrolls have decreed it a proper time for such an act. . . . Worthy individuals have passed from our annals because of being torn between their passion for more than one being. With this device, a man or woman could love and be loved by more than one at a given time, and how could there be jealousy, yes?"

I don't know about that, Carol thought. *But then, I know so little of these people. . . .*

Tanek stopped before Bart and Carol. "Your roles are quite simple, and, unfortunately, dictated by ancient prophecy. Your plaything here, this thin little male, is to help us decipher one section of the prototype's plans that will allow the construction of a null field, rendering this device useless to all. Your Soloman will help configure that device. And you, Abramowitz, will assist in the ritual of Unity, in which the Varden and the heathen Nasnan will put aside their differences and at long last become one."

"What about the prisoner?" Carol asked. "His name was not given in my report, but he is a Federation citizen, and his release—"

"That is negotiable only if it can be proven that he is not a murderer. Otherwise, he is subject to our laws and punishments. If your Federation attempts to interfere or intervene, there will be war between Vrinda and all your allied races."

"Then . . . who is working to prove his innocence?"

Tanek stared at her blankly.

"Who defends this man, who seeks to uncover the truth?"

He merely frowned. "I'm afraid I don't follow. His fate is in his own hands. He does not show remorse. He does not show elation at the kill. This makes him a Hollow, a killer without a soul. As of this moment, his guilt is proven in our eyes. He does nothing to defend himself. Why should that burden be placed on us?"

"You were about to commit genocide. He stopped you."

Tanek continued to stare uncomprehendingly. "What of it?"

"Their passions run wild, they're more animal than human, their ritualization, the foundations of their culture, is based on madness." Carol stared down at the ugly mess she had been served as a late dinner. Bart sat across from her in a huge, empty room that looked like a mead hall of ancient Vikings.

Bart looked equally displeased with the stew of guts and other unmentionables bubbling before him. "Their species has achieved warp drive, but it seems more for the purpose of conquest and colonization than peaceful exploration and the expanding of cultural and intellectual horizons. Yet there is something here, something about them, that offers a promise that they might embrace reason, they might ascend beyond their aggressive mind-set, just as humankind and so many other races did long ago."

"There's more to this. So much more than has been revealed."

"I agree. The identity of the prisoner, for one. Why would Starfleet keep it a secret from us?"

Carol set down her ladle. "I don't know." She rose from the table. "But now seems as good a time as any to find out."

"What about this ceremony? You are to officiate, yet—"

"It can wait," Carol said, storming away.

"Carol, it's this time tomorrow!"

She slammed at the wooden doors to get the attention of the guards posted on the other side. "Then by this time tomorrow, I'll be ready."

It took until dawn for Carol to negotiate an audience with the prisoner. By the time she was taken to his antiseptic steel chamber eight floors beneath the keep, she had come to wonder if she had somehow passed from one state of reality to another. The design of this underground prison was patterned after one used on a dozen warworlds, and there was no trace of "medievalism" to it. Every cell on this, the lowest level, was empty, save one.

A man sat in the bright recesses of the cell. Tall, dark-haired, haggard, but possessed of a sly smile and a near-boundless reserve of contempt.

Martin Mansur. Her hated rival.

"What took you?" he asked.

The guards left her with him, an invisible wall of energy separating them.

"So," Carol said, "it's a question of scandal."

Martin's smile was as smug as ever. "Even you can't think things are that simple and straightforward. Not after being around these people for any length of time."

"You're an important symbol for Starfleet. So far as most people are concerned, you teach independence, existence without self-limitations. You and I know better, but that's not the point. So what are you doing here, anyway?"

Martin eased himself back against the wall of his cell. It was lit by some inner fire, just like the floors and ceiling. His clothing was white, pure, just like the sheets on his cot and the waste disposal device set discreetly in the corner.

He laughed, taking in her discomfort. "Why am I here? Um—because I got caught?"

"You know what I mean. Why did you come to Vrinda in the first place?"

"Well, you know what they say. You're only as good as your last big triumph." His smile faded, but only a little. "It's been some time for me. I have competition. I'm not about to retire, not at my age—"

"So you were out to prove something," Carol said.

"Again, things are not so simple."

"A man is dead," Carol said. "Did you kill him?"

Martin said nothing. His expression didn't change. He was too well versed in neurolinguistics to reveal himself in any way through conventional body language. There would be no looking to the left when he was lying or looking to the right when he was telling the truth. No concealing of his thumbs to indicate he was concealing other information. None of the thousand "tells" that she knew so well, which also made her a lousy choice for a poker-playing partner . . . and a cynic when it came to human nature.

"All right, I'll ask another question. Why disrupt the

natural order of a world that isn't even Federation aligned?"

"Why? That's simple enough. If your skills were as sharp as you say they are, there would be no need for explanation from me."

Carol barely had to think twice about it. "This is all about your standing in the community. Your fame. That's all you think about."

"Oh, but you *do* go on. The question is, are we really so different? Is the life you have the one you really wanted, or just your way of dealing with disappointment, of trying to be someone, anyone, rather than owning up to your failures."

"You mean when I trusted you."

"Exactly. Look at the basis of the work you claim I took from you: Trust no one, depend on no one, but yourself."

"Yet here you are, depending on me."

"No. Here I am, knowing full well that you will follow the dictates of your nature—that you are weak. You were afraid to go forward with your findings. Left up to you, they would have sat in a drawer all these years. Even now, you don't have the courage to own your own mistakes. You have to have a 'bad guy.' Your weakness is your enemy."

"Maybe I was wrong in what I believed," Carol said.

Martin gestured expansively. "Maybe you were. I never said I agreed or disagreed with your notions, only that I felt they had merit. In other words, profitability. A universal enough statement that those in need of a moral compass, those, like you, who are weak, would seize upon *in droves*. And in that, I was correct."

Carol nearly staggered under the weight of the sudden realization that struck her hard and fast. "You don't care if these people go to war. You don't care if they all die."

"I 'care,' as you put it, in terms of how it will affect

me. This prison is proof from the weapon they've created. None of the ghosts can enter here. And if they employ any of the conventional weapons they already possess in mass quantities, I'll also be safe from the blast and radioactive side effects."

"But you'll starve."

"Not at all. I could leave this cell and get to the mess any time I wish."

Carol didn't bother to ask how this was possible. "You knew they'd send me."

"I was counting on it. I knew that if I canceled my appearance at the conference, you would be en route there when this situation turned critical. That would make you the only likely choice."

Carol's anger was boiling over. *"Why?"*

"It's a win-win for me. If you succeed and help this ceremony of joining to go off without a hitch, if the null-field device is installed, and so on, I will be given a slap on the wrist by Starfleet for my actions, but lauded publicly as the savior of this world. If you fail, you'll die, everyone dies, but me. I lose nothing either way. I only stand to gain."

"I could kill you myself," Carol murmured. Even as she spoke, she was shocked that such a thought would cross her mind, let alone leave her lips. Hadn't she seen enough death on Galvan VI?

Again, Martin smiled. He had goaded her well. "You could. But you won't. Too weak. Now, if you will excuse me, I have a paper I'm writing in my head, and I really must keep on schedule."

With that, he sat on his cot, closed his eyes, and tuned her out.

CHAPTER 5

"I've been in touch with Starfleet," Bart said. He walked with Carol through an elegant hedge maze in the keep's enormous central courtyard. A trio of guards—two women, plus the bulky Alhouan—trailed at a respectful distance. An hour had passed since Carol's visit with the prisoner. "By this evening, the *Sugihara* will be standing by to beam us out of here if we raise the alarm."

Carol frowned. "And Martin?"

"The hope is for a diplomatic solution to secure his release, obviously. But if he is indeed guilty of this murder, things become a bit murky. The Federation doesn't have any jurisdiction here. Even if we decided to throw protocol out the window, scans from previous vessels show that a transporter beam can't penetrate to the underground level where he's being kept, and sending in an extraction team could touch off an incident that would be . . . unfortunate. Particularly with these people being in possession of a technology that absolutely baffles the top minds in S.C.E."

"You transmitted the schematics?"

"No, I simply described what the device can do. Martin

had the chance to do so but elected not to. I suppose he had his reasons."

"He always does." She shuddered. "Have they shown you the plans?"

"Only passages that have been copied from the original. Menzala Trivere was a genius on every possible level. His linguistic encryptions are among the best I've ever seen, and that was nothing but a sideline to him. Still, I've already cracked some of the code, and I'll have the rest in time, I'm sure."

"Is the *Sugihara* going to be able to back us up on-planet?"

Bart shook his head. "Again, this is a delicate situation. Farhan Tanek authorized the intercession of three outsiders, and he has made it clear there will be no more."

"Their scrolls . . . They must have a library here. I'll need to see it."

"I doubt they'll allow that. They've been bringing items to me, and to Soloman, on a need-to-know basis."

Carol hugged herself. "Then I'll tell them, what I need to know is all of it."

"I think you would have to put on quite a display to get anything accomplished in this place. And there are other concerns . . ."

"Assassins who can pop up anywhere, anytime? We can't touch them, but they can hack us up into bits?"

Bart swallowed. "Right. Yes. That. Not so graphic, though, the way I would have phrased it."

"We should each have one of those devices Tanek was wearing."

"I've already suggested it to Soloman. He'll do what he can."

They navigated the remainder of the maze in silence. Every now and then, they passed laughing couples on benches, groundskeepers, or small gatherings of guards.

Any of them, Carol thought, *any* one *of them could be a killer. Any one of them might be real . . . or an illusion.*

Tanek, what were you thinking when you approved the development of this technology? We can, therefore we should? I can wipe out my enemies? Then what?

What about your new enemies, your new rivals? How can you hope to control or contain a thing like this?

It was madness. As Ian had so perfectly prophesied, a true age of unreason.

Three hours later, Carol was hunched over the small table in her quarters, reading one of the scrolls that had been approved for her viewing. This was insane. She couldn't possibly learn all that she needed to know in the narrow margin of time allotted to her. Did Tanek want her to fail? His paranoia would destroy them all. . . .

Or she could go see Martin. He had been on this world for well over a month. She had questions and he could certainly provide the answers. But could he be trusted? Naturally not. It might amuse him to give her some measure of truth mixed with just the right amount of lies to make her falter at a crucial moment in the ceremony.

Did he really care so little about the lives of others that he might do such a thing? Or was she allowing her own emotions, her feelings about what he had done to her, how he had broken their trust, to command her?

Rubbing her eyes, she leaned back and wondered if that might be the case.

"Excuse me," said a rumbling voice.

"Gah!" Carol shouted, nearly falling out of her chair. Alhouan stood before her. Or did he? Was he real, or a projection? She hadn't heard him come in.

"I need to talk to you," the guard said.

Carol nodded slowly. "Ah . . . there's a custom on my world. In the part that I'm from. We shake hands *every* time we see each other. A little odd, I know . . ."

"You want to be sure I'm not a phantom. I would,

too, given the circumstances." He held his hand and she shook it. His grip was firm. Carol felt her body relax, then immediately tense up again as she remembered the doppelgänger sitting upon Tanek's throne, and how he had been solid to the touch when he willed it. This was no test at all.

Maddening.

"You are doing nothing to learn the truth about the killing," Alhouan said.

That startled her. "I thought you and Tanek and all the rest had already decided what was true."

"No matter. The man being held is one of your sect. For that reason alone, his welfare should concern you."

"I don't have the time to play detective, all right? It's out of my realm of expertise. After tonight, if all goes well, I'm sure Tanek will allow Federation investigators to come and examine the evidence and attempt to build a defense, if one is warranted."

"Not so. There will be an accident tonight. When you are at the ceremony, the accused will meet with misfortune. It has been decreed."

Carol stepped away from the table. "By Tanek? By—what do you call them? The highborn? Your council?"

"It has been decreed, and it will be done. Unless the truth is uncovered in time."

"And what if the truth is that Martin killed that man?"

Alhouan was rock steady, and his silence filled the room with a fiery fury. His upper lip twitched and he said, "Blood calls to blood. And 'that man'? He was my friend. If the betrayer below did not kill him, then the guilty party will be able to rest easy after tonight. Unless something is done."

"So tell other people. You can't just leave this in my hands."

Alhouan's gaze narrowed. "Everyone else *knows.*"

Carol stared as the man turned his back and left her chamber.

How could she stop this? How could she possibly play her part in the evening's events, while also preventing Martin's murder. Was she supposed to be in two places at once?

Then it came to her: Perhaps that was *exactly* what she would have to do.

Carol entered the wide, opulent throne room where Tirza Sirajaldin paced like a caged, mad animal. The man was wiry, his head shaved and littered with tattoos, and he wore a scarlet robe with strips of deep blue in the form of lightning bolts. Jade jewelry adorned his flitting form: rings, bracelets, even a gleaming headband. His boots scraped along the stone floor and he held a golden goblet in his hand.

"They seek to mock me," Sirajaldin said.

"Sir, my name is—"

"I know who you are. The pawn."

Carol's ire rose at that one, but she held her composure.

"They keep me here, in the seat of power of my enemy, as if to rub my nose in what I may see, but never have."

"Then power's all you're after, too?" Carol asked. "As leader of the Nasnan, I would have thought your position somewhat different, at least based on what I've read."

"Even this goblet is Tanek's!" Sirajaldin screamed, hurling it across the room, shattering a glass statue. Carol found herself reminded of the glass of brandy she broke on the *Lionarti*.

Sirajaldin stood before an open window, golden sunlight streaming in, clutching at his form with its searing fingers. Finally, he hung his head. "Power is not what I want. *Control* is what I'm after. The right to live my life as I choose."

"Isn't that what tonight's ceremony is all about? A

peaceful accord between former enemies? Freedom to live as you wish?" Carol crossed her hands behind her back. "Or am I not the only pawn in this game?"

Sirajaldin faced her. "Ah. The enemy of my enemy must be my friend. So that's what this is. No, I wouldn't count on any such thing if I were you." He nodded at the rafters. "They are listening, you know. Watching and waiting. Devices so small, one couldn't possibly see them with the naked eye."

"Then they already know who killed the scientist."

Sirajaldin shook his head. "They know all save what is in your heart and mind, and that is what maddens them. *That* is why they manipulate, that is why they ritualize emotion. What they seek is truth, and to them, the only truth is what you feel."

"You didn't answer my question."

"He was intelligent enough to evade their devices. In point of truth, he may have designed many of them. There are no records of what went on in that chamber. All that is known from surveillance in the hall is that Martin Mansur entered the chamber, fled shortly thereafter with the schematics, and delivered a communications device to Tanek's advisor."

"I've seen no advisor."

"His advice wasn't taken well, it seems. He met with an accident. Note the tower in the distance," he said, pointing at a ruin on a hill. "It accidentally had its upper levels blasted off by one of Tanek's ships. It just doesn't pay to be a stationary object on some planets, I suppose. Oh, and the advisor was standing on the roof at the time, I should have mentioned that."

"I want to talk to you about the device."

Sirajaldin laughed. "This weapon of theirs. Imagine what it must be like to divide yourself, to be in more than one place at one time. One would have to be mad to imagine actually doing such a thing, madder still to master the skill."

"You can do it. You're not really here."

Sirajaldin stopped. "Pardon?"

"It took me a little while to see the tells," Carol said. "Look down. Sometimes you cast a shadow, like when you threw that goblet. Sometimes . . . most times . . . not."

"If I'm mad, it's because they made me this way."

"No doubt."

Sirajaldin frowned. "What is it you want, anyway?"

Carol smiled for the first time that day. "To go a little mad myself."

CHAPTER 6

The device fit firmly on Carol's wrist. Sirajaldin had refused to meet Carol in the flesh, and she was beginning to think his paranoia justified. However, he had led her to a chamber in which another of the weapons could be found.

Thinking makes it so, Sirajaldin told her. *It may also drive you mad. . . .*

The contraption on her wrist was slightly more complicated than Sirajaldin had let on, but although she was no technical adept like Soloman or the various tech heads on the *da Vinci,* she quickly deduced what each control might allow her to do. It was all a matter of degrees. In the first stage of "removal"—as Sirajaldin had called it—one might travel outside his or her body with no awareness of the corporeal form that was left behind. Traditional "astral travel."

She touched the control and felt as if she were taking a nap. The sensation wasn't jarring in the least, which surprised her.

Seductive little thing, aren't you? she thought as she thought of the hall outside—and suddenly found herself whisked through solid matter, into that other space.

"Yow!" she hollered, despite herself.

The sensation, admittedly, had been a rush. So long as she could think of this body, this new body of hers, able to pass through walls, able to be seen or not seen depending upon her will, as her one true form, she would be all right.

But just thinking *that* had made her visualize her true body back in her chamber, open-eyed and staring at nothing—and suddenly she was seeing through two sets of eyes, her mind processing more images, more tactile sensations, more thoughts, than she could possibly handle. She almost screamed—

And it was over. She was back in her room. Back in her body. Simple as that. For a moment she had feared that a return to her true form would not be possible, that she would grow confused as to which form was which. . . .

That she would, indeed, go mad.

Steeling herself, she tried again. This time, her second form made it down the corridor and even passed through a couple of walls, breezing past guards who had no clue she was anywhere nearby, before her anxiety once again mounted and she recalled herself to her primary form.

Mastering the skill of being a ghost took much less time than she expected. Then she set to work on duplicating herself. In other words, maintaining control of both forms at once, multitasking, studying the scrolls and learning what she could in preparation for the ceremony with one body, while traveling, listening to conversations, processing information with another.

The whole thing became second nature to her so quickly that she wondered what she had feared. There was a sense of freedom, of empowerment, that went along with this business that was greater than anything she had ever experienced before. Why had she been so afraid?

Remember, they know you're doing this. They want this.

You have to figure out why. . . .

She found Bart working hard in his chamber on the translation. He was surprised to see her, but he didn't realize that she was just a projection; the device on her wrist was hidden under the billowing sleeves of the long ceremonial robe given to her for tonight's service. Soloman sat beside him. They exchanged greetings, then Bart filled her in on their progress.

"We're having to extrapolate some," Bart said wearily as he shoved the scrolls away. "Fill in blanks. It's the only way we'll have any chance at all of activating the null field in time."

"I bet you could use two of you right now," Carol said, smiling inwardly.

Bart bit his lip. "Hmmm . . . I don't know. I worry about the side effects of the device, even if I had one to wear. I think Tanek is right in having this null-field generator employed."

A sudden rush of anger coursed through Carol. She had no idea why Bart's words had struck her so disagreeably, but she suddenly wanted to be elsewhere. She flickered in and out of existence for an instant—fortunately at the exact moment when her comrades were looking to the window, distracted by the sound of laughter outside—then controlled herself once more.

Side effects? Ridiculous. The only side effect she had felt was the confidence brought about by finally having some control over circumstances. Even as she stood here, information was flowing into her mind . . . her other mind . . . her true mind. Or was this her true mind . . . ?

Enough, she commanded, banishing the chaotic flow of thoughts.

"Will you be ready by tonight?" she asked.

"Absolutely," Bart said.

Nodding, Carol turned and left the chamber. The guards outside snickered as she passed, one of them raising his wrist and flicking his own device in her way. She shrank from him, remembering how Tanek had destroyed the doppelgänger assassin in his quarters.

No, not Tanek. Another ghost . . .

They know . . .

Walking down the corridor, she wondered why she hadn't told Bart what she had learned from the guard about Martin's upcoming accident, and that she had secured a device herself. It was curious that she would keep such things to herself. Against her better judgment, against her nature . . .

But what need did he have to know? She would resolve all of this by herself. She would find the answers.

She even knew right where to look.

Gaining access to the dead man's chamber turned out to be a simple matter; what surprised her was that it had been cleaned out completely. Bared wires dangled from the ceiling and from otherwise cleverly disguised ports in the walls, all rugs and wall hangings had been removed (though she could tell from the accumulated dust in certain areas that such items had once been in evidence), and all furniture, files, and such were gone.

She heard laughter from just behind her, a kiss of shadows upon her neck. Startled, she whirled just in time to see another hooded figure—dressed identically to her—leaping through the wall overlooking the courtyard. Racing to the window, Carol peered out and saw *nothing*. The robed and hooded figure had vanished before hitting the ground.

A ghost. Another ghost!

What would happen if they met? If they fought?

She wanted it. She wanted to *know*.

Stepping back, she gained some distance on the window and *leaped* through the wall. She laughed as the cobblestones launched themselves up at her, exalted in the thrill of executing the impossible and knowing full well she could survive it, survive anything . . .

It was like being a god.

"Someone's had enough, I'd say," someone whispered behind her. "I wonder if she'll even feel it."

Carol's mind was suddenly overturned. She was plummeting to the ground. In a second she would strike, yet not die. How could anyone be behind her?

Then she understood. The voice hadn't been heard by *this* body, it was her true form that was being threatened, her frail prison of flesh that was about to be attacked.

Withdrawing instantly, she found herself back in her chamber, launching herself away from her desk as a crackling energy blade soared down at her, slicing into the billowing hood she wore, but missing her head completely. There was a crackle and a *thunk* as a very solid blade buried itself in the desk. Her phaser was in her hand, aimed and ready to fire as she turned to face her assailants.

A boot kicked the weapon from her hand and a fist struck her in the mouth, the pain sending her reeling. All she glimpsed was the hooded figure—*her doppelgänger, was that possible? It wasn't, yet—*

And someone else's leg swept under hers, tripping her, sending her smashing onto the floor, her back and skull ringing with pain as she smacked down hard. She wasn't trained to be a warrior, didn't have the savage will, even, of these barbaric, mad people. That was what Corsi and her security people were for. But she wouldn't die here, not here, not like this, not with that bastard Martin smirking at her from his cell down below, not with the lives of so many depending on her.

The energy blade was back in the hand of the first hooded assassin. There were two, she now saw, both with shadowed faces, both dressed identically to her. Yet the shimmering material worn by the killer who went after Tanek could be glimpsed from beneath the robes. Were these ghosts? Flesh?

Did it matter?

Carol's left hand went to the device on her wrist. All she knew was rage: an almost divine fury at the idea of losing control now that it had been granted to her, of losing in any way, of causing grief to others . . .

Then they appeared. Two more doppelgängers. Another four behind them. Six in all. She could see through each of their eyes. Move through each of their forms. The sensory overload was staggering.

She didn't care. Her doubles descended upon the intruders, pounding, kicking, breaking chairs upon them. One laughed, scooping up her phaser. Her—its finger twitched as she aimed at the killers hunched nearby—

"No," all seven of her forms said at once as she realized what she had almost been tricked into doing: The phaser's line of fire was directed toward the intruders, and beyond them, to her own sprawled, corporeal, original form. If these were ghosts, and she now thought they were, the blast would pass right through them and she would kill only herself. Instead, she activated the disruption signal Sirajaldin had pointed out to her, and grinned with savage delight as the intruder ghosts were shattered like screaming glass.

She looked to the ceiling, to the recording devices she could not see, but knew were there somewhere. *You can see,* she thought. *Watching. However many of you there are. Whoever you are.*

Like what you've seen? Have I done as you've expected?

Carol considered trying to find them. It would be fun seeking out the avatars of insanity, the nameless, faceless gameplayers who were driving her so desperately to the brink. And when she found them . . .

When she did . . .

No! This isn't me. Not me.

Then who?

Struggling to regain control, she looked to her wrist and felt the gnawing, hungry weight of the device strapped to her. With it, anything was possible. Reality was just a silly word, nothing more.

In that moment, it all came together in her mind. She knew what had happened. *All* that had happened—and why.

All that was left now was to stop it before this world was plunged into a greater sea of madness and destruction than even she had dared to contemplate.

CHAPTER 7

Night had fallen, the tapestry of stars spread wide over the horizon. Carol stood upon an ornate stage erected near the newly restored tower where Tanek's advisor had met his fate. She was surrounded by thousands of onlookers, including two dozen of the so-called high-born, as well as Tanek and Sirajaldin. Bart and Soloman were high above, on the tower's rooftop, the machine they had been working on all day rising next to them, reaching another ten feet into the air. The machine was an uncomplicated affair from the look of it, bearing the shape of a trident with curling talons.

Carol had never been so terrified in her life. Oh, she *knew* the *Sugihara* was in orbit around this world, and that she could be beamed out at a second's notice . . . but she also knew Tanek and all his insane compatriots must also have that information. That meant they could have made arrangements to block any transporter beams, any communications.

She was on her own, and that likely meant she would die on this mad world. And for what? A people she didn't understand, a race she cared nothing about, beings whose beliefs brought nothing to the surface within her except contempt? Loathing?

Who am I angry at? she wondered. *These people, for being true to their own nature, or myself, because I see all my own weakness mirrored in their acts?*

Soon, Martin would have his little "accident." Time was running out. She gazed upon the sea of distrustful faces that made up her audience. They looked at her with unabashed hatred. An outsider should not be here, no matter what the scrolls said. That was what their expressions suggested to her.

That . . . and a desire for annihilation before accepting the beliefs of others. Yet they were followers. Two men controlled the masses, and both needed to be called to the stage.

She tapped the Scepter of Truth twice, and Tanek and Sirajaldin approached.

"I face my fears," she said, her voice quivering slightly. "I face them openly and honestly, and I share with you my terror."

Her heart raced and she pictured Kieran Duffy, wondering what thoughts went through his mind in those final moments, and how he found the strength to do what had to be done.

Love. For him, it had been love, she decided. The face of another was before him.

For her, only Martin's face came to mind. As Tanek and Sirajaldin approached, then bowed before her, Carol felt only hatred. "I wear my emotions like this cloak. Its colors are many, its shading varied. I have forgotten the souls of my ancestors. I am enraged because I see the faults of myself reflected in all of you, and rather than direct that anger inward, I find myself loathing each of you. Since coming here, I have let myself be ruled by emotions, and while that is strength for all of you, for me, that is weakness."

A roar of outrage came from the assemblage, but Tanek and Sirajaldin turned at the same moment, raising their hands for silence, and the crowd acquiesced.

"Our traditions center on truth," Tanek said. "And she speaks truth. We don't have to like what she says, but we must respect it."

"I mourn for lost comrades," Carol said, moving forward and nodding to Tanek and Sirajaldin. "And I mourn for all of you. Because the truth—"

Carol yelped as something unseen struck her leg. She tripped and fell, a collective gasp rising up from the audience. She had never stood before so many people in her life, and right now, she wasn't standing at all. Sprawled at the feet of the dissident leader Tirza Sirajaldin, a man she had never truly met in the flesh until this moment, Carol considered the device on her wrist.

A ghost was up here with her, a ghost that could take corporeal form but still be unseen.

It's evolving, she thought. The technology, its uses are becoming even more frightening.

She could warn the others. A part of her felt she must.

Yet . . . something was not right.

Helped to her feet by Sirajaldin, she continued the ritual. "Unburden yourselves," she commanded. "Free yourself of your hatred for one another in the only way both your factions will recognize." She lowered the staff. "Touch this relic, sacred to both your orders, and tell if your intentions toward peace are true or false."

It's here, she thought, feeling the breath of the invisible intruder upon her neck, nearing a snicker as it darted from one side of her to another, then vanished. *It might kill me. Kill either of them. Set off a riot, touch off a war.*

Or is it in my mind? Has all this put me over the edge?

Tanek went first. The brawny barbarian clutched the staff. "I believe the teachings of the Ancients should be upheld. Blood calls to blood. But a world at war because of a division of beliefs, while appealing on many levels to me, is not what is best for my people. I ordered the creation of the device we have come to nullify today in order to kill Sirajaldin and all his people. That is no longer an option. We must live together, if we are to live at all."

Carol nodded. According to tradition, the staff would splinter and break if either man lied. She could see no physical reason why that should happen, but there was much more to the physical world, at least so far as this planet went, than she had ever dreamed possible, and so she considered it might be true. Or that the ghost might make an attempt, not on the men, but on the staff.

And she was prepared.

Sirajaldin grasped the staff. "I have never wished for genocide. Only control over my own destiny. That is a gift I would share with my people. This accord is true."

Carol drew back as both men released the staff and tapped it twice. She was about to speak, when the ghost slipped its hands on her from behind, the cold edge of an invisible blade pressing against her throat.

"Say anything other than the words from the sacred texts and I will slit your throat," the ghost whispered. "I saw your eyes. I know you have a sense of what's happening here. Speak anything but what you were brought here to say and you will be silenced."

Carol said nothing. Instead, she willed herself away, releasing hold of this doppelgänger form, drawing back into her true body, buried deep in the crowd.

"What?" shouted the invisible assassin upon the stage.

Tanek whirled—and disrupted the ghost's essence, his own device turning it visible as it shattered the wraith like an ancient mirror.

The scepter dropped to the stage, bouncing once upon the wood floor, and then Carol was back, grasping it, startling all who had gathered here, even her friends high above.

"It doesn't kill the original, does it?" she asked. "It only makes it difficult for that person to gather his wits and his will again for some time."

"Yes," Tanek said. "That is true."

"You have *all* been deceived," Carol said. "And you have all willingly participated in that deception."

"Madness," Sirajaldin said.

"That's right. And we live in an age of unreason."

Carol had known that it was far more than a coincidence that attempts had been made on her life, but none on Bart and Soloman. She had been the one wearing the device. She had been the one to leap forward into the same madness engulfing so many of these people.

And her would-be assassins . . . how serious were they? If someone had actually wanted her dead, there were cleaner and more efficient ways of going about it, particularly considering they had access to the same technology that was practically branded to her wrist.

That was how it felt now. A part of her, a thing that had been seared into her flesh, her soul, a mark upon her sanity.

She aimed the scepter at Bart and Soloman. "It was all a trick. Menzala Trivere couldn't transform all his theories into reality on his own. He needed our help."

"With what?" Bart called.

"You haven't created a null field at all. This is a mass amplification module. It will make the power available to any and all on this planet . . . possibly even beyond.

"Power for its own sake."

"What are you accusing us of?" Tanek demanded.

"She's simply stating truth," came the voice of Alhouan, who dragged the chained form of Martin Mansur with him through the crowd.

Carol said, "This was about potential. It never had anything to do with your planet joining the Federation. The man behind this wanted to know what we might do with your technology. If we could be stronger with it than yourselves."

"The murderer," Tanek breathed.

"He's not," Carol said. "Because there was no murder."

Alhouan stopped before the stage, removing a small projection device from his pocket. "See for yourself."

A screen rippled into existence behind Tanek and Sirajaldin. Images with specific dates and times played. Carol looked at the footage of the scientist entering and leaving his chamber, all that could be found after she had appeared to Alhouan and communicated all she could to him by covering her hands from view and tracing ceremonial symbols upon his arm to secretly pass along her suspicions.

"The man you see before you was my friend, or so I believed," Alhouan said. "And no one killed him. He had all that he needed in his private chamber to assemble his own working prototype weeks ago, and that is what he did. View the holos yourself. Seventeen days ago, he entered his chamber at night, left it in the morning . . . then left it again in the afternoon. The corpse we found was a duplicate, one he maintained until ritual cremation."

"The device already existed?" Martin said, his eyes wide with fury. "I was manipulated?"

"We had no knowledge of this," Tanek maintained. Sirajaldin agreed.

"Not consciously," Carol said, holding up her arm, exposing the device. "But you've felt it, haven't you? The lure of it. The power it offers."

"It's an addiction," Alhouan said. "One that drives its victim mad. We were all in it with him. All of us. But it seemed like sanity. It still does."

Someone in the crowd gasped as a figure fled from its ranks and burst into the tower. It was the scientist. The dead man.

He was desperate. Crazed.

Tanek's face flushed crimson. "You have no right to secrets," he hissed at Carol. "The ritual has been tainted. This union—"

Sirajaldin struck him, and suddenly, dozens of wraiths burst into existence all about them, the crowd multiplying, doubling, tripling in number with every beat of Carol's heart.

"The only thing you can't control is what is in my heart and mind," Carol said, touching the device on her wrist, willing her doppelgänger into existence beside the startled Bart and Soloman. It reached the device seconds before the lunatic scientist, who was still intent on seeing his will inflicted upon all on this planet.

Carol touched off the null field from her wristlet, causing the energies within the amplifier to overload. Crackling blue-white energies reached for them all, wiping the doppelgängers out of existence.

EPILOGUE

Tanek ordered them offworld immediately, of course. Although there were isolated bits of fighting here and there, the civil war on Vrinda never materialized. The people thought they wanted mass destruction, chaos, bloodshed; what they truly wanted was the power of the device. Without that, without its addictive abilities to re-create oneself, the desire had been lessened.

Martin was in the *Sugihara*'s brig, and the first thing Carol noticed when she went to visit him was his mad eyes. His mind, upon taking in the possibilities of all she had experienced, the power and control she had possessed, then tossed away, had snapped. In his head, he was still planetside, living in a world in which he could be anywhere, everywhere at once, and even transform his appearance to be a dozen, a hundred, a thousand individuals at once. More than that, he could be idolized by countless admirers, and they could all be himself.

"Why would I leave? Why would I ever go?" Martin said, laughing and telling her she was again the failure . . . but now she knew differently.

"Fine, Martin . . . you *belong* here," she said.

"He had been right," Martin whispered. "Tanek. He

visited me. Tortured me. Said it was the end of the world. He was right. The end of the old world, the beginning of the new. And it is *glorious.*"

Martin was right, of course, but not the way he thought. Once, Carol might have taken pleasure in Martin's fall from grace, but now she just pitied him.

From there she went to the mess hall to find Bart and Soloman.

As she sat down to join them, Carol said, "I'd say their emotional honesty isn't all it's cracked up to be. In the end, they were just as self-deluded as the rest of us."

"Not all of us," Bart said, taking a sip from his coffee. "You wound up being the most emotionally honest person on Vrinda because you recognized the device for what it was."

Carol almost smiled. "Not something I've been accused of in the past."

Soloman added, "Now the people must go cold turkey—which is, I believe, the best way to recover from an addiction." He frowned. "I have never understood that phrase."

"Later," Bart said with a grin. "I think you should be proud of what you've done here, Carol. It may not be what Starfleet had hoped for in terms of the mission, but it's probably best for Vrinda in the long term." He gave her a look. "And maybe for you, too."

"Maybe."

"And best of all, we've got a week and a half left. It's not the vacation I was hoping for, but Captain Demitrijian is gonna be able to drop me off at Starbase 92."

This time, Carol's smile was genuine. "Good."

"I will be returning to McKinley Station," Soloman said, "to make sure the *da Vinci*'s new computer is up to standard."

"I'm sure it will be," Bart said.

"Up to *my* standard," Soloman amended.

Laughing, Bart turned to Carol. "What about you?"

"Oh, something will turn up," she said. She thought about an angular face framed by raven hair, and wondered how long it would take to get to Pacifica, and if it would leave enough time to get back to Earth in a week and a half. She really liked Ian, and it was about time she started being a bit more honest with herself—and her feelings.

BALANCE OF NATURE

Heather Jarman

CHAPTER 1

Fear consumed her, muting her voice, bleeding all color from her vision. P8 Blue clung to a railing as the mother-tree world trembled and heaved. In her mind, she cried out to her friend Zoeannah, encouraging her to hold on tight so she wouldn't fall, but her throat trapped the words. A shadow sliding past caught her eye. Instinctively, without thought to the danger, she released one limb, catching the duffel strap before the bag went shooting over the edge. *My legacy . . .*

Indifferent to the chaos, evening breezes wafted lazily through the open sides of the passageway, stirring fine splinters and dirt into blinding breath. Unwilling to release her grip to rub the dust out of her eyes, Pattie blinked rapidly, trying to clear her vision. She winced at the sharp pains caused by the scraping scratch of dirt trapped in her eye membranes. Letting go would be easy. To curl into her protective shell was her instinct, but doing so would certainly mean death. She gripped tighter with each drunken sway.

A flash of flame, a metallic buzz, and all lights within seeing distance were snuffed out. The inky silhouettes of the surrounding rain forest blurred in the deepening darkness. Flickering green power surges crackled angrily, offering only the stingiest light to see by. Even if they survived this quake—the first in her lifetime, the first in several Nasat lifetimes—Pattie worriedly wondered what damage the township had sustained: from cracked struts to bearing beams, delicately balanced between branches, collapsing as structural weight shifted, every possibility was an engineer's nightmare. *If I make it through, there'll be work to be done.*

The shaking stopped. Silence squeezed into the void left by the quake, swallowing all sound and filling the empty space.

The fleeting pause gave P8 Blue a moment to breathe. And another. She allowed herself to relax enough to consider more than survival. *Maybe it has passed,* she thought. Though poor lighting made seeing difficult, she pivoted her gaze to the side, still maintaining her tight grip on the railing. She listened for a groan, a sigh, a breath—any evidence that her companion had survived the quake. *If she's been injured . . .* Pattie clicked worriedly. *Zoeannah would have been home in her paddock if she hadn't met my transport. She would have been safer there with walls that surround and protect her.* She cursed whatever stupid shell architect had decided that leaving a few open-sided corridors contributed to the township's aesthetic. A misstep here would send one careening hundreds of meters through a tangle of vines, fungi, flowers, and animal nests into the understory layer, several kilometers below the township. *Zoeannah could have fallen. And what about Tarak? What will I say to him?* She shook off the troubling thoughts, knowing that guilt and worry could be paralyzing. If only she could reach the tricorder on her belt, she might be able to scan for Zoë's Betazoid lifesigns—

A tremor erupted, sending the mother-tree lurching from side to side. Each sway dislodged transport carts from the tracks and tossed carrypacks into the air like flotsam. Feeling a slight give in her grip, she strengthened her hold. Her fear-sharpened senses absorbed the sickening crunch of shells hurtling into kiosks, the acrid smoke rising from exploding consoles. Falling building debris hit those Nasat too startled to curl into defensive postures or maneuver out of the way.

She mustered up enough humor to be darkly amused by the placid computerized voice reciting an emergency message over the comm system, alternating between lingual clicks and Federation Standard. *"Please remain calm while Central Services examines the situation. Automated systems will be restored to full capacity as soon as possible. Thank you for your cooperation and have a nice dark cycle . . ."*

Startled by an ear-shattering crack, Pattie swiveled her gaze toward the forest. A severed tree limb plunged like a battering ram toward their corridor. A quick mental calculation placed impact within thirty seconds. *A breath and we'll be obliterated,* she thought. Time staggered, slowed.

Please be calm while you're being squashed flat. Resistance is futile . . . she thought, putting her own spin on the computerized message.

There has to be an escape route, she thought. A passageway, less than a hundred meters ahead, cut through the mother-tree core to an adjoining branch sector. Assuming they could reach the passageway without being thrown into the forest, they would be out of the path of the oncoming limb. As the tree deck beneath her convulsed, she nixed that idea. *Other options.* Heading back up the conveyor to the canopy-side transport station? Same problem. So P8, her friend Zoeannah, and others unlucky enough to have chosen this traveling route were effectively trapped. Nothing they could do would prevent the impending blow. With luck, they might survive impact.

After all she'd been through of late, Pattie had to believe in survival. She stared at the ton of devastation plunging toward them, growing closer, ever closer by the second, unable to look away.

A few more steps. We only need to make a few more steps. Galvan VI should have taken me. To end this way feels like an epilogue, she thought, amazed at fate's arbitrary whims. *Any second now it'll hit . . .*

The broken limb gained speed and momentum the closer it came. Undeterred by the back and forth swaying, the ridiculous message repeated. If Pattie could reach her phaser, she'd take out the comm system speaker without hesitation. There was something ignominious about facing death while a computer calmly insisted there was nothing to worry about. Breathing deeply, she braced for impact—

The quaking stopped.

With a jerk, the creaking mother-tree righted itself into a solidly vertical position.

The tree's abrupt shift counteracted the limb's momentum; a resounding thwack, a twitch, and it tumbled leadenly down through the surrounding tree layers.

No one moved or spoke.

Relief was slow in coming. Pattie waited. Watched.

The breeze tossed leaves with a silvery rustle. Branches bowed. Avian squawks echoed in the distance, punctuated by the whirr of furry *laito* monkeys swinging from vine to vine collecting a nocturnal snack of fruit and seeds.

Time elapsed.

Though it appeared that normalcy had been restored, Pattie sensed that no one—herself included—dared move, fearing the quake would resume. She was loath to be the first to risk it; she would wait.

The sound of limbs shuffling along the floor came from behind a tipped-over maintenance terminal. A panicked clicking from a Nasat looking for a missing friend followed. Rubble fell from the ceiling. Reinitiated conduits whined, gradually revving up until the familiar hum throbbed steadily. The computer message sped up to garble, then halted mid-sentence; a new message replaced the old one. *"Planetary science council has issued an all clear. No apparent seismic activity in the area. Repeat: no apparent seismic activity. The cause of the quake is unknown. Please return to your paddocks for safety lockdown and to receive up-to-date reports on township status."*

A fleshy humanoid hand touched her primary pincers.

Inhaling sharply, she closed her eyes, her limbs quivering with relief. *She's alive.* Pattie's respirations came quickly and irregularly as she at last allowed herself to process the emotions that she'd pushed aside since the quakes started. *We're alive.*

"Pattie"—Zoeannah coughed, involuntarily clutching tighter—"you all right?" Without letting go of Pattie's hand, she crawled up closer where they could talk face-to-face. Planting her elbow on the floor, she rested her chin in her palm. "Not like I would notice a dent or two in your shell in *this* light."

The warm weight of Zoë's hand comforted Pattie more than anything else could have. Gratitude filled her. *She's fine,* she thought, repeating the phrase over and over for reassurance. Pattie reciprocated the squeeze, touching her antennae to Zoë's forehead. "What about you? Are you hurt?" She twisted her head to get a better view. A piece of plating that had fallen on Zoë's lower body worried her; Pattie pushed it aside. Her acute vision, now adapted to the darkness, scanned her teacher-friend for broken bones, bleeding, or any other evidence that she'd sustained serious injuries. She looked her over again—and again—before allowing herself to relax. Though she needed a tricorder to confirm her assessment, she could discern enough to determine that Zoë had suffered nothing more serious than a few scrapes and a head-to-toe coating of dust and dried moss. Pattie reached over and plucked a twig out of her friend's tangled curls. Humanoids required so much maintenance. *What a nuisance it must be to have all your fleshy parts on the outside!* "Your telepathy must be short-circuiting if you need to ask me how I'm doing."

Zoë half-coughed, half-chuckled, her shoulders shaking. "It's always good manners to ask how someone is feeling—even if I already know, Pattie." Rolling over on her back, she pulled an arm across her chest in a stretch, repeating the gesture with the opposite arm. "As for being uncomfortable, I just need some ointment for my sore hands. Honestly, I didn't know whether I could hold on any longer." She paused, brushed her fingers through her hair, dislodging bark flecks. "And a bath. I'd really like a bath."

Pattie didn't know why the fleshy species bothered with their multitudes of cleaning rituals; a coating of rotted bark dust and fungus on their epidermal layer might improve their natural state. In the years she'd served around humanoids, she decided no amount of sonic waves, water, oil, perfume, soap, or scent improved upon the sour musk that permeated every corner of their living spaces. But she'd adjusted. Being tolerant of the quirks native to other species was expected of a member of a multiworld community. There was a reason, however, why the Nasat avoided living too close to Zoë and Tarak's lab and it had nothing to do with them being noisy neighbors. "The evening rains will start soon," Pattie said, noting the rising mists, the slight shift in air pressure. "You won't even have to go back to your paddock. Take a walk on the verandah over there"—Pattie cocked her head toward a porch protruding off the walkway—"and wait."

"That's not a bath, that's asking to be encapsulated in mud." She massaged her hands, alternating between right and left. "Pattie . . . do you think you could use your communicator to check in with Tarak? He usually keeps the transmitter on when I'm out." Her voice quivered slightly.

Pattie touched her combadge. "P8 Blue to Dr. Tarak."

A crackle, static, and then: *"Tarak here. Because you have contacted me, I presume that you have survived the quake in fair condition, but Dr. Xanfer—is she also well?"*

"Yes, Doctor. She's fine. Dirty, but fine."

"The minimal inconvenience of filthiness is preferable to other, more potentially serious injuries to her person. I wish you both continued health and clear thinking. I will anticipate your presence when circumstances allow it. Tarak out."

Sighing deeply, Zoë placed a hand over her heart. "I sensed that he was fine, but I couldn't be certain if my wishes for his well-being had misled me." Contented, she sighed again, her shoulders slumping with relief.

She's in love, Pattie realized with happy surprise. She'd seen something of humanoid romantic relationships lately, and recognized the signs. *What a time to find out.* She had questions for Zoë, but they would wait for a more opportune moment.

Zoë assumed a cross-legged position, brushed dust off her tunic and craned to see what was going on around them. "Are these quakes common? And if they are, will there be more tremors?"

"Haven't had one in my sixteen seasons—or eight years by Federation reckoning. If memory serves, it's been more than a score of seasons since we've had any kind of serious tremors."

The groan of circuitry far below announced the power systems restarting. The groan also informed Pattie that she could feel safer about resuming an upright posture. Zoë followed her lead, scrambling to her feet.

Beyond the obstacle of an overturned kiosk blocking their path, Pattie saw some Nasat uncurl; others hobbled toward the closest exits. Most were too dazed to move, let alone escape to safety. A few cowered against a railing, trapped behind a dangerous power surge arc between computer terminals; either machine could explode without warning.

"You think we should stay put? Wait for security services to evacuate us?" Zoë asked.

"I'm not sure." Pattie carefully picked her way around the kiosk, holding on to the sides of the structure for balance. Zoë followed behind.

Without the kiosk to block their view, they discovered more than a dozen injured Nasat—a few fatally.

"We'll need to help," Zoë said, stating it as a fact instead of a request.

Pattie nodded.

"I'll start assessing the wounded. My telepathy might help us where our training won't." She jerked her head in the direction of the public information terminals. "You see if we have any medical supplies to work with. I wouldn't have a clue as to where to look."

Pushing aside debris covering the floor, Pattie searched for any signage that indicated compartments where emergency medkits might be stored. *I hope the government implemented the latest building regs in their recent reconstruction.* Drawing on her years spent studying Federation construction and building codes, she made a guess where the supplies might be and found them where she would have expected to find them on Vulcan, Trill, or Andor. *At least we've standardized a few things since joining the Federation.* Nasat tended not to fuss over details. She opened up the floor panel and removed a couple of wrist-lamps, the medkit, and a medical tricorder.

Zoeannah took a wrist-lamp proffered by Pattie, clicked it on, and muttered, "What a mess!" when the beam illuminated their surroundings. She knelt down beside an unconscious Red Nasat who had lost chunks of his chorion shell. "Quite a dramatic entry you made,

Pattie. Maybe bring a bottle of Ktarian merlot or a piece of Risan pottery next time. Save the theatrics for the engineering corps," Zoë said dryly.

"And to think I was worried you wouldn't like the show. I admit that a quake's a bit dramatic, but the homeworld hasn't seen one in a while," she deadpanned. "I always liked to shake things up."

"I'm not even going to comment on that pun."

Pattie answered with her equivalent of a wink: curling one of her antennae in Zoë's direction.

Zoë felt for a pulse in the shell's forehead. "Sarcasm suits you, P8. I always suspected you'd be witty once you mastered communication basics." She sat back on her heels, looked over at Pattie, and grinned. "Either that, or spending time around 'softs' is rubbing off on you."

Tamping down a snappy retort, Pattie paused reflectively. Various scenes from her life over the last three years flashed by in an instant; it had been a long journey—not without complications—but she'd triumphed. She said quietly, "If I gained anything from spending time around softs, it would be the belief that I could do anything I put my mind to. Being around softs is what gave me the confidence to join Starfleet in the first place. Thank you."

Zoë's eyes smiled. "Of course."

They settled into a pattern of business intermingled with small talk as they attended to the wounded. Working with Zoë—to whom she owed so much—made Pattie's tasks much less stressful. Pattie hadn't enjoyed Starfleet's required medical training course when she enlisted, nor had she discovered a natural knack for it during her time in the S.C.E. To have Nasat lives dependent on skills she hadn't enthusiastically cultivated would have been nerve-wracking without Zoë's steady, even-tempered approach. Pattie, knowing more about Nasat physiology than Zoeannah, focused on the mechanics of fixing injuries while Zoë used her telepathic skills to ease shock and sense pain. Her offer of comfort and kindness to the traumatized made Pattie's task easier.

Think of them as sentient machines, she thought. *Medicine is just engineering the physiology of a biological organism.* They had been working almost a half hour when the first security services officer rode down the conveyor from the transport center.

"Evacuate the premises," the Yellow shell clicked authoritatively. "Township Council wants all open areas cleared. Proceeding to lockdown mode as soon as all public areas are secure. Move along." The Yellow shooed several limping Nasat toward a mother-tree passageway before meandering over to where Pattie and Zoë had set up a makeshift triage station.

"Proper medical attenders will be dispatched shortly. You can leave them be," the Yellow said to Pattie, using secondary limbs to indicate those Nasat yet to be examined. "On behalf of the Council, thank you. Be on your way now. Follow proper evacuation procedures and return directly to your paddock by the shortest possible route."

Pattie continued working. "I've had field medic training, Officer. I can be useful until the attenders arrive."

"Best to comply with the Council's orders," the Yellow insisted. Squatting down on his haunches, he plucked the medical tricorder out of Zoë's hands and dropped it into the medkit. After collecting chemsutures and exo-plaster and depositing them alongside the tricorder, he snapped the kit shut, scooting it close to his forelegs.

With one of her limbs, Pattie nudged the kit across the floor until it rested beside Zoë. *How dronelike is this officer? I'd forgotten how mindlessly compliant some shells can be,* she thought, reopening the kit. She tossed the tricorder back to Zoë, who continued working. "I'm confident the Council wants to save lives."

The Yellow's throat bristles tensed, his antennae curled downward. "Naturally. But they have more knowledge than you or I do."

"If we can contribute to the emergency efforts, we will. 'With many small limbs large tasks are done.'" She quoted a Nasat proverb. Sorting through the hypos in the medkit, Pattie settled on one that would stabilize the respirations of the wounded Nasat.

The Yellow waddled past Zoë and tapped her on the shoulder. "Reason with the Blue, or I'll call for backup."

Zoë and Pattie exchanged glances. The Betazoid shrugged, yawned. "She's in charge."

Pattie appreciated Zoë's vote of confidence. Her teacher would stand by her if she decided to be stubborn; Pattie knew that from experience. But she didn't want to cause trouble; few softs lived in this township. A disgruntled peace officer could make it difficult for Zoë to approach potential subjects or access semirestricted databases. She stood upright; Zoë followed suit.

"Fine, then, but let me leave my paddock code with you so that the Council can contact me when the repairs start," Pattie said. "My career training will be useful to them."

"Cocky, aren't you, Blue?" The Yellow's mandibles twitched with suspicion as he grudgingly removed a scanner from his utility vest. "Designation?"

She paused for a minute, shifting her thought processes out of standard into the clicks, chirps, and pitch of Nasat. The Yellow wouldn't find a Nasat record for "Pattie." "P8 BlueTS27Q6. Starfleet Corps of Engineers."

He tapped her name and waited for the computer to retrieve her ID file. "Starfleet doesn't have jurisdiction in local matters, but I'm supposing their training should be mostly applicable here." Clutching his scanner in his pincers, the Yellow swiveled his eyes from the data on the screen toward Pattie. "Hmmmm. Haven't been home in a bit, P8. Suppose it's understandable that you've forgotten how things are done around here."

Choosing to ignore the Yellow's personal insinuations, Pattie persisted in constructively dealing with the emergency situation at hand. *Give me a terminal with access to the sensor data and I could map out every weakened bearing branch or cracked floor,* she thought. "My training would be invaluable in determining whether the township's sustained any damage from the tremors," she protested—though she'd have better luck arguing with a replicator than a Yellow. Eons of natural selection had given the Yellows their steady, methodical ways. From time to time, she'd heard stories of Yellows that had abandoned their larvae instead of finding a nursery, or those who'd up and left the township to hitch a ride on a starship. Those exceptions notwithstanding, you went to Yellows when a task required relentless, often repetitive, perseverance.

"Confirming ID," he said, activating the neuro function on his scanner and waving it over her forebrain to confirm her bioelectric signature with the population database. His antennae shot up. "Interesting. Chatty for a 'quiet'—"

If the officer had continued nattering on, Pattie hadn't heard it. She froze, rooted where she stood, her blood chilled. She willed her mouth to move. Her thoughts stuck and stuttered. Hearing it again after so many years shouldn't matter. *It shouldn't matter.* One cycling thought refused to go away; she grasped it, clung to it. *Quiet? I have conquered that!* But her mouth refused to comply with her will to speak, and a sinking sense of humiliation drained her energy. She stood before the Yellow, helpless.

If I can pull up my record in the township database, I can prove to him that he's mistaken! She stepped toward the officer, gesturing with her limbs, attempting to communicate that she wanted to borrow his ID scanner.

The startled Yellow misread her intentions as aggressive and staggered back. He pulled his limbs tight into his abdomen, preparing to curl into a protective ball; his reactionary behavior further fueled her frustration.

She took another step toward him. *I can make him understand. I mean no harm. If only I can find the words. I know how to say this!*

At the crest of her frustration, her mind blanked.

In a breath her muscles relaxed, her limbs collapsed to her sides like snipped puppet strings. She breathed deeply, blinked, and shook her head. A wide-eyed Zoë held her tightly with her trembling hand pressed into a soft spot beneath Pattie's mandibles; she hadn't had to do this since Pattie's early learning days. Pattie, as a young Nasat, had been so conditioned to anxiety whenever her fellow Nasat misunderstood or humiliated her, that Zoë had worked extra hard on helping Pattie overcome the emotional reactions that interfered with her cognitive processing.

Today, the technique worked the same on her adult body as it had on her nymph body. Steady pressure on the nerve bundle acted like a circuit breaker, forcing Pattie to relax. Interrupting the anxiety allowed the instinctual emotional/biochemical reaction triggered by the Yellow's words to ebb. If Zoë hadn't intervened . . .

Cognition of what she might have done dawned on her. She glanced off at an angle, away from Zoë, into the dark rain forest. *I've gone and given credence to the very point I was trying to dissuade him from believing: that "quiets" are misfits.* She muttered a potent curse she'd picked up from Corsi, doubting if the officer could claim the ability to curse in multiple languages. Ironic.

She winced inwardly when she saw the officer had backed up against a wall, all limbs extended, poised for offense—his aspect indicating he still expected Pattie to attack. He clicked an angry warning, jabbing a pincer toward her. He was a shadow of hundreds of other fearful Nasat that Pattie had met in her youngest seasons.

But he had nothing to worry about. Pattie had never intended to harm him—or lay a pincer on him. Persuading the Yellow to believe her was another case entirely. Worried, she looked at Zoë, who still held her loosely. She willed her Betazoid friend to interpret her conflicting emotions.

With a gentle smile, Zoë briefly touched her thumb to the center of her forehead, then placed the same thumb on the thin, sensitive tissue behind Pattie's antennae. That her teacher so easily employed the Nasat gesture of affection comforted her immensely.

Zoë whispered, "Let me handle this." She squared her shoulders and extended a hand to the officer. Tentatively, he placed a limb in her palm, indicating he would listen, though his eyes darted frequently in Pattie's direction.

"P8's not a 'quiet,'" Zoë explained. "At least not as you understand quiets to be. She has full lingual abilities—both of communication and comprehension—after graduating from the Federation's neural-electric linguistics project. A physiological marker might register her as a quiet on your scanner, but I assure you that's a technicality."

The officer's eyes darted between Zoë and Pattie several times before he spoke. "I've heard rumors about that neural-electric memory process. So it isn't just Federation sap and fog. P8 seems to be able to communicate just like the rest of us."

"Obviously," Pattie retorted. "Or we wouldn't be able to have this conversation, would we?"

Zoë shot a warning frown in Pattie's direction, but the sarcastic tone appeared to have been lost on the officer.

"Learn something every day. Guess membership in

the Federation has its perks." The Yellow shell clicked his scanner back onto his utility strip.

"You'll let the Council know that I'm available to assist in the structural evaluations?" Pattie asked.

He tapped his pincers irritably. "Back to that, are we?"

"Well?"

"You won't go having a fit or anything like you quiets are prone to do, will you?"

Biting back a caustic reply, Pattie waved her antennae, no. Zoë squeezed Pattie's limb in a gesture of support.

"Assuming you can behave yourself, I'll give them your paddock number." He returned the ID scanner to his utility belt. "But I wouldn't plan on much. While citizen support is greatly appreciated, at a time like this, repair efforts are best left to the experts." Pattie restrained herself from pointing out that she *was* an expert in exactly this sort of repair effort. "In the meantime, return to your paddock and remain there until the 'all clear' is issued. Excuse me," he said, wandering off to shoo *laito* monkeys away from chewing on exposed power cables. After checking in with the other Nasat tending to the wounded (presumably giving them the same lockdown lecture he'd given Pattie and Zoë), he vanished up the transport center conveyor.

"What about the injured?" Pattie said.

"I think we've done what we can," Zoë replied. "And I'm not just saying that because we've been ordered to go. I honestly think we've helped those that we could and they'll be fine until the attenders arrive."

Pattie curled her antennae in acknowledgment. She checked the duffel where she'd stowed her larvae and, satisfied that the precious cargo was undamaged, followed behind Zoë on the path she picked through the wreckage. With the duffel secured on her shell, she could maneuver with little difficulty, simplifying the five-or-so-kilometer journey they had to the lower-level branch sector where Zoë's lab/paddock was located. Pausing at the doorway through the mother-tree, Pattie looked back on the wounded they had assisted, feeling grateful that her exit was far less conspicuous than her entrance.

Welcome home, P8 Blue.

CHAPTER 2

Not surprisingly, Pattie and Zoë discovered that few conveyors and turbolifts had resumed operating. Any functioning automated transport was used to move wounded and security personnel. Voluminous civilian foot traffic moved slowly as thousands of night-cycle shift workers emptied out of work centers to return home. Weak emergency lighting further hampered progress; what hadn't been bolted down or attached when the quake hit had been dumped on the floor. When an impatient Red pushing past had tripped her, Pattie nearly lacerated her lower limbs on the sharp edge of a dislodged wall plate. The occasional encounter with an anonymous squish or shattered bits continually reminded them to slow down, move carefully.

Though the mess meant inconvenience, Pattie knew their situation could have been far worse. From what little she could discern, the primary township structures had sustained little or no damage. A good clean-up crew could fix the situation. The farther she moved from the transport center, the more it appeared that new construction zones—near the treetops and spreading out horizontally from the mother-tree—had been hardest hit. Why this was, considering that those zones utilized the latest architectural advances, puzzled Pattie.

Without mechanized transport, traveling between branch levels required that they, and all others returning to their paddocks, climb up and down the peg-poles: meter-wide metal poles with half-circle-shaped pegs protruding off opposite sides. Pattie had used Jefferies tubes and stairs on the *da Vinci,* but she found she adapted poorly to those designs. The peg-poles were better suited to the grasp of her multiple limbs and her body's weight distribution. For Zoë, the peg-poles worked on the same principle as a ladder would, so she had little trouble keeping pace with the queue of Nasat above and below her. Pattie, as she descended, was reminded of how softs used the ladders connecting bunk beds. *Maybe more Nasat might join Starfleet if peg-poles were integrated into starship construction.* She made a mental note to suggest her idea to Captain Gold when she next saw him.

The protracted trip back to Zoë's paddock gave Pattie plenty of time to think about her encounter with the Yellow. Though the humiliation had diffused, she still simmered over the Yellow's labeling her as a quiet. Hearing that word—hearing herself labeled that way—again reminded her why she'd joined Starfleet. In the S.C.E., whatever a Nasat computer said she was, whatever her physiology identified her as being, didn't matter. Her accomplishments defined her, not a defect in the language-processing center of her cerebral cortex. Because she had skills and experience the township needed, a label shouldn't matter—especially at a time of crisis.

Instead of locking down the township, why hadn't the Council ordered every available shell out of their paddock to start working? Clearing the rubble, helping the wounded to safety—whatever was needed. A threat to the mother-tree was a collective threat to all life in the canopy, Nasat, tiny-leafed *neophatra,* or multi-winged avian. All should be vested in finding answers as soon as possible. Waiting around for bureaucratic wheels to grind out an official all-clear notification wouldn't solve the power problems or stabilize potentially damaged buttress roots. Whatever force had quaked the township's mother-tree could resume at any time. Pattie wondered what this townshipwide lockdown would accomplish; she twitched with impatience. *We should be working this problem. Putting our ideas together.*

She imagined their invisible foe, be it a natural force or a yet-unknown predator, lurking beneath lichen-covered branches, through vine curtains and nests, perhaps as far as the muddy forest floor. A destabilized fault in the planetary crust. A rotting buttress root giving way. A deadly infection seeping into the mother-tree's xylem or phloem. Her kindred might have to explore new, nontraditional ways of dealing with the situation. But the problem wouldn't be dealt with by sending frightened Nasat back to their paddocks to curl into protective postures.

A dull crunch—coupled with a groan—startled her. A cloud of bark dust and moss emerged from the ceiling. Looking up, Pattie watched as a synth-wood support beam began bowing. *The quake must have compromised the structural integrity,* she thought pragmatically. She knew the deck above primarily housed residential areas, sparing those below from heavy machinery and equipment, should the deck give way. Still, several hundred Nasat paddocks weren't weightless.

Another groan and the peg-pole jiggled, nearly imperceptibly.

"Wrap yourself around the pole," Pattie called to Zoë. "The ceiling might give!"

Eyes wide with fear, Zoë complied.

Bowing even more deeply, the groaning beam cracked visibly, sending a shower of splinters into the air. The peg-pole swayed. Nasat above and below them panicked, scrambling over Zoë and past Pattie. Others shrieked, waving at the ceiling, pointing and shouting.

With a roar, the beam snapped; a flood of debris filled the air. The weight of the collapsing ceiling bent the peg-pole, severing its connection with the pole above it. The pole tipped, swayed dangerously—but slowly—from side to side. Each sway dipped a bit farther, bringing them closer to the paddock structures below.

As they careened toward the ground, Pattie watched the paddock-huts growing larger with each meter. Her mind's eye transformed the landscape and she saw the *Orion* hurtling toward the *da Vinci* in the turbulent atmosphere of Galvan VI. A wrenching shudder first threw her head back, then threw her forward, slamming her body against metal.

A blink. They'd stopped falling. She looked around. The scene shifted and she again saw the bend and shimmer dance of leaf tufts on supple branches in the forest outside. She respired humid air, air thick with pollen and orchid perfume, not the neutral, recirculated air of a starship. She knew this place. Or thought she did. She was on the homeworld. With Zoeannah. The peg-pole they had been climbing had crashed into a building complex that stood a good ten meters above the deck floor. At least that was where she believed she was.

Deceptive dusk light continually recast the shapes in her mind and she half wondered if some latent racial memory had merged with her present reality. Perhaps she *was* still somewhere aboard the dying *da Vinci* and in the shock and horror of it all, her brain deceived her senses by offering the comfort of home.

Home? To use that word to define this place struck her as odd. She felt more vulnerable, more exposed—more alone—in this elongated moment on her homeworld than she ever had while roaming the stars. *Certainly Zoë must feel similarly.* She dropped her gaze and saw Zoë, her expression pinched, her skin pale. A half-dozen escaping Nasat skittered over her on their way to a rooftop, only a few pegs away from Pattie. Even in the wan moonlight, Pattie could see the whitened skin across Zoë's knuckles as she clenched the pole more tightly.

Not all the Nasat were as discourteous as those that had climbed over Zoë and they had politely queued up behind her. Zoë wouldn't move without prompting.

"Zoë, can you climb?"

Tilting back her head, she turned her dark-irised gaze on Pattie, swallowed hard, and then nodded. She reached a trembling hand toward the peg above her. One more step and Pattie would be able to offer her a limb to hold on to.

"Keep coming, Zoë. I'm here and I'll help you." She watched, noting the extreme concentration etched on Zoë's face as her friend raised a wavering arm, and then another, and another, until her hands were on the peg below Pattie's lowermost legs.

"Up one more peg."

Zoë complied, reaching for Pattie, who grasped her hand in her pincers and pulled the young woman up to stand on the peg opposite her. Pattie used her secondary limbs to maintain her own hold on the peg-pole.

"Let's climb to the roof, okay?" Pattie said. "I'll take a step, then you take a step." They inched upward. Each time the leaning peg-pole vibrated, Zoë clung more tightly to Pattie's pincers.

After reaching the roof, the pair took a brief rest, allowing Zoë a chance to collect herself. Her time in Starfleet had conditioned Pattie to handle ongoing disaster and trauma with relative calm. Steady reactions had become reflexive, even intuitive to her. Working as a civilian scientist provided very few life-threatening experiences for Zoeannah to cope with. For her, dealing with the ceiling collapse, especially on the heels of the initial tremors, took a bit longer than for Pattie.

While Zoeannah rested, Pattie plotted out an alternate—and shorter—route to the lab. *The sooner we have her home with Tarak, the better,* she thought. Zoë could be tough, but many more mishaps would quickly deplete her emotional and physical reserves.

Soon, they resumed their journey, using jokes and small talk as a distraction from the chaos surrounding them. The conversation eventually moved around to Pattie's plans for the weeks she would be on the homeworld while the *da Vinci* underwent repair at McKinley Station on Earth. As they climbed down the last pegpole before the turnoff to Zoë's paddock, Pattie called out to Zoë, "I was serious about helping out with the repair efforts, but I'm afraid if I just show up and volunteer, they'll turn me away."

"Pattie, you know your people," Zoë noted sensibly. "They're very focused on doing things a particular way and once they're secure about an idea or a course of action, they don't like making changes. You like to shake things up."

"I'll have to go to the top, then," Pattie said. "What would it take to get an appointment with Governor Z4 Blue?"

"Hmmm. Might be difficult." Zoë paused on the poles below Pattie to look up at her. "This governor has been slow to warm to the progressive reforms that the Planetary Council embraces. He still considers Tarak's and my work to be a little fringe. He moves cautiously. Doesn't like taking unnecessary risks."

"That's what should appear next to 'Nasat' in the Federation database: insectoid species that doesn't like to take any unnecessary risks."

"I'm not trying to discourage you from trying to help out; I'm just being realistic."

"I know that," Pattie said, her antennae curled pensively.

They touched down on the deck. Zoë looked noticeably grateful to have solid ground beneath her feet.

She circled her head around, stretched her neck, and yawned. Looking over at Pattie, she said, "You okay?"

Pattie sighed. "Shells sometimes don't make sense."

"Neither do softs if that makes you feel any better."

"*That,* I know."

Zoë patted her shell kindly and started down the walkway to the lab.

For a few moments, she stood there, watching Zoë walk away, and thinking. The Nasat's reflexive self-interest had always annoyed Pattie. Upon more thought, P8 Blue acknowledged that some of her present impatience with the Nasat might be a reflection of the time she'd spent around humanoids. Her Starfleet crewmates could be impulsive, but they would never be accused of cowardice. *Better to act when you can choose your course than be compelled by circumstance to react—or surrender,* Pattie thought. She had learned that behavior from watching her friends.

An unbidden thought came to her and she envisioned Commander Sonya Gomez commanding the *da Vinci,* carnage surrounding her on every side. Pattie still marveled at Commander Gomez's single-minded determination to save the crew. What would the commander do if she were here? She wouldn't wilt on the floor, waiting for the bridge's ceiling beams to collapse and bury her. Neither would Captain Gold, poor Lieutenant McAllan, Doctor Lense, or any of the others. *And Lt. Commander Duffy,* Pattie paused to remember. *He chose to make a difference.* She marveled at the number of lives he'd saved because he refused to put his own interests first.

She could choose to make a difference. A meaningful difference. She could be frustrated with this backward, rural township she called home, or she could put the lessons she'd learned aboard the *da Vinci* into action.

She resolved to argue with as many Yellows, Blues, Greens, Browns, and Reds as she needed to—from the civil engineers and the bureaucrats to the officers. She would present herself to the township council. She would use every connection she had to land an appointment with the forest quadrant governor.

To have a substantive reason to be here, the potential to accomplish something constructive, excited her. She'd anticipated finding little more than a distraction from her worries about her crewmates. The more she considered her options—in the present and the future—the more sobering reality intruded. Honesty required she acknowledge that her S.C.E. future held a measure of uncertainty.

Realistically, some members of the *da Vinci*'s crew might be too traumatized to return to starship duty. Corsi and Stevens had struggled mightily when they lost Duffy. Captain Gold faced rebuilding a crew after losing so many, not to mention the heavy repairs his ship required. Even if what was left of the crew reunited, Pattie had no idea whether or not their relationships would ever be as they were before they lost so many comrades. *If I can be an individual of action and help my people, then maybe all the events that brought me here might not have been a complete waste. I might be able to help build something good.*

For the first time since she'd decided to come here, Pattie felt hopeful.

CHAPTER 3

As soon as she'd passed through the paddock archway, Pattie felt safe. With only emergency lighting to see by, she still knew the square shadows of terminals, imagined the computer-generated neural maps marked up with Zoë's notes covering the walls, and recognized the smell of Tarak's favorite *zeeflower* hip tea seeping in a kettle. While Pattie strolled around, reacquainting herself with this favorite place, she eavesdropped on Zoë quizzing Tarak about what he'd experienced during the quakes.

She shared Zoë's relief that none of the lab experiments or data storage had been damaged; the computer had finished the day's final analysis before the first tremor. Tarak, always methodical, had stowed all their equipment and backed up their data shortly after Zoë had left to meet Pattie's transport. He'd even had time to deal with the lighting problem. Ingenious Dr. Tarak had rigged makeshift lighting using the elements from a spare computer and an old transtator. Anticipating (logically) that they might be hungry, he'd lit an old-style lab burner to warm a leftover pot of stewed *kaino* root. Pattie lapped the porridge out of her plate, grateful for the nourishment. They spoke little, comfortable in the silence of friends.

After they'd eaten, Tarak flipped on a fuel-cell powered viewscreen so they could see the updates as they came in. All three settled in to watch; Zoë and Tarak sat cross-legged on a rug they'd thrown on the wood plank floor while Pattie sat in a hammock chair suspended from the ceiling. Tarak had wrapped a blanket around Zoë's shoulders; she huddled against him, her visible relief a marked contrast to Tarak's neutral expression.

They watched without comment as footage played and replayed with different expert analysis. As Pattie had hypothesized, the oldest township branch sectors had escaped almost unscathed. Watching the pictures of various township sectors flash across the screen, she puzzled through possible questions. Why had the lab, for example, sustained no damage even though it didn't benefit from any of the latest engineering designs or materials, and why had sectors like the transport center—which had been designed to withstand a quantum torpedo—nearly collapsed? Conclusions were few: the Planetary Science Council had already ruled out meteorological and seismic causes. A worrisome analysis proposed that the host trees' root systems had become destabilized.

They listened to reports for a few hours before the scientists and officials had nothing new to offer. Commentators indicated that investigative teams would be dispatched to the lowest level observation decks at the end of the night cycle.

"They should go to the bottom and get it over with," Pattie muttered as she watched the screen cut between views from various lower-level cameras.

"An interesting thing for a Nasat to say," Zoë said, raising an eyebrow.

"Just because most of my kindred are phobic about spending time on the forest floor doesn't mean I share their apprehensions." *Especially when circumstances are serious enough to require it,* she thought. *And this might be one of those times.*

"What about the security service teams that go missing when they have to visit the floor?" Zoë argued. "The flash floods, the quicksand. The countless other legitimate dangers that Nasat, hell, that *softs* face if they go down to the bottom. Can you explain those away by phobias and prejudice?"

"You can't live without taking risks. Walking out your door. Visiting the market." She paused, quirked a smile at Zoë and added, "Picking up a friend at the transport."

Zoë laughed heartily. "Point taken."

Pattie had enjoyed this kind of banter with her crewmates and was glad she could have similar conversations with her old teachers. Though Pattie had spent more one-to-one time with Zoë and Tarak than almost anyone else on the homeworld, most of their interactions in the past had been focused on helping Pattie become a fully functioning member of Nasat society. Their discussions about culture or politics had focused on how those issues related to the lab's research or how they impacted Pattie. Now that she'd "grown up" and become a peer, Pattie sensed the shift in their relationship; she enjoyed it.

"I never would make the mistake of lumping you in with the rest of your kindred," Zoë deadpanned. She winked at Pattie, quirking a gentle grin.

Pattie shrugged. "I understand where the traditions come from. My kindred spent a thousand years struggling to rise above our beginnings in the caves and dark places below. Developing the technology that allowed us to live in the canopy instead of in the mud and dark of the forest floor was our first step in becoming a spacefaring people."

"Why 'going to the bottom' is seen as regression has always puzzled me," Zoë said. "The Nasat don't want to preserve their past, their history. Where you've come from. In my twenty seasons here I've never seen a museum, read a commemorative plaque, or met a historian. If a building has outlived its usefulness, the Nasat tear it down and start again, regardless of how significant the location is." She looked to Tarak to add his own observations, but his response was limited to a single nod.

"My kindred have always perceived that cutting ties with the past frees us up to progress. Newer *is* better. If we fully embrace the past, we risk being trapped in it."

"Do you believe that?"

"You're asking the wrong Nasat." Pattie laughed. "I've spent the last few seasons working with species who tote four-hundred-year-old relics around from posting to posting simply for sentimental reasons. And from what I've seen, that's not such a bad thing. Maybe some of their craziness is rubbing off on me."

Tarak reached over Zoë's lap and clicked the viewscreen off. "The comnet is no longer broadcasting any new or useful information. Should the township have further delays in fully restoring power, we need to preserve our resources." He stood up to stow the portable viewscreen in a cupboard.

Zoë yawned. "Right now, we don't have any students living here. You can choose any nest you want if you're ready to conclude your waking cycle," she said, pushing down another yawn.

"If you require sleep, please don't stay up on my account," Pattie offered. "I'm a full cycle away from needing to rest."

Tarak and Zoë exchanged glances; his eyes narrowed, she shrugged.

"Understanding the situation at hand would be of greater benefit than what would be gained by allowing our physiological processes a regenerative period," Tarak said. "We will remain awake until such time that the need to rest is equivalent with the need to gain knowledge."

Grinning gently, Zoë patted Tarak on the thigh.

"What he's trying to say is that we'll stay up with you if you want."

"I haven't heard an update on your research," Pattie prompted.

"No new breakthroughs, if that's what you're asking," Zoë said.

"It appears that 'quiets' hatch at a uniform rate planetwide, regardless of shell color or geography," Tarak explained. "When all hatchings are statistically analyzed, one can hypothesize that there will be approximately one quiet in every seven hundred and fifty hatchings."

Pattie had always wondered whether her own limitations would be passed to her larvae. She felt relieved knowing that her offspring might escape the struggles she had acquiring communication skills. Impressions of her own early days in this lab floated into her consciousness.

Oh how afraid she'd been at the prospect of having her mind probed by aliens. The stories she'd heard! That quiets were being offered to the Federation to be experimented on. In the end, however, her fear of being condemned to a life of silence overcame her fear of the alien softs. She'd discovered a petite Betazoid redhead who had been the first to give words to her feelings. And Tarak: a silent, methodical Vulcan with his neural scanners and his endless hours in the nurseries, watching the nurturers pass information to their charges.

That was where he'd found Pattie, in the nursery. Two seasons old and still mute. She had only vague memories of Tarak asking a nurturer if he could "talk" with her. The nurturer had laughed at the ridiculousness of the request. And then the gentle probing of Tarak's telepathy had been the first time someone had understood *her* thoughts and fears, though her mouth couldn't form the words. How many lives had they touched since hers?

She hadn't seen any Nasat around the lab tonight, though. "How many students do you have?"

"We've recently graduated thirty-five," Zoë said, pouring herself a cup of *zeeflower* tea. "Recruiting has been slow, but I'm confident that the Planetary Council will encourage more quiets to take advantage of our program."

"You'd have more support in the capital township," Pattie said. "The Federation has a stronger presence there—new ideas are embraced with less skepticism. Nasat and alien live side by side and no one questions it."

"But what about those quiets who don't have anything close to the resources offered in the capital? They'll be forever consigned to menial tasks, to being alone. We can't abandon them just so we can go where our work would be better received."

I owe these two so much, Pattie thought. *How can I ever repay them?* "I'll see if I can search out quiets among the newly hatched. I'm sure the nurseries would be happy to be rid of them."

Zoë smiled. "Now then, why would the nurseries want to be rid of their quietest charges? At least they can find a cycle's rest with the quiets."

"What else are you planning for while you're here?" Tarak asked.

Pattie's mind shifted back to the thoughts she'd had on her journey from the transport to the lab. *I will make a difference.* "These quakes. I'm confident my engineering training could help in the ongoing repairs. If not my skills, my limbs. I can work a plasteel seamer with the best of the construction workers."

"I could sense your mind moving a mile a minute on our way back here," Zoë said. "But I thought you were on vacation. Your last communiqué was ambiguous—I had the impression you'd been under a lot of stress."

"Our last voyage ended . . . badly. We lost many crew members."

"Communicate our regrets to Captain Gold when you speak to him," Tarak said.

"I will. In the meantime, the best way for me to work through my experiences is to stay busy."

"We'll help in whatever way we can. Right, Tarak?"

He nodded his head affirmatively. "If your need for our assistance has diminished, would it be permissible if I retired for the remainder of the dark cycle? I believe I will be more efficient if I can rest before the light cycle begins."

"Please," Pattie said, waving him in the direction of the sleep room. "I still have several cycles before I require rest. Don't stay up on my account."

Tarak nodded politely in Pattie's direction. He looked to Zoeannah.

"If you don't mind, I'd like to talk with Pattie for a bit longer." An almost imperceptible exchange passed between the softs—Pattie almost imagined he smiled—and he exited the room.

"So . . . you're probably wondering about—"

"How long have you and Tarak been—"

"More than research fellows?" Zoë finished with a wry grin. "About a year, though we'd gradually been heading toward being involved since his mate Tu'vara disappeared with the *Cairo* near the Romulan Neutral Zone. You never would have known by watching him, but the psychic bonds Vulcans have with their mates . . ."

"Having touched minds with Tarak as a pupil, I can guess at what might have been between him and his mate. You must have been a great comfort to him."

"I don't know about comfort, but our work gave him an outlet, a place to focus his efforts. With both of us so dedicated to our work, developing a more interpersonal connection was a natural evolution of our work relationship."

She studied her friend, the softness in her eyes, her almost-smile. "You seem happy. Though I wouldn't have ever put you two together. I have to admit that as soon as I realized that you had feelings for him, I was a little surprised."

"I knew you had it figured out as soon as I observed your body language when I was talking to Tarak over the comm," Zoë said, blushing.

"Body language? I'm a Nasat. We don't really have body language."

"I'm a Betazoid," Zoë teased. "I sense body language."

"Of course," Pattie said dryly.

She dropped her eyes to the ground. "As you might expect—he was very logical about proposing our . . . um . . . uh . . . partnership." She adopted a matter-of-fact tone, mimicking Tarak's speech patterns. "'Establishing a mutually beneficial domestic arrangement with me is more practical if I decide to live here permanently,' and so on. Very carefully thought through. Not quite the emotional exuberance that most Betazoids expect from their partners"—she blushed—"but he compensates in other ways."

"Oh." Pattie felt comfortable about not asking Zoë to elaborate further. Softs placed an importance on their romantic—and by corollary—their sexual relationships that was completely foreign to Nasat. The idea of emotions and sociological connections forming around copulation wasn't anything Pattie could figure out. Reproduction was like eating or resting—a bodily function that was carried out at the appropriate time.

Yawning again, Zoë stretched and rubbed at her eyes with her fists. "You mind if I sleep?"

Pattie smiled. "Of course not. I spend all my time working around you weakling softs so I'm used to all the pampering you require. Sleep, food, water—"

"Yeah, yeah, yeah," Zoë said, laughing.

Once she'd vanished into the private quarters, Pattie turned the viewscreen back on, hoping that new information had come to light. During the fifth time through a particularly heavily damaged branch sector, Pattie's sharp eyes noted something she hadn't picked up previously. "Computer, save newsfeed TS2, channel 4, 0212 to 0220 to lab database." The computer squawked an acknowledgment. She replayed the footage, sharpening the resolution on specific shots, pulling the view closer and closer until she could see the rivets in the floor, but the anomalous characteristic was fully discernible. *What have we here? Certainly not evidence of seismic activity. Maybe defective building material? Or . . . something more dangerous.* Satisfaction suffused her; she had her first lead. *We have ourselves a mystery.*

CHAPTER 4

In my youngest seasons, never would I have dreamed that I would be received into the governor's office, Pattie thought, taking in the banks of computers, the holo-projected map of the homeworld, the ornately carved planters overflowing with white orchid blossoms and opalescent vines. Mid-sun cycle mists carpeted the lower branches and tree decks. She watched a brilliantly colored keel-billed avian sitting on a knobby branch outside the governor's window, grasping hard yellow *hermoorsia* fruits in its beak. Considering how difficult it had been to secure this appointment, Pattie decided she'd better enjoy the experience while it lasted.

Pattie had spent the remainder of the night cycle downloading whatever tremor data she could procure into her tricorder, running various analyses using the Starfleet databases, and studying the conclusions. She hadn't uncovered much new information by the time the sun rose, but she had determined that whatever had struck her township didn't match any conventional parameters. The irregular tremor patterns and resultant damage weren't typical of weakening buttress roots, nor did they appear consistent with past problems with erosion or other ground-based problems.

After reviewing the frames she'd found unusual, she did wonder if a new systemic infection might be attacking the mother-tree. If a new virus or parasite had invaded the forest, the mother-tree might be vulnerable to assault. Some organisms could decimate a mother-tree in a matter of weeks. Regardless of what had caused the tremors, Pattie had renewed interest in both identifying the source of the problem and finding a solution.

Beginning with Zoë's acquaintances, Pattie had contacted every shell she could obtain a comcode for, dispatching messages every few minutes for hours, until she'd determined that none of the local officials would assign her to an investigation team. Their replies sounded remarkably similar to the security services officer she and Zoë had encountered the night before. So she had started in on messaging her contacts in the capital. This had consumed the remainder of the day after the tremor and into her second night at home.

By the following morning, she'd located several Nasat Starfleet personnel, based on the homeworld as part of a Federation detail, who knew of someone who knew someone who might be able to bend the governor's ear. Apparently, while visiting a nearby starbase several months ago, the governor had become quite friendly with the base's commanding officer. Commander Emon had been in his first year at the Academy when Captain Gold was graduating and wanted to know how the captain was faring since the *da Vinci*'s horrific mission to Galvan VI. After an exchange of stories, Emon contacted the governor on Pattie's behalf, arranging for an appointment the following day. She hadn't expected to spend most of her first week on leave working Nasat bureaucracy, but if it gave her the chance to help the township, it seemed like a small sacrifice.

The Green shell monitoring the governor's schedule alerted Pattie that the governor was ready to receive her in his office. She approached the door chime with some trepidation, knowing that she wasn't exactly a *welcome* visitor. *Here goes nothing,* she thought, and pressed the door chime.

The door hissed open.

"P8 Blue," the governor said, clicking his pincer politely. "I am pleased to associate with you." Behind his half-moon-shaped console, he stepped out of his seat-hammock to greet Pattie formally.

Pattie reciprocated the polite gesture by clicking her own pincers, and assumed a spot in the visitor's seat-hammock.

"You didn't have to go to such lengths, P8. Contacting Commander Emon. I would have seen you," the governor said as he took a seat behind his console.

"I apologize, sir, but until I talked to Commander Emon and asked him to contact you, I couldn't even procure D5 Green's comcode to *ask* for an appointment. Those officials beneath you do an excellent job of making sure you aren't bothered."

"Every Nasat believes the problems of his deck sector or paddock group are the most pressing item on my agenda. I would never have a chance to govern if I took every appointment that was requested." The governor scrutinized Pattie from head to foot and limb to limb.

"Point well taken," Pattie said.

Leaning over the console, he looked directly into Pattie's eyes. "I know who you are, P8. You're unusual by Nasat standards, but you're even more unusual in this forest quadrant. A quiet that can speak thanks to some alien scientific tinkering, who then enlists in Starfleet and becomes an engineer."

"That pretty much covers it, sir," Pattie said, unable to read the governor's perception of her life history. Some Nasat—especially those in the capital—found her choices novel, even fascinating. Here, in the rural part of the homeworld, she was seen as one of those crazy shells that wasn't hatched quite right. "But I believe I have something to contribute in this situation. Whatever I've been able to pull off the feeds and out of the databases, I've analyzed. I have an interest in this situation."

"When I heard your chosen profession, I thought you might," Governor Z4 said, fanning his limbs out to indicate the whole of their surroundings. "All this shifting and shaking. You're an engineer, after all. The damaged buildings and broken equipment. Just your type of tree bark, if you know what I mean."

Pattie's antennae curled her assent, hoping the governor would grant her a position on one of the teams.

"Circumstances have become more complicated in the last few days, though," he said. "Consider this latest development." He directed Pattie's eyes toward a bank of monitors. Pattie recognized the comnet footage from the previous days as well as a few pictures taken more recently. He tapped a command into his desk panels, making the commentary audible. Pattie followed the governor's lead, turning her attention to the reports, watching the latest development—a security services investigation—with keen interest.

Dozens of Nasat had gone missing during the quakes. Whether they'd fallen from the township or had been killed by falling debris wasn't readily discernible from the evidence. Most puzzling to investigators was where the now-missing Nasat had been when they'd vanished. A graphical map indicated that all of the missing had resided on the township perimeter where virtually all structures were enclosed. That the two- and three-hundred-year-old open-air corridors and paddocks near the township center reported no accidental falls from the decks or missing individuals seemed illogical to investigators, and to Pattie, though she conceded that the greater structural damage on the perimeter might figure into the analysis. Security teams hadn't ruled out abduction, though that was the least likely of all their scenarios.

The governor folded his center limbs over his abdomen, flexing his pincers thoughtfully. "Tremors that don't have seismic causes. Nasat, who reportedly had been at home in enclosed paddocks, vanishing. We're seeing strange times, P8."

"These missing shells, assuming they've fallen, how will they be found unless security goes to the bottom?" Pattie posed the question tentatively, assuming she'd be barraged with the usual list of reasons why Nasat didn't travel to the rain forest floor.

What might have passed as a smile in a soft filled the governor's face. "Since you left for Starfleet, we've installed hundreds of kilometers of security netting. Mostly to keep out the strangler vines and parasitic plants that threaten life in the canopy, but also to catch anything or anyone that might fall from the township decks."

"Netting?" Pattie asked, puzzled.

"Something the Federation developed. A translucent, lightweight, loosely woven fabric. Spun metal threads are virtually indestructible. A force field would be unsafe for avians, monkeys, and many other species that live in the canopy. The netting provides us a measure of protection while allowing air, mist, and rain to circulate, and about seventy-five to eighty percent of the light to filter down to the understory levels. Our scientists assure us it's quite safe. Virtually no impact on the lower level biosphere. We're testing the concept in our township. If it works, it will be implemented planetwide."

Pattie pondered this last revelation. *A security net. I suppose it makes sense, but we haven't utilized anything of the kind in hundreds of years. Why now?* Something about the scenario nagged at her, but she couldn't identify what. For the time being, she decided to keep her concerns to herself.

"It's possible our missing kindred are somewhere on

the netting," the governor continued, "but scouring the nets will take hours—maybe days—depending on how far out they have to go. In the meantime, we have the question of the tremors and their effects."

"Yes, and that's what I want to discuss with you." Pattie slipped a padd off her belt, activated a file, and passed it across the desk to the governor. "If you'll examine that newsfeed picture, you'll notice a dark residue on the floors of the paddock. I've improved the resolution so you could better see it."

"Hmmmmm," the governor said, rubbing his chin with a pincer. "No one has mentioned it yet, but the teams in the field have their hands full trying to prevent decks from collapsing. You think this residue is related to the tremor?"

"I'm not sure. But I took the liberty of comparing that visual with several databases—botanical, engineering, historical—and couldn't find anything similar. From what I can tell, this residue isn't related to any construction materials or pest infestation—" Pattie paused. "And if you'd give me access—"

"Let's get to the point, P8," the governor interjected.

"Sir?"

"I expected you'd ask for a position. Why else the appointment? If I didn't want to give you the opportunity, I wouldn't have seen you today."

"So?"

"So. I'll grant you a *provisional* position on the team."

Her expression must have been quizzical, because the governor continued with an explanation. "Provisional because you're coming from the outside. Starfleet ways aren't necessarily our ways. If your presence proves disruptive, I'll revoke your credentials."

"Of course, sir," Pattie said. She searched her fellow Blue's face, watched his limbs, wondering if he was truly open to giving her a chance, or whether he was merely doing Commander Emon a favor. She sensed no malice or suspicion from him. *This might turn out fine.*

Reaching behind him, the governor shifted a lever, closing the office shutters. He then tapped in a sequence of commands on his console. A metallic sizzle announced the activation of a privacy shield.

"I don't need to tell you, P8, how serious this situation is. Whatever you learn out in the forest has to remain confidential."

She nodded.

"A lot is riding on this investigation. If we can't assure the safety of the population, the Planetary Council will order an evacuation," he said soberly. "We have to find the enemy. Whether it's a mutated virus, an enemy's weapon, an evolved strain of the *c'kh* fly—any of these could drain the life from the mother-tree. We can't take that risk."

"Excuse me, Governor, but I'm not a biologist," Pattie said, shaking her head doubtfully. "I know how to reinforce an off-balance deck, but I'm not sure what to do with *c'kh* fly infestations."

"I have biologists and botanists and chemists, P8. What I need is a fresh pair of eyes. I'm going to take a chance on yours." He folded his limbs over his abdomen and leaned back in his hammock-chair. "You're one of the kindred who have lived on the outside and seen more of life than many in this township. I had Commander Emon check out your Starfleet file. You've witnessed stranger things than I can conceive of. Perhaps you can find answers where all my experts cannot."

Pattie bowed her head. "I will do my best to honor the trust you've placed in me."

"I'll upload your security clearance and passwords to the networks as soon as you leave. I've already informed the team leader you'd be joining him"—he looked down at the screen—"in township sector 9A, deck 6."

"Would you have offered me this chance without Commander Emon's intervention?"

"Truthfully? I doubt I would have known you were here had you not been so persistent. That being said, I know how to recognize an opportunity when I see one. Don't make me regret my decision."

The governor's response didn't surprise Pattie. She was accustomed to being treated like an outsider, an oddity. "So why take the risk, when so much is at stake?" she said at last, seeking to assuage her own curiosity.

Leaning back in his hammock, he placed his hands together and flexed his fingers thoughtfully. "We came out of the same nursery, P8, though I doubt you knew me. I watched you from afar—like when you joined that alien research project—and have been curious what you would become. Let's hope for the sake of both of our reputations that satiating my curiosity doesn't prove to be poor judgment."

CHAPTER 5

On her way to rendezvous with the research team, Pattie discovered she had a bit of extra time, so she decided to check into a handful of nurseries. The governor had offered her the use of his personal transporter, but she decided she'd enjoy the opportunity to become reacquainted with her hometown. After all, the research team was only a turbolift and a few conveyors away from the governor's office. She scrolled through the maps on her padd as she traveled, occasionally glancing up to check the signage at each intersection of conveyor with side street, plaza, or branch sector. After passing the markets and the township's research quarter, she hopped off a conveyor in an older branch sector where the map indicated she'd find a nursery that interested her.

Pattie passed through the security checkpoint without even a curious glance. *Maybe the governor's endorsement on my ID record will simplify my life,* she thought. She took a leisurely pace, surveying the neighborhood as she walked, imagining what it would be like to spend the first season after hatching in a sector that predated her own hatching by probably a hundred seasons. But Pattie preferred the red-brown clay plastered walls, wood slabs, and rock floors more than structures that used syncrete and plasteel. Maybe her experience being raised in a modern neighborhood comprised of replicated materials biased her expectations for her own offspring. *Will they be successful here?* she wondered.

As she walked, she saw a cluster of paddocks abutting an attender health center. Off a side street, she noticed a learning pavilion for shells in their third or fourth seasons. Even the youngest nymph Nasat had been considered. A plaza built around a ten-meter-wide branch was filled with fruit-bearing vines, edible flowers, climbing shrubs—all providing an excellent playground. Crowded food centers bustled with activity as the local workers took their mid-cycle meals. Pattie wondered if these food centers used replicators or whether they cooked their root-aphid puddings and seed-pod pilafs the old way. Climbing up a ramp, she looked down into the kitchen and saw flashes of red, yellow, brown, and blue as the feeder shells rushed between steaming pots and thick casseroles. She knew that neighborhoods that continued to operate without the latest technology did it more out of pragmatic necessity than a reverence for tradition. Retrofitting branch sectors with the proper wiring, power conduits, and equipment was a slow, cumbersome process. Still, Pattie liked the thought of her larvae hatching here, taking early meals in that kitchen where the old ways hadn't been completely abandoned. *The softs are rubbing off on me,* Pattie thought, annoyed with herself. *I'm starting to sentimentalize the past.* She moved past the hungry crowds down the corridor to the nursery.

A retinal scan allowed her to pass through the exterior gate, through an archway, and into a hive of confusion. A Green rushing between hatching sacks, a Red nurturer filling thin plastic feeding tubes (shaped like the flower stamens ancient Nasat young fed on in the forest) with fruit-pollen pulp. A Brown attended to wall-to-floor-to-ceiling hexagon-shaped hatching tubes, a swollen pupa residing in each tube. The Brown fussed with the temperature/humidity controls in an effort to assure that the maximum number of pupae hatched. Pattie watched interestedly, never having spent much time in the nurseries, and no one noticed her for a few minutes. A Yellow shell, holding a newly hatched charge, clicked the nonsense rhythms of Nasat nurturing songs as he swayed back and forth in his seat-hammock. Pattie had a vague recollection of those chants. All Nasat nurturers knew them; they aided newly hatched shells in language acquisition. *I wonder if that young one he's rocking will be able to click back those words,* Pattie thought.

The Yellow looked up from his charge. "Greetings, Blue. Can I be of assistance?" he asked.

"I'm examining your facility. That's all I need if you don't mind me observing for a few minutes. Are you taking in any larvae this season?"

"Of course," answered the Brown shell that was tapping commands into the hatching tube console. "While at present our nests are filled to capacity, we expect our young nymph shells will soon move into their own paddocks. Are you ready to deposit today?"

Pattie shook her head. "I'm on shore leave from my starship. I had hoped to find a nursery before I had to return to duty."

"If you're interested, take one of our datachips." She gestured at a bucket sitting beside all the feeding gadgets. "Everything we need to know to properly gestate your larvae. How long since they'd been laid, if you know any information about the fertilizing shell. Fertilization isn't such a big issue unless there are specific genetic markers we need to be concerned with. Once you've filled out the forms, submit the request to our database. You don't even need to be planetside. We can retrieve your larvae from wherever you've stored them."

Pattie removed a chip from the bucket and dropped

it into the pouch mounted on her belt. "Fertilization happened so many seasons ago that I don't recall who the partner might have been, but as a rule, I tend to avoid partners with shell degeneration or impaired limb function."

"Always a wise precaution," a Brown shell said sagely. "I hope we can be of help."

She asked a few rudimentary questions, primarily to get a sense of what types of shells her larvae would encounter once they hatched. The odds were against her ever knowing her progeny after they hatched, so she wanted to make sure she could look out for them while she could. When she felt she had enough information to make an educated decision, she said good-bye to the nursery workers and went on her way to the research site.

Though she knew she'd be checking out other facilities, Pattie had a good feeling about this one. One thing she'd learned from softs was to trust intuition. More times than she cared to recall, one of her crewmates had said something along the lines of "I have a bad feeling about this," and the feeling had proved to be an accurate barometer of the situation. As she walked down the corridor, she fingered the pouch containing the datachip. *Yes, I definitely have a good feeling about this.*

Noting the cracked floor planking, Pattie stepped gingerly onto the sector of deck platform, wondering how long the damaged structure would hold the weight of all the shells working in the area. She saw a repair team equipped with plasteel seamers hiking up a peg-pole; she supposed they were starting to mend the cracks in the ceilings and walls. Several shells stood around with computers, laying down protective sensor grids that would warn of minute shifts in the structure that might indicate impending collapse. In the corner, issuing orders, she saw a Green shell—M9 Green was her designation, according to the governor. She had squeezed a plasma clipboard between a pair of limbs and was frantically scribbling notes with a stylus. Pattie watched for a few moments, reluctant to interrupt, when she concluded that this was an individual who would continue working until she was forced to shift gears.

"P8 Blue reporting for duty, sir."

M9 looked up from her clipboard. "Ah yes. The governor let me know you'd be working on our team. Structural engineer?"

Pattie nodded.

"Tell you what, P8, we've pretty much surveyed every damaged paddock for ten kilometers. Why don't you join the squads rappelling below the decks to check out the mother-tree? Your skills are too valuable to waste with tasks any shell with a seamer can handle."

M9 produced a security ID that Pattie clipped to her utility pocket, explained the basic layout of the worksite to her, and introduced her to the various team leads. Pattie's team was headed by a young Brown, Y29, that Pattie instantly took a liking to. Pattie's job would be to survey the branches beneath the lowest township deck for structural integrity. Though the decks were built from fabricated materials, the architects utilized some of the mother-tree's massive branches as support struts. A compromised branch could doom a sector to collapse.

Y29 and Pattie passed through rows of ordinary residential buildings to the outermost rim of paddocks. When they passed the last paddock, they turned into an L-shaped hallway with a maintenance door at the end. Exiting through the door, Pattie discovered that she was walking on a narrow plank path that followed along the building's edge. A railing, about limb height, with thin, fibrous netting was the only barrier between Pattie and the forest.

With wonder, she gazed out into the verdurous curtains, the tangle of scarlet flowers and twig nests, the delicate, mottled petals of fungi growing in branch hollows as slivers of sunlight tessellated on leaves larger than she was. Pattie felt small and alien in this wild, grand landscape. *This has surrounded me most of my life, and I feel as if I've never seen it before. . . .*

While she had lived most of her seasons on the homeworld, Pattie, like most Nasat, had matured from nymph to adult with the rain forest surrounding her. Her earliest nymph-songs had been animal squawks and tweeting and the gentle shush and plink of the late-day rain splashing on waxy leaves. During class, the overripe sweetness of rotting fruits and moldering leaves had wafted through windows. Wherever she roamed, she felt the forest's presence. But in actual, measurable time, Pattie had been outside the protective township barriers only a limbful of times in all her seasons. The Nasat brought the forest into their dwellings, but rarely ventured out into the open forest. Even with their position as the dominant sentient species on this world, the Nasat remained vulnerable to the aggressive predators that lurked in the world beyond the township. Being a peaceable species, they preferred keeping to themselves instead of aggressively colonizing or controlling the forests. All manner of animal and plant life coexisted, relatively undisturbed by the Nasat presence.

So for all her otherworldly experience, Pattie had never truly known her home planet. This deficit hadn't been obvious to her until now, as she meandered along the farthest rim of Nasat civilization, gazing out at the gaping maw of wildness.

Y29 provided her with equipment and a brief set of instructions on how to use the gear. A flush of excitement filled Pattie as she fastened climbing crampons onto her lower limbs, strapped herself into a harness, and waited in line for her chance to go over the edge.

Dozens of Nasat managed the climbing lines. Each

line was attached to one of hundreds of hooks mounted along the platform's outer edge. The hooks were ostensibly provided for botanist-attenders (those who cared for the mother-trees) and maintenance workers, who routinely rappelled beneath the township decks. Accessing power conduits or examining the tree's health was more easily accomplished outside the township.

Pattie's turn came. She paid close attention to the orientation when her group assumed the frontline positions.

"We're looking for abnormalities. Evidence of sabotage," a Yellow clicked. "Malfunctioning equipment. Infection. Anything that looks like it isn't supposed to be there." She pointed to a flat computer panel built into the harness. "If you find something that needs evaluation, this sensor panel can take a reader and transmit both picture and analysis to the base team up here. This companel also functions as your communicator. Questions? No. Then good searching."

Pattie surrendered, a little nervously, to a brusque Green who snapped the rope into place on her harness, demonstrated to Pattie how the automated controls worked—how to take up the line slack, how to let out more line—and told her it was time to drop over the side.

Not that different from zero-G, Pattie thought as the air whistled past her ears. She worked her way down the trunk with measured jumps, covering the equivalent of two or three decks of distance before she reached her assigned branch. Peering down the length of the branch, she guessed she had a kilometer or so to cover. Giving herself enough rope slack to move comfortably, she began slow, deliberate switchbacks, surveying the mature branch as she walked, holding her tricorder out in front of her.

Pattie was pragmatic enough to know that her study would take time. Like a complex piece of machinery, a mother-tree's health was subject to more variables than could be swiftly assessed. Minor bark beetle infestations or leaf rot didn't warrant a call to base camp. What Pattie kept foremost in her mind were the images she'd seen on the newsfeed last night.

Pictures of the damaged sectors (the one she presently worked in being the worst) showed evidence of scarification on the building and tree surfaces—almost akin to an acid spill—but the color, pattern, and characteristics of the scars resembled nothing she'd seen in her labs. She looked for the small, almost unnoticeable puddles of the same residue that appeared to be related to, if not the cause of, the scarification. It was a stretch, she knew, to assume such a minor thing could be related to the massive destruction she'd experienced last night; but Pattie knew to never rule out any possible evidence until you had to. *Patience,* she admonished herself as she walked back and forth.

How long she'd been walking, how far away from the trunk she had gone when her tricorder finally flashed a match, Pattie didn't know. As the permutations of the brown and green landscape had begun to blur to her eyes, the beep startled her. She shook herself back to awareness and studied the reading.

The tricorder had "seen" a marking similar to the one Pattie had noticed on the footage. *What if I'm onto something?* she thought. Nervously, she squeezed her pincers together. She squeezed her eyelids down hard a few times to help her alertness and then she read the tricorder reading. And reread the analysis. Dropping down on all her limbs, Pattie studied her discovery.

A pocket of dark brown—almost black—stickiness oozed out of a crusty laceration in the branch's bark. She nudged it with a gloved finger and a puff of smoke erupted. *Whatever it is, it's nasty,* she thought. Using a small, sterile slide from her harness panel to collect a sample, she ran a preliminary analysis and transmitted the specs to the base team. When they knew how they wanted her to proceed, they'd contact her. In the meantime, she decided to see how widespread this symptom was. She activated the wood adhesives on her crampons, assuring that she could walk the circumference of the branch without falling, and gingerly crawled over the side. Steadying her breathing, she moved one step at a time until she hung, shell down, beneath the branch.

The attack hairs on her neck bristled; she gasped.

For as far as she could see, similar pockets of black-brown ooze dripped off the branch. Thick ropey vines and ferns prevented her from seeing too far into the jungle, but the dark shadows staining the pale ochre faces of upturned flowers that grew below the branch were unmistakable. As the substance dried, scars formed on the bark surface. She activated her computer panel and began transmitting pictures.

After she'd passed most of an hour hanging upside down and accumulating sensor data, her signal receiver crackled.

"P8 Blue, this is base. We want as many pictures as you can manage. Follow the branch as far as the rope line will let you. Copy."

"Acknowledged, base. I'll head deeper into the forest."

Scrambling back on top of the branch, she activated the control that slackened her climbing line and began her hunting expedition.

She walked until the tree trunk and her teammates had long since passed from sight. In her aloneness, she jumped at the echoing chirps and animal skrees, wondering if a sharp-toothed sloth, prepared to pounce, waited in the next hollow. Rope or no rope, the prospect of dangling in midair, several kilometers off the ground with only a finger-thin rope to hang on to terrified her. Gradually, she acclimated; the hollow thumps of nuts falling from higher branches stopped startling her. She stopped worrying if a misstep would send her careening off the branch so she moved more swiftly, with confidence. Parting tangles of plants, stepping over furry mosses, and skirting the edges of *laito* monkey nests, she hunched over her tricorder, diligently taking readings. Life seethed on every side. Instead of fearing it, she found her environs comfortable, cozy.

When she reached a fork in the branch, she decided to take a break. A water seep trickling daintily from the upper reaches had smoothed a hollow in the bark where she could sit. For a late-cycle meal, she ate her fill of orange *jahang* berries and sipped beads of water off a leaf. *Let's see whether all this walking is getting us anywhere,* she thought, transferring data from her harness companel to her tricorder.

As the sensor input was received, the data was broken down and cross-referenced with every available Federation database, a time-consuming process. Consequently, Pattie didn't expect conclusive results would emerge until later. The rudiments of the problem, however, had begun to take shape. Sensors identified the unusual substance, not surprisingly, as an organic toxin with no known link to any disease, pest, or invasive organism native to the homeworld. She read the computer's prognosis with concern:

LONG-TERM EXPOSURE TO TOXIN CAN RESULT IN IRREVERSIBLE DAMAGE AND/OR DEATH TO ANY ORGANISM.

A rustle.

Startled, she turned to the side. *Must be the wind.*

She turned back to her tricorder. NO KNOWN ANTIDOTE EXISTS.

The shadows deepened. She looked up at the sky where clouds had blanketed the sun. But the forest—the forest felt . . . darker.

Another rustle . . . scraping twigs . . . soft squish . . . fruit falling . . .

Leaves trembled as if a wave had passed through the tunnel of gnarled twigs behind her. *Something's here,* she thought. *Maybe someone caught up with me. Or a team member transported down.*

Cautiously, Pattie eased into a standing position, cocking her ear toward the deep forest. At first low and intermittent, a hum rose, gradually increasing in pitch until the sound's acuity made her wince in pain. She tried raising two limbs to cover her ears, to block the horrifically sharp noise, but her limbs stayed fixed—paralyzed at her sides. Unwillingly, she listened, and while no words came from the sound, images formed in her mind. Warm dizziness suffused her. Her eye membranes dropped, bounced up, and dropped again. Around and above her, long reeds rippled and waved; the light dimmed as the green ceiling lowered, coming closer. . . .

Abruptly, the hum stopped.

The warm feeling abated. Pattie stirred from the trance she'd been in; panic engulfed her. She spun around, checking the forest on all sides of her; she saw nothing unusual. Whatever presence had been here had departed. Sunlight sliced through the clouds, refracted through mists, and painted sprays of rainbows in the air. Snippets of jewel-blue glowed bright between wisps of clouds. *Maybe I drifted to sleep for a few minutes,* Pattie thought. *I have been awake for three straight cycles. I should probably check in. See if anything new has come up.*

She touched her combadge, which she had tied into the companel on her harness. No response. Only a few kilometers separated her from the base station, so distance wasn't an issue. She shrugged off the equipment problem, assuming that her sensor transmissions must have depleted her power supply. Maybe the combination of humidity, minimal nutritional intake, and the stress of the past few cycles had resulted in a little forest madness. Heading back to base before the hallucinations started seemed to be a good idea. She'd only covered a short distance when the companel crackled to life.

"P8. Is that you? We lost you on our sensors for a minute. What happened out there?"

She opened her mouth to speak, but no sound emerged. Not a click or a squeak. A garble of words flashed through her mind. Moving her jaw back and forth, moving her teeth up and down, pushing her tongue against the roof of her mouth—none of it created sound. She massaged her neck in hopes that relaxing the muscles around her gullet would help.

Nothing.

"P8? Are you there? We're sending down a team if you don't copy this message."

Covering her eyes with her limbs, she opened up her throat, willing a squeak, a scream, a click, to emerge.

Silence.

What's happened to me?

CHAPTER 6

"Whatever it is that happened out in the forest seems to be temporary," Zoeannah said, attaching the neural sensors to Pattie's head. Sitting on a wheeled stool, she scooted back and forth the length of the bed, adjusting the biobed settings and checking the readouts. "You seem to be communicating just fine now."

"By the time the pair dispatched by the base team found me, I'd regained most of my language skills," Pattie explained, feeling more than a bit frustrated. "Before that, though, I can't explain why I couldn't speak. I tried all my usual techniques, but nothing seemed to work."

Prostrate on a biobed, Pattie had spent the last hour submitting to examination by Zoeannah and Tarak. Tarak, who had undergone Nasat attender training, had worked her up medically. Not surprisingly, he had found nothing. Tarak had taken possession of Pattie's tricorder, hoping that her discoveries in the forest might give him a clue as to what caused Pattie's muteness.

From where she sat at the computer, Zoeannah twisted back and said, "Go ahead and initiate the scan, Tarak." To Pattie, she said, "No talking. You know the rules."

P8 pivoted her eyes in annoyance. From where she

lay, she watched Zoë's panel lighting up as a map of her brainwaves appeared on the monitor.

"This is unexpected." Tarak removed a stylus from a desk drawer and was marking points on the computer screen. "The central cortex has been hyperstimulated."

"What?" Pattie clicked.

"You." Zoë placed a hand over Pattie's mouth. "Quiet. Now."

Anxiously, Pattie contemplated Tarak's revelation. Before she learned to speak, her upper brain functions were primarily based in the central cortex. Nasat scientists believed the central cortex was the most primitive part of the Nasat brain. Whatever functions it had served had become obsolete as the species had evolved. In an average Nasat, the central cortex might show low-level brainwave activity a handful of times during a day. As a result of her work with Zoë and Tarak, activity in her central cortex had slowed to normal levels. To have it activated again couldn't be a good sign.

"My readings are complete, Zoeannah," Tarak said. "Both of you should examine this data."

Zoeannah rolled her stool over to Tarak's terminal, with Pattie following close behind. He projected a holographic representation of Pattie's brain with color being used to map concentrations of brainwave activity. The hologram showed color variation from blues and greens (mildly active) to reds and oranges (extremely active). Just as Tarak had said, the central cortex glowed red-orange, indicating that it had been heavily stimulated.

"Out there in the forest, you were exposed to stimuli you'd never encountered before, Pattie," Zoë noted. "It's possible that your sensory intake was overloaded and it activated this cortex."

Brow creased, Tarak studied the readout on Pattie's tricorder. "The toxin, perhaps, when inhaled or touched, could provoke a violent nervous system reaction. I will generate models that will allow us to study the toxin's effects without having to reexpose you or other Nasat."

"But it's the humming thing I keep coming back to, Tarak," Zoë said, chewing on her fingernails. She shook her head. "Sounds at certain frequency can potentially impact neurotransmitters." She shook her head. "Too bad your tricorder didn't pick up any readings."

"I couldn't activate it," Pattie said, throwing out her limbs helplessly. "It was like whatever was there had numbed me up. Lulled me into a trance."

"You should consider giving up the investigation," Zoë said. She touched Pattie's shell.

Pattie knew Zoë was looking out for her interests, but abandoning the investigation when the threat appeared more serious than before went against her nature. "We don't have any proof that what happened to me resulted from anything in the forest. It could have been a random confluence of factors."

"Random?" Zoë threw up her hands and drew in a sharp breath. Abandoning her stool to futz over the computer terminals, she moved with a restless energy that betrayed her concerns.

Tarak stepped to her side, calmly placing a hand on her arm. "Pattie is correct, Zoeannah. We can hypothesize the source of her muteness, but we cannot say for a certainty that we know the causation."

"I don't want to lose my language abilities either," Pattie said. "But I think proceeding as normal would be best. At least if it happens again, we'll know there's an underlying reason. That it wasn't random."

Sighing, Zoë slapped her thighs with her hands. "Fine. But I want all the data from the investigation team. If this toxin has anything to do with your neural readings, more than just you could be in trouble."

"What do you mean?" Pattie asked.

"If something lurking out in the forest can hyperstimulate neurotransmitters to the degree we've seen in you, every Nasat in this township could be vulnerable. All of our studies have shown, without question, that an overactive central cortex is related to communication deficits. This holds true for any Nasat—not just quiets. With concentrated exposure to this stimulus, the township could regress a thousand years in language ability in weeks, maybe days. Still, I'm not willing to sacrifice you to find out, Pattie. Got that?"

To show affection, Pattie touched her thumb to her forehead, and touched the thin skin behind Zoë's ear. "What I learn, you will learn."

Pattie arrived at the briefing just before it began. Security services had posted guards at every entrance to seal the doors as soon as the meeting started. The discussions had been classified and would not be carried on the comnet.

Her team leader, Y29, waved to her from his seat in the front row. Pattie also noticed the governor reclining alongside the head of the Planetary Council. Other officials from the capital wearing brightly colored honor sashes chatted with investigation team heads, a few of whom Pattie remembered from this afternoon. The governor's rotunda was filled to capacity, but Pattie located a seat in a back corner. Based on her earlier conversation with the governor, she felt that keeping a low profile would be a good idea. She managed to slide into her row as the chief investigator, T4 Yellow, rose from his seat-hammock to speak.

"We've assembled here this night cycle to review the results from today's investigation. I think I speak for all who have studied this problem when I say that we are facing a threat more serious than any we've seen in a hundred seasons."

Reactionary clicks and crowd noise erupted. Based on Pattie's personal experience in the forest, she wasn't surprised by the announcement. She was curious, however, to see what the team had identified as the threat. The chief investigator hushed the group and began his presentation.

The lights dimmed and a holographic projection of the Nasat township appeared in the center of the rotunda. Each of the twenty decks was outlined in a different color, allowing P8 to distinguish the various township sectors.

"As most of you know," T4 began, "the damage from the tremors occurred in the township perimeter."

The computer filled in an irregular red border around the perimeter, indicating the damaged areas. Pattie could see that the destruction was more far-reaching than she'd previously known. One sector—the most recently built—had collapsed entirely several hours before the meeting.

"Data from our investigation teams indicates the presence of an organic toxin, origin unknown, in and around the damaged areas. Our chief botanist-attender, having received and analyzed the data, has a diagnosis."

T4 moved aside for a Brown shell that Pattie assumed was the botanist. She tapped commands into the rostrum terminal and the picture changed. Pattie recognized the projected pictures as the views from her harness sensor; she felt some measure of pleasure knowing that she'd made a contribution to the discovery.

"Because this substance doesn't have any known match in our databases, coming up with an ID has been challenging," the botanist said. "Several hypotheses have been put forth. Perhaps the toxin is a result of introducing new, off-world construction materials into our buildings. As we've been more actively involved in trading with other Federation worlds, it's possible we've also imported a mutagenic virus or bacteria that our trees don't have a defense for. I assure you all that we're working to find an antidote to the toxin as quickly as possible. Unfortunately, the toxin has already invaded several mother-trees."

The projection shifted, becoming a rendering of the mother-tree overlaid with a graph. More than a dozen sections of the tree glowed yellow, sections in close proximity to damaged decks.

"The yellow indicates necrotic tissue. Under normal circumstances, we can surgically remove the damaged areas and graft healthy tissue in its place. In this case, however, we fear the toxin has already penetrated the tree's circulatory system, thus compromising the tree's immunity. The tree might not be strong enough to withstand the surgery."

The governor raised a limb, requesting to be recognized. "So the mother-tree has an infection. But it *can* been contained?"

The botanist exchanged looks with T4. "No. I expect we'll have branch death within the week."

A collective gasp sounded from the gathering. Pattie glanced at the tree structure and mentally superimposed the township decks. *If those branches go, the deck loses critical supports. I suppose we could construct artificial limbs to replace them—the way they do in the capital city—but what if the construction materials are the problem?*

"We are surveying the primary trunk and limbs for similar cellular damage. Botanists have been dispatched in hovercraft to study the understory region. However, we are not optimistic. All indicators point toward weakening buttress roots. There are few other explanations for the severity and irregularity of the tremors. We are in danger of losing the mother-tree."

Pattie, along with everyone in attendance, sat in numb shock. To a Nasat, the mother-tree represented all aspects of living: food, shelter, and protection. When the brutality of life on the forest floor nearly wiped out the Nasat, it was to the trees that they escaped to survive. In the trees, they built settlements where they could finally move past the sustenance life of their ancestors, developing tools and ultimately technology that opened up the stars for exploration. The loss of a mother-tree was unthinkable.

Once the botanist-attender had made her sober pronouncement, few in the audience found the remainder of the presentation nearly as vital. Pattie believed she heard something about security services being unable to locate any of the missing Nasat. A Federation official announced that a research team from the closest starbase had been dispatched and would be arriving in a few days. Finally, a Green shell stood, interrupting the Planetary Council member, and said, "What do we do about the mother-tree?" His inquiry was echoed by hundreds of other voices.

The Brown shell botanist stood. "We don't have any plan of action until we know the severity of the poisoning."

"But what about the dying branches? What about the decks built in those sectors? Will all those Nasat have to evacuate?" someone else called out.

"Why aren't we *all* evacuating?" another shouted. "The moon base could easily host the township population until this problem's solved. Why wait until every deck collapses into the forest?"

The last comment provoked controversy. On every side, discussions erupted. Pattie eavesdropped on bits of conversation, but found no one asked the question she felt needed to be asked. *In their fear, they're all being swept away by reaction. We need to take charge—make preemptive decisions.*

She waved her hand, seeking recognition from the rostrum. The confusion in the room made it nearly impossible to be noticed. She stood and waited for the chief investigator to recognize her.

Grateful for a chance to distract the crowd, T4 nodded to Pattie, indicating she had the floor. Attempts to shout above the noise proved futile, so T4 waved Pattie up to the rostrum. When the audience noticed a new shell had joined the group, the talk gradually stuttered to a halt, and the attention shifted to Pattie.

The governor gave Pattie a meaningful look, his

antennae taut. Pattie understood his meaning: *Behave yourself.*

"I am P8 Blue. I work as a structural engineer for Starfleet. And while I have a multitude of ideas for how we might construct supports for the weakened decks—even for the buttress root systems, I'm concerned that our focus is too narrow."

"When we're literally working every conceivable angle, I don't know how you can say that," the botanist said, thrusting her padd at Pattie. "Take a look for yourself."

"I've seen it. Up close," Pattie said, politely refusing the padd. "I was in the forest today and I saw how widespread the toxin is. Whatever it is seems to have invaded the mother-tree without being noticed until the damage is too extensive to correct. We can't afford to solely depend on the tried-and-true approaches. Every option needs to be open."

"Clearly you think we're missing something, P8," the governor said coolly.

Here it is. Swallowing hard, Pattie said, "We need to go to the bottom and set up a research outpost."

Those on the rostrum exchanged glances. Pattie noticed more than a few sets of pincers tightening. A wave of clicks and chirps rose up from the audience.

"We don't need to risk going to the bottom, P8," the chief investigator said dismissively, "unless the buttress roots require structural assistance. Our botanist-attenders and security services use hovercraft. Our sensor nets are extensive. What do you believe we can learn from going to the bottom that we can't learn far more easily? Why risk more lives?"

An unnerving stillness settled over the audience. Every Nasat in the rotunda awaited her answer. She couldn't read the governor's mood, though she guessed he didn't appreciate the controversy.

Pattie considered her reply carefully. She had more

arguments against T4's statement than he would give her time to share. She needed to say the words that would be most helpful. Of all the reasons she had joined the S.C.E., the one that stood out the most was her thirst for diversity, a willingness to explore new methods of solving problems. Now here she was, standing before the elite of her world, confronting the ridiculous taboos and prejudices she'd witnessed her whole life. She could say what they wanted to hear or she could say what she thought. *I, alone, can't fix this. I can only do the best I can.* Taking a deep breath, she said, "One of the lessons I've learned in my seasons in Starfleet is that you can't solve a problem from a distance. You have to be willing to get right in the thick of it. This problem is serious enough to warrant exploring every path open to us. Why not go to the bottom?"

"Because we don't have any evidence that this ailment comes from below the canopy," one of the investigators said. "And what if we go to the bottom and it spreads the infection?"

"We still need to eliminate the forest floor as the source of the problem."

The botanist leaped from her seat, limbs gesticulating angrily. "You're asserting that we are failing to do everything in our power to assure the safety of Nasat and our mother-tree!"

Before Pattie could reply, many in the crowd scrambled out of their seats, evincing outrage, confusion, fear. Pattie reciprocated their feelings. "This isn't about assigning blame! This is my home too!" she shouted, but the commotion smothered her words. As Nasat crammed into the aisles and up to the rostrum to make their voices heard, Pattie allowed herself to be pushed to the rear. *I've done it now,* she thought, fully expecting to have her clearances revoked. Quietly, she slipped away as anonymously as she had come.

* * *

From the shadow darkening the floor, Pattie knew that Zoë stood in the doorway. The Betazoid would want to talk. It was difficult to hide a bad mood from a telepath, but Pattie didn't feel like talking. She'd had quite enough discussion, thank you. Upon arriving at the lab, she'd gone straight to a nest. Though she wasn't feeling tired, she wanted a chance to think without being disturbed. Using a padd, she'd conjured up a facsimile of the tree projection the botanist had put up. Repeatedly running her eyes over each branch and leaf tuft, she imagined what type of engineering wizardry would be required to save the township. She wasn't as optimistic as she'd hoped she could be. The circumstance wasn't unlike what happened to a starship when a deck became severely damaged. Once structural integrity was compromised, the safest course was to lock off the deck and shore up protective shielding in the still intact areas. In the township, the seriously damaged areas would have to be dismantled before they weakened more stable structures. What troubled Pattie was how to save the moderately damaged areas. Shifting weight from one branch or installing artificial supports for one sector might require modifications in other sectors. No matter how she played through the scenarios in her mind, they always ended in a chain reaction.

"You can ignore me all night. I'll sleep in the doorway," Zoë said finally. "The bad vibes you're putting out will keep me up anyway."

"Close the door, then," Pattie said.

"Very cute. But that doesn't cut it."

"The summary version is this: nothing looks good, for the mother-tree or for me. Whatever I ran into in the forest is more potent than even I imagined."

Dropping down on the floor beside Pattie, Zoë looked over Pattie's limbs at the padd she worked on. "I take it this is a graphical representation of the damaged areas."

Pattie nodded. "And while I seriously doubt that I'll be invited to continue participating in the investigation—"

Zoë's eyebrows shot up.

"—if I can help work a solution on how we can save the township, I'll feel useful."

Peering intently at the graphic, Zoë tipped her head to the side, frowned, and tipped her head to the other side. She reached for the padd. "May I?"

Shrugging, Pattie passed it over.

"I swear I've seen this before." She gnawed on her lip. "I *know* I've seen this before." Sitting back on her haunches, she thought for a long moment before slapping her thighs. "Got it!"

Zoë disappeared into the adjoining room. The clatter of padds being tossed aside and Zoë's mutters amused Pattie. She returned shortly, grinning triumphantly, with a padd tucked beneath her arm. Thrusting it at Pattie, she said, "I knew I'd seen it before!"

Assuming that Zoë wanted her to activate the tablet, she did so. When a nearly identical township map appeared on the screen, Pattie wasn't surprised, but she wasn't sure what this had to do with their present dilemma. She turned a questioning look on Zoeannah.

"Several years ago, we worked with a loremaster to find any records that might be pertinent to our research. Census, birth data—anything vaguely anthropological that could give us clues about the quiets. This map you're looking at might be five hundred years old."

Pattie studied the maps more closely, noticing that indeed, many similarities existed between them. Each map had similar chunks of the township perimeter outlined. *Just how similar is the question.* Butting the padds against each other, she transmitted the data from the older padd to the newer one. With a few quick commands, she had pulled up a projection of the maps: the overlaid trees appeared in the air. The highlighted sections appeared as virtual concentric circles, with the younger tree forming a blue perimeter just inside the yellow perimeter of the older tree.

"Even when you figure in tree growth, the resemblance is uncanny," Pattie said finally. "What was this map for, anyway?"

"Population distribution," Zoë said. Sensing Pattie's confusion, she continued, "In previous centuries, quiets tended to be isolated from the general population. Why? I can't say, but this old map indicates that the quiets' paddocks are clustered together in the highlighted areas."

"So, long ago, the quiets lived along the perimeter, but specifically near these areas that have been recently damaged."

Zoë nodded.

Pattie's mind raced through possible connections between the events of the past few days and a faraway time. "Can we even *make* a connection between these two maps?" she said, thinking aloud.

"On the surface, the two scenarios don't appear to be related, but I think the similarities are too uncanny to be ignored."

"We might find answers in history—"

"If Nasat were better about keeping their history. Your kindred don't believe in preserving the past," Zoë said philosophically. "And yet, here you see that there might be a link, however tenuous, between whatever is happening now and what happened then."

After her disastrous appearance at the meeting, Pattie had resolved to walk away from the investigation—especially since it seemed like she was bringing more confusion than clarity to the problem. But seeing these maps . . . She considered her options and made a decision.

"So, do you have any other records that might be of use?"

* * *

How far into the dark cycle they worked before the door chime sounded, Pattie couldn't say. Neither of them had known precisely what they were looking for. Before long, Pattie's nest area was overrun with padds, hand-drawn charts and graphs, scrolls, data chips, and holos from Nasat history. She had been deeply absorbed in the earliest recorded township map when Tarak appeared in the doorway.

"The governor's here," he said.

"I have to apologize to—"

"He's not here for you, he's here for Zoë and me."

Pattie and Zoë exchanged puzzled looks. Zoë shoved aside the census data for Nasat Year 1647 and followed Tarak into the receiving room.

Resisting the impulse to spy, Pattie dropped her gaze to the map she held with four of her limbs. Though the primitive rendering failed to offer a computerized map's precision, the proportions and scale were such that she could approximate what the mother-tree (and township) looked like nearly a millennium ago. The cartographer had inked in the outlines of where future decks would be built. Pattie noted with amusement that the mapmaker had only anticipated another eight decks after the original four. *How could they have foreseen the day when we'd have more than twenty?* Nasat pictographs formed the map's border, providing a narrative or instructions. She was far from an expert in interpreting pictographs, but she could translate enough to figure out the general idea.

". . . and on this day, we raise this township, mindful of the promises made by kindred past . . ."

What promises? Pattie thought.

Muffled voices came from the receiving room. Pattie wondered what problem the governor had brought to Zoë and Tarak. *It doesn't matter to me anyhow.* She forced her attention back to the map.

An idea occurred to her. She waved a scanning wand over the old parchment and loaded the scanned record into her padd. It took only minutes to convert the drawing into three dimensions. A press of her thumb and all three map projections—each outlined in a different color—appeared in the air, spinning side by side. Overlaying one tree atop another was simple. Pattie gazed at the intertwined multi-colored lines, muttering aloud, "What am I supposed to see? It's right in front of me, I know it is. . . ."

"Pattie?" Zoë poked her head around the corner.

She looked up from her maps.

"I need you to come with us. I'll explain later."

Not much was said on the way to the attender health center. No one had offered an explanation on why this was relevant to Pattie. For Zoë and Tarak, however, she would comply without question. The governor had acknowledged her once, briefly, when he said, "You certainly know how to stir things up, don't you?"

She assumed he was referring to her outspokenness in the investigation briefing. Before she could reply, he'd moved ahead on the conveyor to stand with his aides.

As soon as they arrived, Pattie recognized the health facility as being the preeminent research center in the forest quadrant. Tarak had done his attender fellowship here when he'd first started his research. On their way in, they passed by a pair of security services officers, which struck Pattie as strange. *Since when do health facilities require protecting?* A turbolift and back hallway later, the group arrived at another security checkpoint before entering a patient's room.

A Red shell Nasat lay on the biobed, body rigid, neural-feedback sensors attached along the ridges of his skull. With eye membranes rolled nearly into his sockets, his coal-black eyes stared, unblinkingly, at the ceiling. Attenders stood on various sides of the bed, each monitoring different physiological functions. Tarak approached one of them—a Green shell—and began talking in hushed tones with her.

Surveying the room, Pattie gathered that whoever this Nasat was, he had sustained serious neurological injuries. On a monitor, she studied the color patterns that showed brain activity, discovering that every quadrant glowed red and orange, indicating that every neuron and synapse was firing steadily, without respite. *You can't survive that kind of biochemical overload,* she thought. She shifted nervously, remembering her own brief encounter in the forest. *Maybe that's why I'm here.*

Pattie watched as Tarak used his own tricorder to take readings. Gesturing for Zoë to begin her work, he examined the monitor readouts while Zoë wrapped her hand around the injured Nasat's, studying him intently. After a few moments, they conversed quietly. Zoë gestured animatedly with her hands; Tarak shook his head.

"I'm afraid we don't have much to add to your diagnosis," Tarak said, spinning a monitor around for the governor to see. He pointed to the erratically fluctuating brainwaves scrolling across the bottom of the screen. "Resequencing cannot address this degree of neural chemical breakdown. Given time, the brain might be able to restore equilibrium. Time, I'm afraid, is all we can offer."

"What about stabilizing the cortical activity?" one of the attenders asked. "I know part of what you've done in your research involves building new neurochemical pathways—"

"With a conscious, willing subject who has the ability to apply focused effort over an extended period of time," Tarak said. "We could work with him if he recovers—"

"To put it simply, Governor," Zoë interrupted, "this Nasat's brain has been so overstimulated that irreparable damage might have been done to the tissues. As Tarak said, waiting is the only option."

Pattie didn't generally consider herself to be obtuse, but she remained unclear as to precisely why she'd been included on this visit. Her soft friends were well known in the forest quadrant for having neurological expertise. Why the governor would call them was obvious. Maybe they thought she might lend some insight based on her own experiences, including her most recent bout of muteness. Or maybe, she considered cynically, the governor didn't want her to get into trouble if they left her at the paddock unsupervised. The thought tainted her mood with a bit of petulance. Intending to find out once and for all, she leaned forward, raising a limb to get Tarak or the governor's attention—

Zoë shot her a look that admonished patience.

Tarak, Zoë, and the governor clustered with the attenders, talking for a moment longer.

When the group broke, the governor said, "Let's go outside and talk, shall we?"

They filed behind an orderly who guided them to a vacant suite. Once the orderly had returned to duty, the discussion began.

Pattie opened her mouth to speak, when Zoë quickly cut her off.

"Where did you find the Red in there?" She glared meaningfully at Pattie.

"On the security netting about two kilometers from the township," the governor said. "Not much improvement from when we found him, unfortunately."

"And you know for a fact that he was one that went missing during the quakes?" Zoë persisted.

Now it becomes interesting, Pattie thought, becoming intrigued.

"We were able to confirm ID when we found him. He had been in his paddock—in his nest. One of his neighbors confirmed that when he vanished," one of the governor's aides said. "How he came to be in this state . . . well, that's the part that worries us."

He felt a presence. He felt a presence and heard a sound that pierced him to the core, Pattie thought. *And the part where I come in . . .*

"Excuse me, but I think I might have some insight to offer here," Pattie began. She related her experience while working on the investigation and the resultant symptoms.

The governor didn't bother hiding his surprise. "Could other Nasat have had similar experiences?"

Pattie waved her antenna. "Possibly. Based on what we saw in the Red shell, I'd say definitely. Any clue what happened to the Red?"

No answer. The governor looked to his aides for a response. They both raised their limbs in frustration. "Fine, then," he said, "I'll tell them. Security services discovered several holes in the security netting. Cut from beneath. From the bottom." He paused to let Pattie digest the information.

"How soon do you want me to go down?" Pattie asked.

Because of the general population's concerns about trekking to the forest floor, the governor had ordered the team's formation to remain secret. The group would meet at Zoë and Tarak's lab and would head down to the observation decks in smaller groups to avoid incurring public attention. Several from the investigation, such as Y29—who had, incidentally, agreed with Pattie at the meeting—would be going, along with security services. The team risked encountering the same force that Pattie had, so the governor had asked Tarak if he would join the team's attender in providing health services. Equipment would be beamed down to the spot beneath the break in the security net. Because of unpredictable conditions on the floor, the team would hike on foot to the equipment. The most recent surveys of the floor were loaded into their navigation equipment, but all of them knew that the whims of nature constantly changed the territory.

Pattie, Y29, and Tarak were the last to leave. Pattie had touched her thumb to her forehead, and to Zoë's ear before Zoë's eyes welled up. She threw her arms around Pattie's shell, squeezing her tightly. "Come back," she whispered, then disappeared into her private rooms, with Tarak following close behind. Pattie pulled Y29 out into the public passageway, offering a little privacy to the couple. After a few moments, Tarak emerged, his carrypack secure, walking stick in hand. "We should be leaving."

And they began the long journey into the dark.

CHAPTER 7

The weathered observation deck felt slippery beneath Pattie's feet, the splintering planks wet with dew. Nervously, the team huddled near the center of the deck platform, all of them wanting to avoid the rickety railings. Here, beneath the security netting, the eerie, gray twilight that passed for day had to suffice until night fell when wrist-lamps could be used. None of them knew how far they would travel or how long they would be gone. Even if new supplies could be transported down, the feasibility of doing so was unknown. Conserving resources was a paramount concern.

On the team commander's signal, they began silently filing down the well-worn steps to the bottom. When Pattie's turn came, she descended, all the while marveling at the work of her ancestors. The platform—these steps that had been carved into the tree itself—predated the township by several hundred years. If the stories were true, the Nasat of the last millennium had scrambled up into the trees to escape their predators' pursuit. A lookout, stationed up on a makeshift platform, would warn the kindred of impending danger. *They did everything they could to climb up, so we're climbing back down. Maybe we haven't learned as much as we hoped,* Pattie thought wryly.

They traveled slowly, pausing occasionally when one of the team members would lose footing. Pattie used these opportunities to study the verdant mosses growing in the crevices of the tree bark. Seemingly innocent vine tendrils crawled tentatively around shrubby brush, twining over and under, slowly strangling their host. Pairs of glowing yellow eyes appeared in the shadows. A noise would send the creature scampering off. The wall of humidity rising around them took the most getting used to. Pattie, in particular, after living in the regulated atmospheres of starships for so long, had some trouble adjusting. The deeper into the understory they traveled, the more sodden, the more thickly dense the sweltering air became. Condensation dripped off the shell of the Nasat above Pattie; she was certain drops rolled off her own shell on the Nasat below her. The sheer volume of decomposing plant life and sour animal wastes, the overripe perfume of rotting flowers and fruit nearly overwhelmed Pattie.

When they reached the bottom, the team leader, a security services officer named D6 Blue, organized the group into smaller units of five, assigning one individual in each group the responsibility for keeping track of the others. He dispatched several security shells into the forest to survey the perimeter. While they were out on reconnaissance, he checked all the tricorders in the group, making sure that everyone had the same coordinates programmed into their navigational sensors. A locating beacon had been attached to the equipment about twenty-five kilometers from where they'd descended, making it simpler for the team to fix on their destination. The plan was to set up camp once they arrived. Where and how far into the forest the team would go the following day had yet to be determined. They hoped that they would find some kind of clue that would help them track whatever had invaded the township, but they couldn't be certain.

The scouts returned, reporting nothing unusual. D6 ordered the group to move out.

Each step required caution. Low-lying mists carpeting the marshy ground hid elaborate crisscrossing root systems. Pools of algae-laden waters lurked in every hollow and divot. Tarak perpetually kept his hand in front of his face as clouds of gnats swarmed in his eyes, nose, and ears. A constant chorus of *neek-breek, breek-neek* rang in Pattie's ears until she had little room for her own thoughts. But staying focused on the path was critical. One misstep could result in a soaked carrypack, a broken limb, or other, more serious injuries. Long, feathery leaves shrouded the path ahead. Other rubbery textured fronds were large enough to smother Pattie—or any other Nasat—should they fall. Brimming with sticky nectar, pitcher leaves (the size of starship consoles, Pattie noted with awe), temporarily blinded any kindred unfortunate enough to trip and stumble into a pollen-heavy stamen. Whatever awaited them on the forest floor was well hidden.

Pattie, Y29 Brown, Tarak, and their other team members, F2 Red and W37 Yellow, said little as they walked. The heavy humidity sapped Pattie's energy, and she assumed the others felt similarly. The smallest movement seemed to require such concentration that Pattie felt like she trudged along at a *skagoh*'s pace.

A stagnant pool. A reed bed. Step beneath the gnarled root nodules. Careful there—don't lose your pack. Another pool. Duck down to crawl under another root.

Time dragged by. The decaying leaves of the variegated ferns blurred together in one fetid, brown-green swamp.

Over the hours, daylight dimmed slowly, from dank grayness to murky dusk. As the rotting quagmire became more difficult to discern from the mud, Pattie nearly slipped into a peaty bog. She picked wet leaves off her limbs but was unable to scrape the slime out of her joints. *Maybe this wasn't such a good idea,* she thought. Pushing aside her discomfort, she trudged on, counting on the promise of her tricorder that base camp was only another kilometer away.

Finding stable ground to set up equipment had proved nearly impossible. D6 Blue ordered most work surfaces suspended between roots or laid over fallen trees. Usually, Nasat sleeping nests could be easily made up using the forest materials. Under these circumstances, however, there was a fear that an unexpected thunderstorm or ground shift would endanger any Nasat resting in a nest. Makeshift hammocks where they could curl up would have to suffice. As an additional protection, Tarak had devised a type of neural shielding, modeled after an instrument he used in his lab to limit the brain's ability to respond to certain stimuli. While not entirely foolproof, the shielding would scatter any large concentrations of specific energy frequencies. He'd chosen what frequencies to protect against based on Pattie's encounter.

The business of organizing camp consumed the rest of daylight. By the time Pattie was ready to take her night cycle meal, darkness had fallen and they were sipping their plates of fruit pulp by wrist-lamps. She and Tarak had been invited to join D6 after their meal, presumably to lay out a plan for the following days. They found the team leader standing behind a table, padds spread out before him, conversing animatedly with a botanist who had come along as a consultant.

"Excellent. P8, Dr. Tarak. Thank you for joining us," D6 said. "As I was just saying to G3 here, I believe our first task is to see if we can find a trail of some kind—any evidence left behind by whatever cut through the security netting."

"Have we come any closer to identifying the toxin?" P8 asked.

G3 shook his head. "No. Because the toxin has

already interacted with the tree's metabolism when we find evidence of it, we're having a hard time isolating its unique molecular components—what's the tree and what's the invader."

"We should start looking as soon as possible," Tarak said. "Waiting for daylight could cost us valuable time."

"Agreed," D6 said, "But we've yet to figure out a consistent method for tracking the toxin scars. Down here, the light and the irregular landscape make it especially challenging. We'll just have to start combing the area—as we did in the mother-tree branches."

While Tarak and the others continued discussing possible strategies, Pattie mulled the problem over in her mind.

"And if we extrapolate a course—" D6 said.

"Wait," Pattie interrupted. "You have a molecular analysis of the toxin?"

The botanist nodded, and transmitted the data to Pattie's tricorder.

Attention fixed on the small screen, Pattie said, as she worked, "If we can figure out what properties these molecules respond to, we might be able to modify some of our equipment to help locate the toxin scars."

"Such as light frequency or sound?" Tarak said.

"Exactly," Pattie said. "My guess is, if we can find the right spectrum of light, we can flash our wrist-lamps over the plants, trees, roots—whatever else might be a likely spot—and see if we can ascertain a direction to pursue. I'll work on this while you all come up with a backup plan."

D6 looked a little surprised to be on the receiving end of an order from an underling. Pattie quickly amended, "If that works for you, sir."

With a tip of his antennae, he indicated for her to continue. The others huddled around him, collectively analyzing the sensor data and land surveys.

While they reviewed potential routes, Pattie fiddled

with her tricorder, her antennae curled in concentration. Biochemistry had never been her strength, but she knew enough of engineering to be confident in her abilities. An hour later, as D6 was ready to dismiss the group until morning, Pattie had a working model of her idea.

She had reworked the light-generating mechanism in her wrist-lamp to emit a narrow spectrum of ultraviolet light. Based on her calculations, one of the submolecular compounds in the toxin would be stimulated by the short-frequency light rays and start to vibrate. As the compound warmed, it would become luminescent. She had augmented the light beam with enough visible-frequency rays to allow the user to see where the beam was being directed. Since none of the other possible approaches would be feasible before morning, Pattie's idea was worth exploring.

To obtain the best result, the group hiked away from the large, standing lamps illuminating the camp and found a fern grove—with fronds twice the height of a Nasat—that was a veritable lagoon of darkness. Pattie flipped the switch on her wrist-lamp, tinting her surroundings a washed-out purple. Even after waiting for a few moments, nothing glowed with a distinctive, white shimmer. She took a few cautious steps deeper into the fern grove. Still nothing.

She turned to the botanist. "Assuming the invader descended back into the forest along a similar trajectory to the one it took to initially break through the netting, where would we start looking?"

"Closer to camp, probably," D6 answered. "I'll take care of it." He scurried back to camp and ordered all the lights dimmed.

Slowly, Pattie walked back toward camp, her wrist-lamp sweeping up and down, across the ground, over plants and saplings. She couldn't understand why she hadn't found anything. Laws of physics and chemistry defined the rules of how compounds responded to specific stimuli.

Wait a minute, she thought. *I devised my light frequency based on the botanist's analysis and she said herself that the sample was degraded. I need to refine the spectrum.* Making a couple of quick calculations, she adjusted the wrist-lamp to higher UVB range. The ultraviolet light winked out for a split second before flickering on again. She held up her wrist-lamp, sweeping the beam across the landscape.

The forest shimmered to life, from the boggy ground, to the blanched roots, to the brush. On every side, the base camp glowed. The botanist raced over to check out one of the lacy, luminous patterns on a fallen tree. A long pause. She turned around, raising her tricorder in the air for Pattie and D6 to see, and nodded.

You can't hide from us anymore, Pattie thought.

Several Nasat had emerged from being curled up, saw the eerie radiance on the bark behind them or the ground beneath them, and shouted out questions to the team leader. Confusion rippled through the group.

Pattie swallowed hard. Imagining something in theory had little in common with knowing something in fact. They had come to this place to find their enemy, whatever it was. To discover that the enemy had been in their midst—might still be in their midst—disquieted her in a way she hadn't suspected it would. Until now, she had been solving a puzzle. The stakes had suddenly become much higher.

"We've found our trail," D6 ordered. "Break camp."

CHAPTER 8

Pattie's first task, modifying a dozen or more wrist-lamps, consumed her time while the others packed up the camp gear. D6 decided that the group would travel with the minimum amount of equipment: food, phasers, medical supplies, and critical gear like the neural shielding devices. The rest would be secured and left to be beamed back up to the township at the appropriate time.

To avoid being disturbed, she sat apart from the others, her tools spread out on a table, intent on the task before her. Each fearful thought that bubbled up from her subconscious was pushed aside. There was no question in her mind of the potential dangers they faced, but letting her imagination run away with her would hardly help matters. The longer she worked, the more rote the wrist-lamp modifications became; her mind wandered, worried. She resolved to direct her energies toward a more productive topic.

Since her visit to the Red shell in the health center, Pattie had rarely thought of the map project she'd been working on. She'd brought the projections with her, fully intending to further analyze them in her downtime, though now it appeared downtime would be rare, if not nonexistent. Conjuring up a picture of the three township maps in her mind, she let them twirl around in her head while she worked. *What's there that I'm not seeing? Each tree is a map of the township, from deep in the past to the present. When you're looking for an answer, focus on their commonalities. Focus on their commonalities, P8.*

The perimeter. Quiets lived near the perimeter. The tremor damage and discovery of toxins came in the perimeter. And on the ancient map? She couldn't recall each pictogram and rendering, but she had a vague memory of a specific directive regarding the township boundaries. What was it? . . .

She had it: the oldest map indicated a ring of territory that was forbidden to build in. No reason was given—at least nothing specific like, "if you build in this area, you'll activate a latent disease." The same territory that now sustained damage. The same territory that had been gradually built up, after hundreds of years of being left alone, in the last twelve seasons.

We violated the edict and we've stirred up something. But what and why? Pattie made an adjustment to the last of the wrist-lamps. *We'd better figure it out fast.*

Amidst the *neek-breek, breek-neek* amphibian choruses, a distracting rustle came from the bushes off to her left. D6 must have dispatched shells to tear down her workspace. *Probably eager for me to finish so we can start moving.*

"If you'll let me pack up my . . ." her voice trailed off.

Not a single shell appeared within five meters of her table. Clusters of them worked on packing up the last of the storage crates. A few scouts emerged from the woods. She twisted to look behind her; she scanned the area but saw only the glints of moonlight reflecting dully off pools of water, the scrubby ground cover, and the scabby buttress roots rising like monoliths. She had a new, keen awareness of her swishing pulse thrumming in her ears.

The forest became expectantly quiet.

A snapping twig refocused her attention. Something was behind her. She sensed it. Like before. Rising from her workbench, she tentatively stepped forward, forcing her leaden limbs to move. She parted the bushes behind her table. A *thwupt-thuwpt* of wings rushed up into her face and in startled shock, she staggered back, watching the avians become dark specks spiraling through the low-lying trees.

Inhaling deeply a few times to settle herself, Pattie leaned back into her seat-hammock. She closed her eyes. . . . *Lack of sleep must be catching up with you,* she thought, suddenly feeling warm, drowsy. . . .

A soft, cool pressure curled around her neck—and pinched!

She flew out of her chair, screeching, clutching at her neck, spinning around, searching. "Where are you? What are you? Show yourself!"

Across the now nearly deserted camp, shells looked up from their work.

"I know you're here!" she cried, continuing to whirl around, trying to peel away, pry away, that thing, the cold fingers—

"Pattie." Tarak's soft voice steadied her.

Turning toward him, she stopped spinning; dizziness convulsed her vision.

His hands touched her face; Pattie instantly felt the stability of his mind melding with hers. The surroundings blurred, her body slackened, and her mind cleared as he probed her consciousness. From Tarak's gentle questioning she instantly knew that whatever she'd experienced had been hers and hers alone, for she felt no recognition from him when she attempted to recall the memory. None of the others had seen or felt it. And for a brief moment she wondered if she was going mad, like quiets were often thought to do. That her defective brain had played games with her, tormenting her with imaginary sensations. Anxiously, she reassured Tarak that she wasn't hallucinating, pleading with him to believe her. And he accepted her thoughts as truth.

Gradually, he broke away from the meld, continuing to gaze deeply into Pattie's eyes. "Be careful," he admonished her. "I do not understand what you see."

Pattie nodded.

A gentle, balmy breath of breeze gushed through the trees. A clatter in the sky warned of a storm. Within seconds, the clouds opened, sending a warm torrent of rain.

Blinking droplets out of their eyes, Tarak and Pattie rushed to gather the adjusted wrist-lamps into a carry-pack to give to D6. The team leader immediately distributed them to the security services officers, who took point at the front of the group. Following the spindly line of Nasat, Tarak and Pattie walked hand-in-hand into the dark, blustering forest.

For a time, Pattie believed she could see ghoulish white-purple shimmers as the wrist-lamps unmasked them. She trudged dutifully behind the others, wondering what horrible place this path led to. Soon, the veil of rain shrouded her view entirely; her world became mud splashing on her limbs, slippery black-green tendrils slapping as she pushed ahead. She kept her eyes down, watching for erupting roots or slippery rock. Tarak walked ahead of her, pushing the low-hanging foliage out of their way. The rain crashed and shooshed, pounding them mercilessly. Lightning crackled, answered by percussive thunder.

Without warning, a Red pushed past, clicking frantically. Pattie couldn't understand what he was saying and stopped to call after him when another shell shoved her aside, hurriedly chasing after the first. Looking up, she saw crisscrossing lavender light streams shooting off in random directions. Muffled Nasat cries pierced the rushing water. Her own wrist-lamp offered short-range illumination, not nearly enough to discern what was happening ahead.

"Sloth!" a Brown hissed as he scrambled past.

She saw vague outlines of shells dropping, presumably into defensive curls, on the pathway ahead; light beams flashed through the trees as the others scattered into the wood.

A guttural howl pierced the air.

Run.

Though her first instinct was for self-preservation, Pattie looked over at Tarak. He had drawn his phaser, but was watching and waiting to see her choice before he moved.

For Pattie, there was no decision to make. She would not abandon a friend.

Indicating the opposite direction from the rest of the group, she shouted over the pounding rain, "This way!"

Without looking back, they picked their way through, over and under every barrier in their path, feet splashing through puddles, limbs scraping on sharp twigs. Y29 Brown chased after, quickly catching up to Tarak and Pattie.

Another howl sounded closer than the first; Pattie felt she had no choice but to pick up the pace. A thorn hedge lacerated her abdomen. Flinching from the pain, she pushed on, with Tarak and Y29 following her lead.

She rounded the corner of a gargantuan bolder when a screech—a Nasat screech—chilled her.

"Pattie!" came Tarak's call. "Y29 has fallen!"

Breathing hard, she hurriedly retraced her steps, dropping on all eight limbs to scoot under a fallen log. When she found Tarak, he was pushing a sapling palm tree down toward a shadowed bog. And she saw Y29. Sinking fast.

Quicksand.

"Stay still!" she shouted, her words nearly drowned out by the rain. Cupping her pincers around her mouth, she continued, "If you move, you'll sink faster. Try to pretend you're floating!"

The ground where she stood thudded beneath her. She smelled the sour, malodorous stench of wet mammal hair. A howl came from around the bend.

Tarak shoved the sapling trunk as close to Y29 as was feasible. Severing the sapling with his phaser wouldn't work because he needed the springy flexibility of the green wood to give the Brown buoyancy once he grabbed hold. Old wood might snap, sending Y29 deeper into the slippery sand.

"I'm going after him!" Pattie jumped onto the limb, crawling carefully along the trunk, trying to avoid slipping into the quicksand herself. Tarak threw all his weight onto the sapling, using his considerable strength to keep it as still as possible. Moving quickly, yet safely, proved difficult, but she could see Y29 thrashing his limbs, propelling himself deeper into the pit. She reached the end of the sapling.

About one body length short.

She gulped. *Not much of a choice.* Gripping the bouncing sapling with six of her limbs, she allowed herself to tip over so she was shell down to the pit.

"Grab my limbs!" She reached toward Y29.

"Can't—breathe—can't—"

"Brown! Do it!"

Y29 gave up thrashing and stretched for Pattie's limb.

She saw him straining to touch her, so she kept shouting encouragement.

A thunderous bellow sounded. Pattie glanced over and saw a pair of glowing green eyes through the grasses.

Extending herself as far as she could, Pattie thrust her arm as far as it would extend. Y29 wavered, bobbled. With one last straining effort, she reached when he reached. Their pincers touched. She grabbed his hand with her own.

"Hold on, Brown!"

Two limbs holding Y29 and six gripping the sapling trunk, she scooted her way back toward solid ground, knowing that the sloth ambled closer by the second. As Y29's fear subsided, he allowed himself to "float" in the quicksand. Dragging him along became easier as the viscous sand lost its grip on him. With one groaning heave, she shoved him toward the bank. Tarak grabbed the Brown by his hands, lifting him to safety. Pattie scurried down the branch in time to see the sloth rising on two legs, mere meters away.

He swiped his claw-encrusted paws, baring his fangs with a snarl.

Pattie met the creature's eyes. Without looking away, she said, "Tarak. Take Y29. Move along the bank. I need you as close as you can safely be to the quicksand. I might need you to catch me."

Dragging the Brown beside him, Tarak ducked into the tall reeds. She heard the rustling as he moved in deep enough to be hidden from view, but close enough that he could see her.

The sloth stepped toward Pattie; Pattie stepped backward onto the bent sapling, testing the bounce with each step. A few more steps and she would be out over the quicksand. While she believed she could jump to shore, she didn't want to test her luck. Hoping the beast would take the bait, she made a quick, jerking fake to the side, knowing that from the beast's perspective she would appear to be running away.

A paw swiped at the sapling. Pattie dove into the reeds. The sloth lost his footing, sliding through the slippery mud into the quicksand.

Without looking back, Tarak, Y29, and Pattie ran, paying no heed to direction or rain, seeking the first sanctuary they could find.

How far they'd traveled when they arrived at the stone mound, Pattie couldn't tell. It wasn't until they had been moving for at least half an hour that Pattie realized that, in her rescue of Y29, she'd lost both her Nasat-issued personal communications device and her Starfleet combadge. The storm hadn't let up in hours. Neither she nor Tarak wanted to check while they traveled and thus risk accidentally losing or damaging a precious tricorder under such poor conditions. Rivulets of water carving through the soil had created unexpected crevasses in the weakened crust, making each step more dangerous than ever.

Tarak had seen the formation first, at the edge of a clearing. In their exhausted state, they had decided finding a safe place to wait out the storm took precedence over locating the other team members. Flash floods weren't uncommon; as they had discovered earlier, rumors of predators hadn't been exaggerated.

Dragging themselves wearily inside, they found a dry, sandy interior that smelled musty, as if the cave had been abandoned for a long time. As tired as she was, Pattie had no desire to fall asleep, only to awaken with a meaner, hungrier neighbor than the sloth. Tarak removed his tricorder from the carrypack and took a reading. The cave was vacant. That was the only news she needed to determine if she wanted to stay. Pattie pushed aside her impulse to drop at the first opportunity when Tarak urged them to go deeper inside, assuring that their presence would go unnoticed to the outside world. They trudged another twenty meters before deciding to stop. Neither Y29 nor Pattie had the energy to chew on a ration bar. Throwing down her carrypack, shutting down her wrist-lamp, and dropping to the ground, Pattie curled up to sleep.

CHAPTER 9

At first, she couldn't tell if a wrist-lamp was on or if the storm had finally passed, allowing the sunlight to seep through the forest. Uncurling her limbs, she stretched, feeling each joint click satisfactorily. She realized she was hungry. Y29 had yet to awaken. Tarak's carrypack sat on the sandy cave floor beside her own, though he was nowhere to be seen.

Fishing through her supplies, she procured a ration bar (normally detestable) that she gobbled down greedily. *How about some water?* Meandering downward, the farther she went, the brighter the light became until she reached the forest clearing. A quick glance around revealed no imminent safety concerns. She climbed up a craggy boulder that helped her to reach a *pledh* fruit vine brimming with tempting clusters of bulbous, ripening seedpods. Sipping water collected on one of its leaves satisfied her thirst. Much to her enjoyment, the mid-cycle sun had heated the stone, so she leaned back to absorb the warmth.

"Pattie!"

She opened her eyes and saw that Tarak had emerged from behind a boulder on the opposite side of the cave mouth.

"I believe I have discovered something of interest. Come quickly. I would appreciate your input."

Hiking a switchback trail carved out of the stone, Pattie followed Tarak into a smaller cave, not far from the larger one where they had spent the night. He activated his wrist-lamp, since Pattie hadn't brought hers. At first, the cave resembled the larger one, but as they went in deeper, Pattie started noticing flashes of color, smoother walls, flattened areas that could serve as tables or benches. *I am in a place of my ancestors,* she realized. Her heart quickened at the thought. *The path we walked to reach this place had not been worn away by rain—tools carved it.*

Tarak paused, raised his wrist-lamp, and illuminated a wall etched and painted in colorful pictographs, the earliest written language of the Nasat. Once upon a time, she knew, these drawings would have been tinted in brilliant hues of green, umber, ochre, and indigo, the colors of rain forest plants and berries. Her trembling hand hovered over the etchings.

"This is astonishing," she said after a long moment.

"I believe it is also relevant to our present predicament." Tarak pointed the light on a section of pictographs and used his other hand to direct Pattie's attention to the text he wanted her to study.

Her eyes flickered over the pictures: swaying trees; an anatomically perfect rendering of a Nasat, but lacking a mouth; clusters of plants with elongated, graceful leaves; ripples emitting from the plants; Nasat, prone on the ground, dead. More pictographs showing destruction. Like Tarak, her knowledge was imprecise, but she, too, could discern a narrative. "This looks like a war," she muttered.

"To me also. It appears the Nasat of long ago were engaged in a great struggle."

She looked up at him. "How far back do these date?"

"Sensors put the paint decay at about seven, perhaps eight hundred years."

Before the maps. Before the promises made by kindred past.

"Who were they fighting? And where did they go?"

"Perhaps they have not gone anywhere, Pattie. Perhaps they are among you still."

Her mind raced through the possibilities. *Promises made. A boundary.* She paused. When factions made war on each other, one of the most oft-disputed causes was territory. Depending on how the conflict was settled, the victor either claimed all, or a treaty dividing up territory, equipment, and resources was agreed to. In the case of the Federation's relationships with her Alpha Quadrant neighbors, demilitarized or neutral zones were established to prevent further altercations.

The realization struck her. *What if my ancestors established a neutral zone and my generation has violated the agreement?*

What if we are at war?

Frantically, she scanned the pictographs, searching for clues to their foe's identity, if indeed, a shadow from the past had once again emerged.

A lost tribe of Nasat, living deep in the uncharted quadrants of the forest? Or perhaps an alien species that once coexisted with the Nasat, but had become extinct, or abandoned this planet for another? She reviewed the pictures repeatedly. Nasat. Tree. Plant. Death. The ripples. And the drawing of the Nasat without the mouth. A mute Nasat.

A quiet.

Among the thousands of pictographs on the wall, not one of the Nasat depicted among the dead had been mute. *Somehow, the quiets had played a role in this conflict,* she decided. A split second later, she shook her head, dismissing her own illogical reasoning. *Of what use would a shell that couldn't communicate be in a war?*

With an enemy who didn't use language.

Snippets of images and sounds fired rapidly, blending together in a soup of confusion. A high-pitched hum coming from deep in the forest. A rustle in a bush. The sense of being watched. A cold, dry arm wrapped around her throat.

Hot . . . wet . . . rain . . . run . . . fear . . . dizziness . . . trance . . .

A throbbing ache began in her neck, and she dropped to the ground.

"We have to find the others," she whispered. "They won't see them coming."

CHAPTER 10

She had done all she knew how to do.

Her relief at seeing most of the team members safely returned to base camp had been quickly supplanted by frustration. In light of her discovery, she had pleaded with the team commander to call for reinforcements, or at the very least, begin the trek back to the observation platform where it might have a safer base. They might have to hike through the night, but considering what they risked facing if they remained on the forest floor, the difficult trip would be worth it.

D6 was unmoved by her arguments. "Pictures on cave walls and old maps?" he clicked derisively. "I have an enemy I can track. Following the trail deeper into the forest will bring us closer to the toxin's origin. That's why we're down here, P8."

"Do you even know what you hunt?" Pattie asked, chasing after him while he unpacked the weapons locker. He slapped phasers into the pincers of every Nasat on the team while she stood by, watching helplessly.

"We don't always have the luxury of knowing the face of our foe," he said.

"But I *do* know what we're searching for. At least I think I do. And we'd do better to—"

"We stay where we are. At dusk we go deeper into the forest. Come with us. Stay behind. Skitter like a little nymph back to your nursery. The choice is yours," he said, "but keep your crazy ideas to yourself. I don't want you panicking the others." In his hands, he held a plasma clipboard where he'd outlined the night's journey, having traced the previous night's efforts with a stylus. Pattie saw that the team would be nearly fifty kilometers from base camp if D6's plan went smoothly.

Too far to escape to the township.

Too far to retrieve protective gear.

Too far to defend themselves if they came under unexpected attack.

Pattie's head had ached since they left the cave; confronting D6's stubbornness only magnified her suffering. As long as the throbbing pain had persisted, she couldn't think or reason clearly. She talked with Tarak about what to do.

D6 had given them permission to leave, though they would have to reach the observation deck before they could call for an emergency beam-out. Flash flooding during the previous night had brought down many trees in the base camp area, including one that had crashed into their equipment storage. Because D6 had no intention of calling for additional support or an emergency beam-out, the communication unit, along with power generators and computer monitors, had remained buried beneath a half-ton of tree trunk and branches. She had lost her personal communicator and her combadge. Y29's was buried in the quicksand bog, and Tarak had used the transducer in his to repair a damaged neural shielding device.

And they had concerns about what would happen if the other team members saw them breaking away from the group. Pattie wouldn't be able to offer an explanation of their behavior without violating D6's order to avoid involving the others.

The three of them were on the verge of making their decision when the last vestiges of natural light guttered, almost imperceptibly at first. As if a dark cloud passed over the setting sun, a strange, syrupy half-light enshrouded them, gradually dimming until dense grayness swallowed them whole. And the ache . . .

Pattie hadn't known she could remain conscious and endure such relentless pounding. If only it would *go away.* She had cradled her head in her hands. A sharp pain stabbed through her forehead; she collapsed on the ground.

Above her, the leafy ceiling dropped, pressing down.

On every side, gaps of light between trunk, root, and bush filled with opaque black-green.

They had come.

A low, dull hum pulsed and it was as if the forest had fallen silent at the command of the invader. Words slipped away, her voice muted; Pattie wondered if she would forever after live in this place of silent, wrenching pain or if this enemy would take pity on her and end the suffering.

From where she lay, Pattie watched Tarak dive for his carrypack. He fumbled for his neural shielding. The hum sharpened, became louder. He pressed his hands to his ears, reflexively curling his legs and arms close to his body. Other Nasat looked on helplessly, paralyzed, teetering and wavering where they stood. D6 reached for his phaser but gave up when the piercing sound became too physically painful to withstand. He tried raising trembling limbs to cover his ears but his pincers locked up, frozen. Drooping, he fell and reflexively curled into a ball.

I can't just lie here and not do anything. Pattie willed her pincers to move. Down. To her side. Where her phaser was hooked to her belt. The excruciating effort took every ounce of strength she had. She found the safety. Deactivated it. Each draining movement took a lifetime. She maneuvered the weapon out to the side, pushing it across the dirt. Tilting it up, she aimed for the trees.

Flame erupted, crackling and smoking. For a brief moment the humming stopped. She fired again, and again, until the perimeter branches flickered yellow-orange. She took advantage of the respite to scramble to her knees so she could face the assault head-on.

She saw them for the first time.

And yet not for the first time, for she had seen them etched into the cave walls. Long, gaunt leaf-limbs, rippling frenetically, their oozing, pseudopod-like feet propelled them forward. She didn't need to see the ground beneath them to know they left pools of toxin in their wake. Her ancestors had not named these creatures; they had only waged war with them. Through her pain, she sensed their fury and saw evidence of it: the skeletal remains of a Yellow, desiccated and thrown aside. Another terrified shell was plucked from a hammock, tossed into the air, and bounced across waving limbs until he vanished in a whirl of green.

Once again the hum rose, this time a rhythmic, wordless chant. They closed in, surrounding the base camp. She knew all chance of escape had been lost.

An agonizing sting ringed the circumference of her head. Dropping her phaser, she stumbled forward, clutched her limbs tight against her shell. The noise pushed into her ears and vibrated her eyes, invading each fragment of her consciousness. She resisted, but her will wavered as the assailant pressed on.

A hand touched her lowest limb and she looked down to see Tarak, who had crawled along the ground. He touched her. She sensed a flash of telepathy. Dropping down where he could better reach her, she felt his hand fumbling on her shell. He touched her cheek.

Don't . . . resist . . . them.

But I have to, she answered. *Or they will destroy me.*

Let them . . . he stammered . . . *speak. Hear their voices.*

She mustered a protest. *They have no voice.*

They have your voice. Listen.

Trust was instinctive between her and Tarak. He who had first given words to her thoughts and had known her. And yet in this thing. . . .

She doubled over in pain.

Don't resist them.

She yielded.

A flood of images washed over her. Prismatic light spinning through misty treetops. Slender leaf-arms opened to receive the beneficent warmth. Quiet groves near cascading water. And the light . . . precious light. Shadow falling. Traveling through the dark. And where is the light? They have taken it. The promise. They have forgotten. Take back what has been lost.

Shaking off the reverie, she came back to her own mind.

Their circle tightened; they squeezed in so close that she knew within moments she could face the fate of the Yellow and who knew how many other shells who had been plucked from their paddocks. The shells that had been devoured by a species starved for light, light that had been taken from them by the Nasat, who had violated their promise to never build beyond a certain boundary. *We have betrayed them.*

Reaching backward, she fumbled for Tarak's hand. She found it: cold, limp. She pressed his fingers to her cheek and felt only dullness. *How can I speak to them without Tarak?* A thought bubbled up. An image of herself as a nymph shell. She had not touched Tarak: he had touched her. And she must do the same.

She took this risk or all of them were lost.

Weakly, she crawled toward the sea of black-green,

uncertain whether they would even give her a chance. Their conflict was palpable. There were those who would destroy her as they had the others. Those who questioned her motives and were consumed with anger. Those, like her, who wanted answers. She pressed on. Extending a trembling limb, she reached toward them, willing one of them to trust her enough to reciprocate her risk.

One leaf emerged, unfurling tentatively.

They touched.

A questioning, frightened consciousness connected with Pattie's. She projected her own fear to the alien. The fragile connection continued as the minds moved in wary circles around each other. Pattie learned their name: the Citoac. *You are named to me,* she said. The Citoac mind named her in kind.

She could not speak for the others, or her kindred in the township. So she spoke for herself; she imaged her sorrow for what her kindred had done. *We have not known of your kind in hundreds of years. The memory has been lost, as has the promise that we would allow the light to pass through the canopy without interference.*

The Citoac she touched wanted assurance that the light would be restored. She caught flashes of the others demanding immediate reparation. Some seething minds would only be satisfied with revenge. Pattie could not sense who would win this struggle of wills. *I cannot speak for my kindred. I can only promise that I will speak for you. I will give you a voice so that this wrong to your kind can be undone.*

A long, silent moment elapsed for Pattie as the Citoac shared thoughts among themselves, determining whether to trust her. She looked around the base camp to see what destruction had been wrought and was sickened by what she saw. If they rejected her . . .

A leaf-limb rippled toward her, touching her hand.

Closing her eyes, Pattie opened up her mind to receive their images. Another curled around her forehead. And another, and still others until she yielded fully to an embrace of cool green.

She smiled. *I am named to them. I am named to them all.*

EPILOGUE

"Are you going to have time to help supervise the deck disassembly?" Zoë asked as the conveyor continued chugging along.

"I gave them my designs," Pattie answered. She switched her duffel from one limb to another so she could better grip the railing. "Most of the paddocks can be easily integrated into other decks. The expansion wasn't really necessary. More like, the township's existing space needed to be allocated more efficiently. The forest quadrant builders can handle it."

"I'm surprised. As an engineer, I figured you'd be jumping at the chance to rebuild the structure."

"The engineering part is fine. I'm just in the mood to do something different for my last week here." Since their return from the forest floor, she had felt like she'd spent more time in politics than she had in engineering. Making a case for the Citoac before the Planetary Council had consumed every waking cycle she had until yesterday.

The Nasat indifference to history had made providing the background of the ancient Citoac-Nasat treaty challenging. She had beamed down to the cave mound with a Federation anthropological linguist and a Nasat loremaster to try to make enough sense of the pictographs to offer a narrative to the Council. Pattie had even transmitted them to Bart Faulwell—en route to Starbase 92 from an assignment he, Abramowitz, and Soloman had taken to Vrinda—for his input. Once all the pieces came together, a story, not unlike the softs' fairy tales, emerged.

Together, they determined that the Citoac and Nasat had once had a protectorate-type relationship. A typically gentle species, the Citoac had no inclination to develop technology or civilization while the Nasat had been more assertive about colonizing the planet. Fearing that the Nasat would overrun their territory, the Citoac had initiated strikes against the Nasat. A truce was made between the two species, allowing the Nasat to build their townships without Citoac interference as long as the Nasat confined their expansion to a predetermined area. Requiring sunlight to maintain their photosynthetic processes meant that the Citoac needed the rain forest canopy to remain in a more primitive state. The Nasat had promised that the Citoac habitat wouldn't be encroached upon. As time passed, the acquisition of technology and the advancement of knowledge dominated Nasat concerns. Maintaining ties with the past became less of a priority; memories of the Citoac faded. Once they became spacefaring, the Nasat joined the Federation's destiny. That they had once had an obligation to a quiet sentient species had been forgotten.

Until the time when Nasat forgetfulness threatened Citoac existence.

Between the security net and extending the township perimeter, the Citoac had been forced into smaller, more hostile territories. Photosynthetic processes became inadequate for feeding; the Citoac had been forced to become carnivorous to survive. From poisoning the mother-tree and penetrating the security net, to invading the paddocks, they had waged war on the Nasat to make themselves known.

What held the most meaning for Pattie had been what she and Tarak had puzzled through after the siege at the base camp. Instead of being genetic misfits or anomalies, quiets existed among the Nasat as nature's way of facilitating communication with the Citoac. Tarak had hypothesized that the quiets concentrated their paddocks on the township perimeter as a way of giving the Citoac easier access to them. How many centuries the quiets had facilitated communication between the two species had been lost. Whether through words or pictographs, the ancient quiets had served a vital role that had helped the Nasat survive into their spacefaring age.

Pattie clutched the handle of her duffel more tightly. *What legacy will I pass to my offspring?* she thought, regretting for the first time that nymph Nasat were raised without knowledge of, or connection to, their parents. But *if* her nymphs inherited her quiet mutation they would be connected to her, and to all the quiets who had gone before. If she took nothing else with her from her visit home when she returned to S.C.E. duty, it would be a sense of belonging to the past. She had never known why softs sentimentalized mementos, old holos, and data chips containing communiqués and journals. Now she thought she might start keeping a personal log once she was back on the *da Vinci*.

Zoë touched her arm when they reached the deck sector. Stepping off the conveyor, they both ran their IDs through the security scanner and entered the crowded plaza. Pattie liked the look of this old place with its clay-plaster walls and playground even more than she had the first time she'd seen it. Inhaling deeply, she could smell the gourd paste cakes being readied for the mid-cycle meal. *Maybe they can find a seat for us. I'd like to meet my offspring's future neighbors.*

"You ready to drop off your young ones?" Zoë asked gently.

Pattie nodded.

The nursery was in much the same chaotic state as it had been when Pattie had visited before. Shells raced around, attending to Nasat larvae in every state of hatching.

Pattie located the director and after a brief interview (a formality), reluctantly passed off her data chip and the duffel bag carrying her larvae. *I hadn't expected to feel . . . empty,* she thought as she watched the director deposit her larvae into a holding chamber. She wanted to leave as soon as possible, to distance herself from her discomfort.

Upon leaving the director's office, she noticed Zoë in intense conversation with a Green carrying not one, but two nymphs. *I hope she knows I want to leave. Now.*

"Pattie!" Zoë waved her over. "Come on over."

Obviously not. She sighed.

Zoë scooped one of the nymphs, a Red, out of the Green's limbs and before Pattie could protest, deposited it in her arms. She took the Green's other charge, a Brown, for herself.

Who have we here? Pattie studied the nymph thoughtfully, guessing he was three or four weeks old. She gave him her pincer to grip; he intuitively clutched at her with all his limbs. In spite of herself, she smiled and clicked nonsense rhymes to the nymph, knowing that he was too young to respond. *Will you be a quiet, little one?* she thought, watching how his eyes focused on her moving mouth and tongue. *If you are, I know exactly who can take care of you.*

Their eyes met and linked. For a long moment, she stared down into the Red nymph's tiny face, wondering who this little one would be two or three seasons from now. She touched his face with one of her limbs. *I name you,* she thought, willing him to feel her words. Whatever was ahead of him, she wanted him to sense that someone, somewhere, knew *him.*

As she was known.

BREAKDOWNS

Keith R.A. DeCandido

Dedicated to the memory of Uncle Cal
and Cousin Calvin

CHAPTER 1

"It is the opinion of this tribunal, after careful investigation of the events at Galvan VI, that neither Captain David Gold nor any member of the crew of the *U.S.S. da Vinci* is in any way culpable for the deaths of twenty-three members of the ship's complement, and that those deaths, while tragic and most lamentable, were in the line of duty. Starfleet considers this matter officially closed." Admiral William Ross looked down from the dais at David Gold. "You're free to return to duty, Captain."

Gold, who was standing before the raised wooden platform in Starfleet Headquarters in San Francisco, said, "Thank you, Admiral."

Sitting between Ross and Captain Montgomery Scott, Admiral Sitak said calmly, "These proceedings have concluded. Dismissed." He then clanged the bell on the dais once.

The declaration and the bell were both formalities. There was no one present besides the three line officers and Gold himself, the former sitting behind the raised wooden desk and in front of the large blue-and-white Federation flag. Gold had requested that the session be private. He saw no reason for the rest of the surviving crew of the *da Vinci* to sit through this, nor did he feel spectators were appropriate. As captain, it was his responsibility and his alone—if any punishment were to be meted out, he would be the only one to accept it. *The rest of them have been through enough.*

Both Ross and Sitak rose and departed the room quickly, but Scotty approached Gold, who hadn't moved despite his dismissal. "Are y'all right, David?" the older man asked solemnly.

"No. For starters, I'm still getting used to this thing." He held up the biosynthetic left hand that replaced his original, lost—along with so much else—at Galvan VI. "It looks and behaves just like the original—hell, it even has that liver spot on my knuckle—but it *feels* wrong." Gold let out a long sigh. "And then there's the whole matter of half my crew's being dead."

Scotty put a hand on Gold's shoulder. "David, lad, you canna blame yourself."

"Someone else I should blame? I'm the captain, Scotty. You know as well as I do where that particular buck stops." He shook his head. "If I'd just done something different—"

Waving an admonishing index finger at Gold, Scotty said, "None of that, now. You start playin' 'what if' games, and you'll run around in circles till Doomsday."

"I know, I know, but if I hadn't moved the *da Vinci* closer to the *Orion* maybe—"

"Maybe the *Orion* would've hit the *da Vinci* at such an angle that it would have ripped your ship in twain and you'd *all* be dead instead of just twenty-three of you."

Gold fixed Scotty with an incredulous look. "You can't assume that."

"You're right, I can't. So why're you?" Scotty asked.

Closing his eyes, Gold said, "I can't believe I fell for that. I must be getting old."

"No, you're tired. And I don't blame you. Come on, lad, I'll walk you out."

Scotty led Gold out of the hearing room. As they proceeded down the corridor, the old engineer said, "I recall something Dr. McCoy said once. Some young person asked him what he thought about death. Leonard looked him right in the eye and said, 'I'm against it.'"

Despite himself, Gold smiled. He had met the aged Admiral McCoy only a few times, most recently when the *da Vinci* brought the old *Constitution*-class *U.S.S. Defiant* home, but that certainly sounded like something he'd say. "Can't say I disagree." The smile fell. "Truth be told, I'm tired of it. One of my oldest friends died in a skirmish with the Klingons a few years back. I seriously thought about retiring then. Rachel talked me out of it—but things haven't gotten any better. Salek and Okha died during the war, and 111 died right after it. My son Nate and his wife died when the Dominion took Betazed. A couple months ago, I was reunited with Gus Bradford just long enough to watch *him* die. And now this."

"Times like this," Scotty said, "I think about Matt Franklin. Good lad, Franklin. Young ensign in Starfleet, fine engineer, had a good career ahead of him. He was assigned to the *Jenolen* a few weeks before that ship was asked to escort some old relic to his retirement at the Norpin Colony."

Gold saw where this was going, but also knew better than to interrupt Scotty in mid-story.

"After the ship crashed, he and I were the only survivors. We worked out a way to preserve ourselves in the transporter buffer so as to not be usin' up all the life support. It *almost* worked."

"The fact that you're telling me this story means it did work," Gold said.

"I am. Franklin isn't. He didn't make it. His pattern degraded. Perhaps we could've done somethin' different. But we didn't, and Franklin died. A young man, his whole life ahead of him, doesn't live, while the old man on his way to retire does."

"You're saying I shouldn't let this bring me down?"

They arrived at the large entryway to Starfleet HQ. "I'm sayin' that life goes on, until it stops. Nothin' we can do about it, except to keep livin'. Until we stop."

"Can't argue with that," Gold said as the massive double doors parted, and the captain felt the cool breeze of a typically pleasant San Francisco afternoon brush against his face.

"About *time* you got out of there."

Gold blinked. He looked at the front steps leading up to HQ's entrance to see his oldest son, Daniel, and his wife, Jessica Silver, getting up from where they'd been sitting on the staircase. They were munching on sandwiches—pastrami on rye bread, from the looks of it, which meant they'd been sent with a care package from Rachel—but moved to greet Gold and Scotty as they came through the doors.

Daniel—a tall, broad-shouldered man who had inherited his mother's brown eyes, his father's brown-gone-white-too-damn-fast hair, but was otherwise the spitting image of his uncle Adam, Gold's giant of a brother—clasped his father in a warm embrace. "It's good to see you, Pop."

Gold sighed. "Don't call me 'Pop,' son."

Breaking the embrace and grinning widely, Daniel said, "Don't call me 'son,' Pop."

"You know," Jessica said, with a grin as wide as her husband's, "that routine wasn't funny the *first* eight thousand times, either."

"Like that's ever stopped anyone in *this* family," Gold said as he hugged his daughter-in-law. As short as Daniel was tall, Jessica's beautiful hair, which now matched her last name, was tied in a simple ponytail that stretched to the middle of her back. Usually she had it tied up in so elaborate a fashion that Gold wondered why she didn't just cut it and be done with it. As usual, she wore her massive gold hoop earrings with a

Spican flame gem dangling inside the hoop. Daniel always said that her green eyes glowed more than the flame gems, and her smile glowed more than her eyes.

"You remember Montgomery Scott," Gold said quickly, indicating the captain.

"Of course," Daniel said. "It's good to see you again, Captain."

"Ach, it's 'Scotty,' like I told you last time. Has your mother tried the haggis recipe I gave her?"

Daniel and Jessica exchanged a nervous glance. Gold had to restrain himself from a chuckle. Scotty had gone to the house for dinner a few months back. Afterward, Scotty had asked Gold if his wife, Rachel Gilman—one of the finest cooks on the East Coast—had ever made haggis. Gold had thought Scotty was joking at the time. *As if Rachel would ever let* that *in her kitchen . . .*

"Not yet," Daniel said slowly.

Scotty laughed, which seemed to relieve the tension. "No surprise there." Sighing overdramatically, he added, "'Tis an uphill battle, bringin' the joys of fine cuisine to the heathens o' the galaxy."

In a mock aside, Gold said, "This from a man who drinks liquid peat bog—on purpose."

Letting out a mock-indignant snort, Scotty said, "I'll leave you to it, lads—and lass. David, I'll be in touch. We'll speak in a few days about the *da Vinci* repairs and, ah, personnel matters."

"Of course." That was a duty he was not looking forward to, but needed to be addressed sooner or later. Luckily, the *da Vinci*'s extensive repair schedule—the ship was all but being rebuilt from scratch—meant it could be later. Still, at some point, twenty-three positions needed to be filled. *Probably more than that,* Gold thought solemnly. A disaster like this almost certainly meant that some crew members might be transferring or leaving Starfleet altogether.

Possibly even the CO. The thought came unbidden,

and Gold banished it back to whatever nether region of his brain hatched it. Now was *not* the time to be making decisions like this.

He looked at his oldest son. *Now is the time for family.*

The house was built in the Riverdale section of the peninsula known as the Bronx—the northernmost part of New York City—sometime in the twentieth century. A two-story dwelling surrounded by a large yard bordered on all sides by a thick privet hedge, the house had been the home of Captain David Gold and Rabbi Rachel Gilman for five decades.

Gold had seen an image of the house that was taken from an old-style photograph, circa 1990 or so on the old calendar, and it didn't look any different now than it did four hundred years ago. Gold knew better, though—in fact, none of the original material used to construct the house was present in the current building, as the march of technology had allowed every aspect of the dwelling's structure to be replaced with something superior. When she was a particularly inquisitive teenager, Gold's daughter, Eden, had asked if that meant it was truly the same house that was constructed four hundred years earlier.

"Maybe, maybe not," Gold had said then, "but it's the same *home.*"

When the Starfleet transporter deposited Gold, Daniel, and Jessica on the front lawn of the house, next to the massive dogwood that Gold planted as a sapling the day they moved in fifty years ago, his first thought was, *I've been away too long.*

Whatever his second thought might have been was lost to the impact of over sixty pounds of golden retriever on his chest. Gold had, of course, braced himself—no one entered the front lawn without being greeted by Freser—so he was forced to stumble backward only a step or two while Freser rested his front paws on Gold's shoulder and proceeded to welcome him home by making sure that no part of his face remained unlicked.

Scratching the retriever behind his ears, Gold laughed between face-licks. It was the first true laugh he had allowed himself since the *da Vinci* got the summons to Galvan VI. "Yes, Freser, Daddy's home."

Freser barked his approval at this state of affairs, and finally got back down on all fours. However, he continued to run in a circle around Gold, even as he, Daniel, and Jessica approached the front door.

"Got another surprise or two for you inside," Daniel said.

Gold raised an eyebrow. "Son, Freser trying to knock me to the ground isn't a surprise, it's an inevitability."

"Fair enough." Daniel opened the front door. "But still . . ."

The first thing that hit David Gold when the door opened was the smell. The kitchen was all the way on the other side of the house from the front door, but there was no containing the olfactory smorgasbord of Rachel Gilman's cooking, especially when she was making one of her patented feasts. From the competing delightful odors of fish, chicken, beef, assorted sauces and soups, and fresh *challah* bread, she had made enough to feed all of Starfleet. That, in itself, was not an indicator of the number of people present in the house—it only took having two nonresidents over to prompt Rachel to cook enough to feed an army—but, Gold soon realized, that the number was fairly high.

For the second thing he noticed was that the massive living room was packed full of family. The first one he noticed was his five-year-old great-grandson, Tujiro, crying out, "*Hi-Ojiisan!*" and running straight at Gold's leg with as much enthusiasm as Freser had.

He looked around and took all the faces in—many of

them slightly altered versions of his own and Rachel's faces. Daniel's youngest son (and Tujiro's father), Michael, and his wife, Hiroko, sat on the couch, along with Nate and Elaine's girls, Danielle Hirsch and Simone Meyer—their respective husbands, Ira Hirsch and Jared Meyer, stood behind them. Gold's pregnant granddaughter, Ruth Graylock, looking ready to have the baby at any millisecond, sat in the big, comfortable chair, with her husband, Rinic Kayven, sitting on the arm, and their boy, little Rinic David Kayven—no longer so little, he was almost as tall as Ruth now—sitting on the floor at her feet. Standing behind the chair was—

My God, it's Eden.

Eden Gilman and her husband, Robert Graylock, stood holding hands, and smiling as goofily as everyone else was at his entrance. He'd seen his oldest daughter maybe three times in the past twenty years, and she hadn't, to his knowledge, set foot in the house in at least a decade. He'd last seen her only a few months ago, at the memorial on Betazed for Nate and Elaine.

"Welcome home, Pop-Pop."

"Good to see you, Dad."

"About time you got here!"

"How long you gonna stand there with your mouth hanging open, Grandpa?"

"I bet he catches flies!"

"Hush, Rinic!"

Gold shook his head. "My—my goodness."

Daniel leaned down to whisper in his father's ear, "Told you, Pop."

A voice came booming from the staircase to Gold's left. "At last, the House head returns! Perhaps now we may feast!"

Gold turned to see a tall Klingon dressed in a long, dark green cassock decorated with several medals. Barely visible behind him was a small woman who had inherited her mother's glowing green eyes and her grandmother's firm jaw: Daniel's youngest daughter, Esther. The man was her new *beau—what's the Klingon word? Oh yes, "parmachkai"*—Khor, son of Lantar. Briefly, Gold wondered how Freser had reacted to Khor—and how Khor had reacted to Freser. Since both Klingon and canine were in one piece, Gold assumed that the meeting went well—or Esther sensibly had the two avoid each other altogether.

"I wasn't expecting to see you here," Gold said, surprised. "In fact, I wasn't expecting to see any of you here. This is—" He wiped away the tears that welled up in his eyes. "This is wonderful. Thank you all for coming."

Then a whiff of matzo-ball soup caught him. "I'll be right back," Gold said, and made a beeline for the kitchen.

No one moved to stop him. They knew better.

Gold almost hesitated before crossing the threshold into the kitchen, wanting to hold the moment of anticipation.

He first met Rachel Gilman at the track at Starfleet Academy. Gold, a champion runner in his day, was part of the Academy track team that was facing off against the team from Columbia University, an institution in New York City that Rachel was attending as an undergraduate, and for which she was also a champion runner. Finding the young student with the curly, light brown hair, almond-shaped brown eyes, distinct cheekbones, and snub nose to be rather attractive, Gold had gone over to talk to her. She had expressed sympathy on his team's upcoming loss, and he had laughed. "We haven't lost yet," he had said.

"Until now." She had said it with complete certainty. There had been no doubt in her mind.

So Gold had made a wager that his team would win hands down. She had accepted, but only on these terms: The loser had to make dinner for the other—from scratch. A product of the replicator age, Gold didn't know how to boil water, but he had been sufficiently confident to make the bet anyhow.

After Columbia's upset victory, Gold had made an attempt to cook a meal, which resulted in the entire dormitory's being evacuated for what was initially believed to be a chemical explosion. As they stood outside the dorm while Security put out the fire, she had looked at him with her brown eyes and the expression that was somehow half-smile and half-frown, and said, "Next time maybe you'll listen to me?"

A week later, she cooked him dinner, ruining him for replicated food for the rest of his life. A year later, they were married. Two years later, he went off to his first posting on the *Gettysburg,* and Rachel became a rabbi and started teaching. Three years later, they moved into this house. And fifty-two years later, he had yet to have cause not to listen to her.

Now he entered the kitchen, which had been remodeled to her exact specifications fifty years ago, and modified regularly ever since. Every type of cooking appliance available—and a few that weren't—had a place in this kitchen, down to a wood-burning stove, which she rarely used (but oh, when she did!). She stood over a pot of soup, stirring it with one hand, even as she added a few spices to another pot with her other hand.

Rachel Gilman's hair was still just as curly, though it had as much gray as brown now. Her brown eyes now had crow's-feet, and her magnificent cheekbones were less pronounced.

She was more beautiful than ever.

As always, she looked at him, gave him that same half-smile, half-frown she'd first given him outside the smoke-filled dorm room, and said, "You're home."

As always, he smiled, and said, "I'm home."

He could tell that she saw the joy he felt at seeing his

family, and that she also saw the great sorrow right behind that at what had happened at Galvan VI. Without saying a word, she reassured him that they would talk about it later, for as long as he wanted, but that for now he should just take joy in being with his family.

"You have five minutes to get out of that uniform and into some proper clothes."

"I forgot to bring my dress uniform."

She held up the wooden spoon threateningly. "Don't make me have to kill you, *Captain.* Go change."

"Yes, ma'am." He turned to leave, then turned back. "How'd you get Eden and Bob to come?"

"I asked them."

Gold blinked. "And?"

"That's it, David. Sometimes it really is that simple."

Before he could reply to that, he heard Freser barking, followed by a distinctive *whooomp!*

Turning to his wife, Gold asked, "Expecting anyone else?"

"Actually, no. You'd better go check." Rachel didn't sound too terribly concerned, so Gold didn't, either. It could have been one of the neighbors, or one of the children, of course.

He went back into the living room, just as Daniel was opening the front door. The rapid-fire pounding of small feet to his right heralded the arrival down the staircase of Anne Meyer and Ike and Jake Hirsch, Danielle and Simone's children. Now standing by the loveseat with Esther, Khor said, "It seems your guard animal has claimed another victim, Captain."

Maybe Esther didn't keep them apart, after all. That was a story for later, however. First, he needed to see who it was Freser had decked.

Gold moved to stand next to Daniel at the doorway. At first, all he could make out was the massive retriever, licking the form of some kind of humanoid lying on its back.

"He's gotten a lot bigger."

At the voice, Gold almost stumbled. Daniel steadied him just in case, but he looked just as surprised as Gold was. Then they both ran out, along with Jessica and Esther, Khor right behind them.

"Freser, disengage!" Khor said sharply.

To Gold's surprise, Freser immediately backed off the figure and ran back toward the privet hedge. *Definitely a story for later,* Gold thought, since *he'd* never been able to get Freser to obey commands so readily, unless they involved food.

Thoughts about the Klingon's ability to bond with his dog retreated as soon as the figure sat upright, leaning against the ground with his elbows. "A *lot* bigger," he said.

His face was almost identical to Daniel's, only with a bigger nose, and his hair was still all brown.

"Joey?"

Gold hadn't even lain eyes on his third child in ages—since before he took command of the *da Vinci,* certainly. He hadn't been able to make Nate and Elaine's funeral on Betazed, and father and son hadn't spoken in years.

Daniel quickly walked over and offered his younger brother a hand up. Joey took it, and Daniel pulled him up into a bear hug. "It's so good to see you again, kiddo."

Joey coughed, but returned the hug. "You're as bad as the damn dog, big guy."

After they broke the embrace, Joey looked at his father. "Hi, Dad. Heard you were home. Thought I'd drop by."

This time, Gold didn't bother to wipe away the tears as he hugged his son for the first time in far too long.

CHAPTER 2

Sonya Gomez sat in the attic of her parents' house in Vieques, staring at a lump of clay.

The attic had been converted to a studio for her mother, Guadalupe Gomez, when they moved in thirty years ago. Sonya rarely came up here after the accident when she was ten years old that ruined one of her mother's most important commissions. In fact, that incident had led to rampant speculation as to the efficacy of Sonya's later chosen career as an engineer.

Now she stared at the clay, wondering if it were some kind of metaphor for the shapeless mess her life had become, or if she were just being too philosophical.

She reached into her pocket and pulled out the ring.

The only light in the attic came from the setting sun through the small window, but it reflected off the diamond, briefly blinding Sonya.

Damn you, Kieran.

Why did he have to propose? Why did he have to die right after he proposed? Why did Starfleet have to test their damn super-weapon on a planet with a life-form on it?

Sonya had gone to the memorial service Starfleet held for the entire crew of the *Orion* and the twenty-three who died on the *da Vinci* at Galvan VI. Aside from Ensign Tony Shabalala, who was still on bedrest after suffering severe burns, the survivors of the *da Vinci* were all there. But Sonya didn't speak to any of them. She just sat stoically through all the speeches and ceremonies. In fact, she hadn't said a single word to any of her crewmates since Dr. Lense officially pronounced Kieran Duffy dead in the shuttle bay.

Least of all Gold.

Her thoughts already dark, they grew darker as she thought of David Gold, a man she had once admired, callously sending Kieran into the atmosphere of Galvan VI knowing full well it was a one-way trip, and then not even doing her—the first officer of the ship, never mind the fact that she and Kieran were lovers—the courtesy of telling her until it was far too late.

The service, held on the grounds of Starfleet Headquarters in San Francisco on a depressingly sunny day, had been a decent Starfleet ceremony. Admiral Ross delivered a eulogy that managed to be poignant despite its necessarily generic nature, given that he had to memorialize over two hundred people. In a touch Sonya would no doubt someday come to appreciate more than she was capable of doing right now, Captain Scott—in his dress uniform and kilt—played "Amazing Grace" on the bagpipes after the eulogy.

Throughout the service, all Sonya could think of was Kieran proposing, and her own indecision.

A squeaking sound followed by the slam of wood on wood heralded the opening of the trapdoor from the second floor of the house, light from the hallway streaming into the workshop in a V shape. A moment later, Sonya's older sister, Belinda, popped up into the attic like an old jack-in-the-box.

"*Here* you are. We were getting ready to send out a search party. Dinner's ready."

"I'm not hungry." Her voice sounded hollow to her

own ears, but she found she didn't care enough to try to modify her tone.

Belinda climbed the rest of the way up the attic ladder and stood before her younger sister. Though they both shared the same hazel eyes, jet-black hair, and sharply defined cheekbones that, as their mother had put it, was the hallmark of the Gomez women, they were aside from that a study in contrasts. Sonya was short and lithe, where Belinda was tall and stocky. Sonya kept her hair long, where Belinda's remained close-cropped. Sonya's face was angular, Belinda's round. Plus, Belinda always wore bright primary colors—usually several at once—where Sonya tended toward more muted earth tones in her civilian garb. At present, Belinda wore a bright blue-and-white linen jacket over a red silk tank top and matching red linen pants. For her part, Sonya was dressed in a simple brown one-piece outfit, mostly because she couldn't be bothered to put any thought into what she was wearing—or, indeed, into much of anything else.

"You're already too skinny, *mija*. If you don't get downstairs and eat something, you're gonna waste away to nothing."

Normally this was the part where Sonya would point out that she had only turned out so skinny because Belinda kept stealing her food when they were growing up, but she didn't have the energy to engage in the usual family banter.

"Just start without me, okay? I need to be alone."

"Ess, you've been alone for a week now," Belinda said. They'd been calling each other "Ess" and "Bee" since Sonya was a toddler and couldn't pronounce her sister's full name, so settled for the first letter. "*Mami* and *papi* might be willing to let you sit and sulk as long as you want, but I'm sick of it. I want my sister back, not this mopey—"

"I'm not in the mood, okay?"

Putting her hands on her hips, Belinda said, "No, it isn't. This ain't you, Ess. You don't mope. I know you and this guy were close—"

"He proposed."

Belinda's entire face seemed to freeze. "What?"

Sonya pulled the ring back out. "He wanted to marry me. He proposed right before we went to Galvan VI. Then—then everything went to hell, and—"

"What did you say?"

"I didn't say anything," she muttered.

"What?"

"I never gave him an answer, Bee. And then he had to go on that damn suicide run, and I never told him and I never got to say that I loved him and I couldn't say good-bye and—"

The words tumbled out of her mouth so fast she couldn't keep up, and then, finally, she broke down. All the tears she had held in check since the *da Vinci* left the Galvan system burst forth.

She wasn't sure when her sister pulled her into the hug, but she welcomed the embrace, sobs convulsing her as she took solace in her older sibling's arms, her tears staining the blue-and-white jacket.

"I'm sorry," Sonya finally said, leaning back so she could see Belinda's face, but not quite breaking the embrace.

"You kidding?" Belinda grinned. "I'm ecstatic! This is the most emotion you've shown since you got here. I was starting to think you were replaced with an android or something. Doesn't that happen to you Starfleet guys all the time, getting replaced with android duplicates?"

"Changelings more often these days," Sonya said with a small smile, wiping the tears from her cheeks.

"Androids, changelings, sentient moss, whatever. I can never keep that stuff straight."

"That's why you didn't last as a news reader." Among Belinda's many abortive attempts at a career was a stint as an onscreen anchor for the North American regional feed of the Federation News Service.

Drawing herself up in mock haughtiness, Belinda said, "I didn't last as a news reader because I got tired of the office politics at the FNS."

"That's your story and you're sticking to it, right, Bee?"

"Damn right, Ess." She grinned again. "Damn, *mija*, it's good to hear you talk like yourself again. I missed you." She got up, pulling on Sonya's arm. "Come on."

Sonya resisted the tug. "I don't really feel like dinner." She hadn't been able to stomach much food since Galvan VI.

"The hell with dinner, you and I are going to walk to Punta Mulas." Before Sonya could object, Belinda added, "And I'm not taking no for an answer. If you won't go, I'll send *mami* and *papi* up here and they'll eat in front of you."

"I—I can't. Not to Punta Mulas. Let's go to the beach, instead."

Belinda winced. "No, not the beach, Ess. There's always tourists there, and they all want my autograph."

Snorting, Sonya said, "What, there aren't tourists at the lighthouse?"

"Not as many, and they're too busy gaping at the lighthouse."

"The beach, or I take my chances with *mami* and *papi*."

Sighing overdramatically, Belinda said, "Fine, the beach, then, as long as I get you out of this damn attic!"

The sand felt warm between Sonya's toes as she and Belinda walked in companionable silence along Sun Bay Beach, each holding their shoes while they walked on the sand. Like the house, the beach was on the southern end of the island. Located just to the east of the main island of Puerto Rico, Vieques boasted several magnificent beaches, but Sun Bay was considered the finest, with its beautiful, crystal-clear water and tilted palm trees, providing just enough shade to keep the Caribbean sun from being intolerable.

I always meant to take Kieran here, but we never got around to it. The only vacation they'd been able to take since they got back together again on the *da Vinci* was that all-too-brief leave on Betazed between the Enigma Ship encounter and the construction of Whiteflower—the latter of which was cut off in order to answer the *Orion*'s distress call at Galvan VI. On Betazed, they had had a lovely picnic in a grassy park. Sonya didn't think she could stand going to the similar park around the Punta Mulas lighthouse just at the moment. At least the beach didn't have any specific connotations that might remind her of Kieran.

Belinda finally broke the silence. "This was the same guy you dated on the *Enterprise,* right?"

Sonya nodded. "It was going really well, too. I felt so—so *good* around him. It's weird, when we dated on the *Enterprise,* it was always—nice, but nothing spectacular. After I went over to the *Oberth,* we didn't see each other for *years.* I hardly ever thought about him—though when I did, I really missed him. Then I was assigned to the *da Vinci,* and there he was. Same goofy smile, same good heart. But now I was his CO. I thought it was going to be hard, but then we went on our first mission together to Maeglin, dealing with the Androssi for the first time."

"The Androssi?"

"Long story. Suffice it to say, we got out of it, barely. But Kieran and I worked perfectly together. It was like we were back on Geordi's team on the *Enterprise* again. And then, after Sarindar . . ." She trailed off. Sonya hadn't told the family about Sarindar.

Sure enough, Belinda asked, "What happened on Sarindar?"

"A lot." She shook her head. "It's funny, I've faced death almost every day since I joined Starfleet. Each posting I served at had an element of risk—on the *Sentinel,* we were on the front lines of the war half the time—but it wasn't until Sarindar that I actually felt like I was going to *die.* It was after that that Kieran and I started getting serious again. It was wonderful—and the work was better, too." Sonya stopped walking right in front of one of the angled palm trees, bent from years of being blown by tropical winds. "We made a good team, on *and* off duty. And then . . ." She leaned back against the tree, the breeze blowing through her curly black hair.

"He proposed."

Nodding, Sonya repeated, "He proposed. And you know what's driving me craziest, Bee? I don't know what my answer was going to be."

That caused Belinda's hazel eyes to go wide, and her jaw to fall open, her mouth in an O. "*You* didn't know? *You* couldn't make a decision?"

"No, I couldn't. What's the big deal?" Sonya asked, confused by her sister's shock.

"Ess, this is *you* we're talking about."

"I know that."

Belinda shook her head. "Remember when you were six and you wanted a cat, and *papi* said that you could only have one if you helped him convert the attic to *mami*'s studio? Every day, after school, you helped *papi* out, doing everything you could, because you wanted that damn cat."

Sonya smiled at the memory of Blanco, the gorgeous white Persian they'd gotten when Sonya turned seven. Blanco wound up staying with Belinda after Sonya went to the Academy, finally dying at the ripe old age of twenty-three a few years ago.

"Remember when you were ten and you said, 'I'm gonna join Starfleet and be an engineer'?"

"Vaguely." She wasn't sure that it was when she was ten, but she knew that she'd had the urge to join Starfleet since she was a little girl.

"You spent the next eight years living, eating, breathing, and sleeping Starfleet's entrance exams. You did everything you could to guarantee, not only that you'd get in, but that you'd be at the top of your class. So when you announced in your third year that you were going to be posted to the *Enterprise* just like your friend Lian was, we all knew that was where you were gonna wind up." Belinda frowned. "What is it?"

"Sorry," Sonya said in a small voice. She had flinched at the mention of Lian T'su, a year ahead of Sonya at the Academy and one of the first friends she had made there, who had gone on from her posting on the *Enterprise* as an ensign to a fine career culminating in the captaincy of the *Orion*—and a nasty death at Galvan VI.

Belinda went on. "I don't think you ever met a decision you didn't like—and didn't stick with. I wasn't surprised you made chief engineer so fast, or that you were so good at it. You were meant to command." She grinned. "Not like your bratty older sister."

At that, Sonya smiled. Besides her brief time in front of the camera as an FNS anchor, Belinda had been, at various times in the last decade and a half, a sculptor like her mother, or, rather, not like her mother, as she was awful at it; a soccer player, until a knee injury forced her out of professional play; a deep-sea diver; an actor; a transporter technician; and now a soccer coach.

"But you've always been the one to jump in feetfirst, to make a decision and stick to it. So what happened?"

Sonya shook her head. The sand suddenly felt cold between her toes. "I don't know."

CHAPTER 3

The meal was, of course, spectacular.

By the third course, everyone in the Gold-Gilman house was stuffed beyond reason. Then the aroma of the roast chicken hit, and they suddenly had room for just a little bit more.

Rachel assured everyone as they each gamely took one more bite of food they were not convinced they'd be able to fit that there was plenty more in the kitchen, as she always did.

Gold found himself sitting quietly at the head of the table, listening to the family talk. Nobody broached the subject of Starfleet or the *da Vinci* or Galvan VI. Instead Daniel talked about his and Jessica's new job jointly supervising the maintenance of orbital habitats. Simone went on at some length about Anne's accomplishments at school, to the latter's great embarrassment. This prompted Michael to wax similarly rhapsodic about Tujiro, and soon everyone was talking about how wonderful their children were, which led to Ruth's pretending to be aghast at the high expectations her soon-to-be-born daughter would have to live up to. This in turn led to everyone wondering what the girl's name would be, which Ruth refused to answer—so everyone decided to ask Rinic, who was even more stoic.

God, I missed this, Gold thought, as even Khor got into the act, telling everyone what he was doing on Earth (some kind of errand for the Klingon High Council that involved talking to some Federation councillors).

After dessert—Rachel's famous cream puffs, which somehow everyone found room for—Khor, Esther, Eden, and Bob all said they had to leave.

The latter two had hardly spoken during the meal, and Gold protested, "Princess, we've barely had the chance to—"

"Dad, I'm not your princess," Eden said gently. "I'm a grown woman with a life of my own. It was nice to visit, but we need to get back home to Montréal."

It wasn't until after they had said their good-byes that Gold realized that he had had no idea that Eden and Bob were living in Montréal now.

"And where are you two going?" Rachel asked Esther and Khor. "I know you gave up your apartment when you decided to go meandering around the galaxy," she said to Esther, "so I know for a fact you don't have a place to stay."

"We will be residing in the Klingon Embassy in Paris," Khor said firmly.

"Don't be ridiculous. You're staying here."

Rachel spoke in the tone that Gold knew would brook no argument. Gold stole a glance at Esther, who looked amused, obviously knowing that the Klingon didn't stand a chance.

"With all due respect, Rabbi Gilman, while we have found your hospitality to be excellent, it is not fit—"

Rachel hit the Klingon councillor with the same half-smile, half-frown she hit her future husband with outside the Starfleet Academy dorm room. "If you find my hospitality 'excellent,' Khor, son of Lantar, then you will not sully it by refusing my invitation."

Khor hesitated. "You realize what you are saying."

"I teach a very popular class in intercultural studies, Khor. I know about Klingon rules of hospitality."

Esther then came to her boyfriend's rescue. "And I also know about my grandmother's rules of hospitality. We're staying here tonight, my *parmachkai.* If nothing else, there's no way, after sleeping on that damned metal slab of yours for the entire trip here from Qo'noS, that I'm passing up a chance at the guest bed here—with its *mattress*—for a night."

The Klingon looked back and forth between his lover and her grandmother. "If that is your wish, then it shall be so. I shall make the sacrifice of sleeping in comfort."

Joey then stepped forward. "I need to get going also. Abigail expected me back home an hour ago."

"You should have brought her with you," Rachel said.

"I don't think that would've been such a good idea."

Gold frowned. "Why the hell not?"

"Just—trust me, okay? Look, I have to go."

"Can't you stay a little bit, Joey?" Gold asked, realizing that, like Eden, Joey had hardly said a word over dinner. No doubt, like his father, he was content to listen and catch up on the family gossip that he hadn't heard in years. But Gold had good reason to remain quiet—everyone knew what he'd been up to. "I'd like to know—"

"Know what, Dad?" Joey asked, suddenly belligerent. "What I've been doing with my life? Now's a helluva time to ask." He took a breath and calmed himself. "I'm sorry. Look—I have to go."

"Joseph Gold," Rachel said, "you can't just—"

"Yes, I can, Mom. And I am. I appreciate you telling me that you were having this get-together for Dad, and I'm glad I came. But this doesn't change anything. You're all related to me, but I've got my own family now. Good-bye."

With that, he walked out the door.

"Damn," Daniel said. "You want me to go after him, Pop?"

Gold shook his head. "There's no point. He's right.

Family this big's bound to have stray threads that get cut off from the rug."

"That's ridiculous," Rachel said. "He's just being a stubborn ass, like he's always been."

"Can't *imagine* where he got that from," Gold said with a smile. "Look, I'm just glad Joey came. And Eden and Bob, for that matter, even if I didn't get to talk to them. Right now, it's good just to *see* them, after all that's happened."

Danielle and Ira, Simone and Jared, and Michael and Hiroko came downstairs. "What *did* happen, Pop-Pop?" Michael asked. "The kids are all in bed—"

"They might even get to sleep sometime in the next three hours," Hiroko added.

"—so I think we'd all like to know what happened to you."

When he walked in the door to his home for the first time in years, David Gold wasn't ready to talk about Galvan VI. Now, though, after all his family had done to make him forget it for a little while, it was time to remember again. The dead deserved that much, and more.

Of course, he left the classified specifics of the Wildfire device out of the story, but he told them all he could. Most of all, he told of the sacrifices so many of the crew made, from Stephen Drew's giving up his own life to make sure the medical staff and their patients made it out of sickbay alive; to Kowal, Feliciano, Friesner, and Frnats, the four members of the damage-control team who got the structural integrity field up and running, thus keeping the ship in one piece a while longer; to Lieutenant McAllan pushing his captain out of the way of a collapsing ceiling, saving Gold's life, if costing him a hand; to Kieran Duffy's ultimate sacrifice that not only saved the ship, but an entire species.

Silence descended upon the living room for many minutes. Finally, Khor spoke up. "They died well, Captain."

"Like that's a comfort," Jared said.

"It should be, human," Khor said sharply. "Death is the one inevitability of life, the one thing on which we all may rely."

"If it's such a foregone conclusion," Jessica asked, "what difference does it make how we go to it?"

"Every possible difference," Khor said. "Captain Gold's brave crew died doing their duty, sacrificing themselves so that others might live. Were they Klingons—and indeed, even though they are not—I can say with pride that they would be welcomed in *Sto-Vo-Kor* among the honored dead." He held up a mug of bloodwine, which he and Esther had brought as their contribution to the meal, and of which only the two of them had partaken. "I salute them."

Rachel held up her own glass of eis wine. "I join the salute." At the surprised looks of most of her family—except Gold—she said, "Khor is right. They did what they had to do, and what many people would not have been able to do. I would rather they were still alive, but if they had to die, it's best that this is how they did it. So I salute their memories."

Quietly, Gold said, "As do I." He held up his own mug, which just had coffee in it.

One by one, the rest of the remaining family also raised their drinks.

The following morning, Gold slept in. He awoke to an empty bed, with the smells of breakfast summoning him to the kitchen. Putting on a bathrobe, he went downstairs to see Daniel, Jessica, Ruth, and Esther sitting around the kitchen table, munching on muffins, with Rachel standing over the oven.

"Morning, Pop."

"Don't call me 'Pop,' son."

"Don't call me 'son,' Pop. Sleep okay?"

Gold smiled. "Don't know, I was asleep the whole time."

Ruth looked plaintively at Rachel. "Gramma, have those two *always* been like this?"

"Only since Daniel could talk," Rachel said.

"Where's everyone else?" Gold asked as he poured himself a cup of coffee.

Ruth said, "Rinic had to get little R.D. off to school, and Danielle, Michael, and Simone had to do the same with their kids, only they all went off."

"Khor had that meeting in Paris," Esther added.

"We've got a few days, Pop," Daniel said, "so we figured we'd stick around, if that's okay."

"To that, I'm gonna say no?" Gold grinned as he took a seat next to his pregnant granddaughter. "You know, they took a pool on the *da Vinci* as to what name you and Rinic would pick for my great-granddaughter. Of course, I'm not supposed to know about that. . . ."

Blinking, Ruth said, "You're kidding." She shook her head. "That's weird."

"What is?"

"Well, aside from that nice Bolian doctor I met that time, and that Scottish guy with the mustache, I don't even *know* any of your crew."

Gold chuckled. "Fewer than you think. The doctor you met has retired, and the Scottish guy is the S.C.E. liaison here on Earth, not part of my crew."

"Yet they're making bets about my daughter?"

Shrugging, Gold said, "It's just the usual shipboard nonsense."

"It's still weird, Grandpa."

Gold considered. "That's not the worst thing my crew's been called."

My crew, he thought. He liked the sound of that. Whatever silly thoughts were telling him to retire had obviously retreated. He wasn't ready. Not yet.

Four years ago, when hostilities had broken out between the Federation and the Klingon Empire thanks to changeling infiltration at the highest levels of the

Klingon military hierarchy, one of Gold's oldest friends, Captain Mairin ni Bhroanin of the *U.S.S. Huygens,* was killed in combat. At Mairin's funeral, Gold had confessed to Rachel a desire to retire.

"You belong in space," she had said.

"I belong with my family."

"You'll always belong with your family, but for now you also belong in space. Someday, it'll just be the one. *Then* you come home."

That day had not yet come. He needed to be home right now, but he knew that he'd need to go back to space soon enough.

"So what's on the agenda for today, Pop?" Daniel asked.

"Research. I need to speak to the families. Khor was right, they all—" He hesitated. "They all died well. Their families deserve to know that. So, since I've got a few weeks before the *da Vinci* will be ready to go back out, I'm going to take that time to track down the families of all twenty-three of my people who died and pay my respects. In person if they're on Earth, over subspace if they're not."

"Anything we can do to help?" Jessica asked.

Gold smiled. "Just keep being here. That's been the best present anyone could've given me. Beyond that—I'll let you know."

The first person whose family Gold tried to find was David McAllan.

For two years, every time Gold came onto the bridge, McAllan insisted on saying, "Captain on the bridge." It was a bit of protocol that had fallen out of favor, though never actually stricken from the regulations. Some captains still insisted on it, of course. Gold had always found such people to be a little too full of themselves. In particular, Gold found it a ludicrous custom to maintain on a ship whose primary purpose was to work in the service of the S.C.E., probably the least spit-and-polish branch of the service.

But McAllan did insist, and it got to the point where Gold actually started looking forward to it.

He'd never hear it again, and worse, the reason why he'd never hear it again was because that brave, ultra-competent, spit-and-polish young man sacrificed his own life for that of his captain. Because that was, after all, the proper thing to do.

To Gold's shock, he realized he knew nothing about McAllan. Most of his crew, he could recite at least one hobby or odd personal habit or *something* about them, but about McAllan he drew a blank.

His Starfleet record, unfortunately, revealed no useful data. His only listed relatives were a mother and father, who both died when McAllan was at the Academy. McAllan's residence was a house in Greece that he shared with four other Starfleet officers. However, a call to that house revealed that all four were away on assignments, with the house under automated care until one or more of the owners came back to Earth.

I owe my life to the man, and I can't even memorialize him to his family or friends.

With an empty feeling in his stomach, Gold called up the service record of Chief Diego Feliciano.

"He won't come out of his room. I don't know what to tell him."

Gold sat in the dining room of the home in Havana, Cuba, belonging to Arlene Rivera and the late *da Vinci* transporter chief. Rivera, a nurse, had been married to Chief Feliciano for ten years. The "he" she referred to was their son, Carlos.

"He turned seven a few days ago. That's when he first locked himself in there. Now he only comes out to go to the bathroom. That's when I've been bringing him food. But he won't talk to me or to anybody." Rivera had been holding a mug full of coffee for the entire time Gold had been sitting across from her nursing his own cup. She had yet to take a sip from it. A petite woman, she had jet-black hair and a round face that was marred by bloodshot brown eyes. "Diego promised he'd be home for his birthday this time. He missed it last year—because of the war, he couldn't get away."

The captain remembered Feliciano talking about having to miss his son's birthday when they had gone on a mission to salvage an alien ship near a secret Federation outpost. Ironically, that had been the mission on which Commander Salek—Gomez's predecessor—was killed.

"He promised that he would be home this time." Tears started to run down her cheeks. "Why didn't he keep the promise?"

Gold's voice was a cracked whisper. "He would have. Diego always spoke fondly of you and Carlos. 'My little Carlitos,' he always called him."

A smile struggled to get through the sadness on Rivera's face. "Carlos hates being called that. I think that's why Diego did it." She shook her head, the sadness victorious over the fleeting smile. "Why did he have to die now? He lived through an entire war; why did this have to happen?"

"I can't answer that. All I can say is that he died saving the lives of his crewmates—and his sacrifice may have saved an entire species. And I also know that that doesn't mean a damn thing to a seven-year-old boy who won't come out of his room. But someday, he will understand."

"Good. Then maybe he can explain it to me." She closed her eyes. "I'm sorry, Captain, I'm not being fair to you."

"Nobody expects you to be fair, Ms. Rivera—hell, you've got no reason to be. It's completely unfair—believe me, I know. I had to bury my own son during the war—he was on Betazed when the Dominion took it."

"Still, it means a lot that you came here. You didn't have to do that."

"Diego didn't have to sacrifice his life the way he did, either. But he chose to. I think the very least I owed him was to let his wife and son know how sorry I am—and how much you meant to him."

"Get out of my house!"

K. E. Bain all but slammed the door in Gold's face when he arrived at the apartment in Juneau, Alaska, he shared with his daughter, Lieutenant Kara Bain, the beta-shift ops officer. "Mr. Bain," Gold began, "I'm sorry, but—"

"You killed my daughter, you son of a bitch. What the hell were you doing flying around a gas giant anyhow? I'm amazed anyone got out alive."

I was trying to salvage a warhead that would've wiped out the planet—and maybe destroyed an entire species—but I can't tell you that. Intellectually, Gold understood the need for classified information, but there were times when it really irritated the hell out of him.

"Mr. Bain, I just wanted to tell you—"

"There's nothing you can tell me that I want to hear, *Captain.* Now get the hell off my property before I shoot you."

Then he actually did slam the door in Gold's face.

"I just wanted to tell you I'm sorry for your loss."

Benjamin Kogleman, the son of Security Guard Claire Eddy, seemed genuinely confused by Gold's words. He was fidgeting with a padd, constantly looking down at its display between sentences. "Well, thank you—I guess. I mean—well, if you don't mind my saying so, sir, why did you come all the way out here?" Kogleman lived in a small tent in the midst of the Gobi Desert, where he worked as an archaeologist.

Gold smiled. "It wasn't that hard, Mr. Kogleman. I have access to a transporter." In fact, it had taken a certain amount of doing—mostly lobbying by Scotty—to give Gold unlimited transporter access during this period for him to visit the Earth-based families of his deceased crew. The initial response was confusion on the part of Starfleet's bureaucracy, which didn't see the need for personal visits. *As if "need" has anything to do with what's right.* "And I wanted to extend my personal sympathies on the death of your mother."

"Again, thanks, but it really wasn't necessary. Starfleet informed me of Claire's death. Honestly, we were never all that close. I mean, I'm sorry she's dead, but—it *really* wasn't necessary for you to come all this way. I mean, you're a Starfleet captain." He laughed a rather fake-sounding laugh. "You must have better things to do with your time than to *schlep* out here to the middle of nowhere."

"Not when it comes to something like this." Gold hesitated, no longer sure that he wanted to perform this duty. He still had the option of leaving and letting Starfleet simply courier the damn thing, especially given this indifferent reception.

Hell, I've come this far. Besides, I give in now, those damn bureaucrats win. Holding out a small box, he said, "Your mother was honored with a Starfleet Citation for Conspicuous Gallantry." He opened the box to reveal a gold pin and purple ribbon. "You're listed as her next of kin, so you're the one who gets it."

Kogleman blinked. "I am? I mean, she listed me? That's—odd. I didn't think—uh, thank you, of course, Captain," he said quickly, taking the box and closing it. "That's very considerate of Starfleet. Believe me, I'll treasure this—uh, this honor. Look, I have to get back to work, unless there's anything else, some kind of ceremony or something?"

Gold shook his head. "No, Mr. Kogleman, that's all. Thank you for your time."

"Right, of course. Thank you, Captain."

* * *

The second-to-the-last trip of the dozen or so that Gold had to take on Earth was to Dublin, Ireland, where Susan and Edward Drew currently lived. They had raised their grandson Stephen Drew, one of the best security guards on the ship, since his parents died when he was a boy.

Their house was located in the midst of a series of paved walkways, with a lovely stained-glass window taking up much of the upper portion of the front door. Gold rang the bell, and was greeted by a woman of medium height and wide build, paper-white hair framing a round, friendly face. This had to be Susan.

"I'm Captain David Gold," he said.

"Of course you are. Please come in, Captain," Susan said in a musical voice with an accent Gold couldn't place. He knew that Drew's family had lived all over Earth—Susan's work as an engineer took her all over the planet—until they retired to Dublin after Drew joined Starfleet. Gold remembered Drew saying once that his grandparents had always thought it ironic that he was assigned to an S.C.E. ship, given his grandmother's occupation.

She led him into a small kitchen that, surprisingly, had an old-fashioned stove next to the replicator (Rachel, of course, had one just like it, but she was a special case) and a lovely wooden table, in the center of which was a tea set.

At that table sat two men, one quite familiar: Vance Hawkins, one of the few surviving security guards from the *da Vinci* and, Gold knew, Stephen Drew's best friend. The tall, dark-skinned man was wearing civilian clothes, and immediately stood up at Gold and Susan's entrance.

"Sir!"

Gold waved his arm. "At ease, Hawkins."

A short, skinny man also rose, offering his hand. Like Hawkins, he was bald, though Gold assumed that it was a more natural condition than the fashion choice of the security guard. "Young Vance here was payin' his respects, Captain. I'm Edward Drew."

Returning the handshake, Gold noted that Edward retained an Irish accent. "A pleasure, sir. I'm only sorry I couldn't meet you both under better circumstances."

They all sat down, except for Edward, who asked, "Would you like some tea, Captain?"

Not normally a tea drinker, Gold nonetheless accepted the offer. Edward retrieved a mug from the cupboard, then sat and poured tea for them both.

"It's good of you to come, Captain," Susan said. "Such a terrible, terrible thing. Vance was telling us what happened."

"It must be even worse for you," Edward added. "To lose so many. You have our sympathies, Captain."

"Thank you," Gold said, surprised.

"Stevie spoke well of you—of all the people he served with." Susan smiled. "His letters were full of stories about your adventures."

Edward chuckled. "Of course, he had a few choice words for that Commander Corsi of yours."

"But he respected her. And you, Captain," Susan added quickly. "And all the people he worked with. He said it was much better than the usual Starfleet ship because—how did he put it? 'The officers don't have poles up their asses.'"

Gold somehow managed not to sputter his tea.

"He was even sweet on one of them—one of the engineers, a woman named Norma. He said on any other ship, he wouldn't have even thought of asking out an officer, but that you, Captain, fostered such a pleasant atmosphere that it seemed perfectly natural."

Drew was interested in Weiland? Gold shook his head. Too often the captain was out of the gossip loop.

Hawkins said, "Yeah, he was finally ready to work up the courage to ask her for a date when we were putting

Whiteflower together—then the crisis hit, and he backed off. He figured there'd be time afterward. It's not like he was in any—" He hesitated. "Excuse me."

With that, Hawkins suddenly got up and left the kitchen.

Also excusing himself, Gold went after him. He found the large security guard standing in the middle of the living room, surrounded by some rather tacky-looking furniture, even tackier-looking statuary and other *tchotchkes,* and a rather nice painting of a much younger Susan and Edward in a suit and wedding dress.

"You all right, Hawkins?"

"I'm fine, sir, it's just—" Hawkins took a deep breath. "It doesn't make any sense."

"It never does, son."

Hawkins shook his head. "No, not just death—I'm used to seeing people die. Comes with the territory, especially in Starfleet security. No, what I mean is that Drew didn't make it."

"What do you mean?"

"Sir, I don't know if you noticed, but Steve *never got hurt.* Since we signed on to the *da Vinci* together back during the war, I've been thrown into bulkheads, shot, stabbed, beaten up, cut, got turned into a lunatic by a thousand-year-old computer, and hit repeatedly on the head. It became a running joke, to be honest—I was spending more time in sickbay than Dr. Lense. But Steve, no matter what, came out fine. Never got hurt, not even a scratch. But this time—this time, I come out okay and he *dies.*" He shook his head again. "It's just *wrong,* sir."

Putting a hand on Hawkins's shoulder, Gold said, "You won't get any argument from me, son."

Susan's voice came from behind them. "Is everything all right?"

Gold turned to see Susan and Edward standing in the doorway.

"I'm fine, ma'am," Hawkins said. "I just needed to—it isn't—"

Susan walked over and embraced the—much larger—Hawkins. "It's all right, Vance. I know how close you two were. I know how much you miss him. We all do." She broke the embrace. "Now come back into the kitchen before your tea gets cold, and you can tell us some more embarrassing stories about Stevie."

Hawkins smiled. "I don't think I've got any left—at least, not any that I could tell you."

Edward chuckled. "D'you think it's anythin' we haven't heard before?"

"No, just that Steve made me promise never to share the stories with anyone—least of all the three of you."

"If it's about that practical joke you played on Stevens and Faulwell while we were at Whiteflower, I wouldn't worry about it." Gold spoke lightly, though Hawkins's dark face suddenly went gray.

"You *knew* about that?"

"It's a small ship, Hawkins." He grinned. "And the old man wasn't born yesterday."

Susan led them back into the kitchen. "Now this we *have* to hear."

For most of the rest of the afternoon, the four of them sat in the kitchen, drinking tea, and sharing stories.

"You ever plan on coming to bed?"

Gold looked up from the workstation in the study to see Rachel standing in the doorway. It took him a second to focus on her—he'd been staring at the screen for quite some time, and his eyes weren't as young as they used to be—and even when they did, Rachel still looked a bit foggy.

"What time is it?" he asked.

"Two hours after you said you'd be in bed within half an hour."

Gold shook his head. "Sorry. I forgot about the time differential on Betazed, so I'm waiting for it to be a reasonable hour on the part of the planet Deo's family's in."

"And it can't wait until tomorrow?"

Having visited all but one of the families of his Earth-based crew, Gold had spent an entire day contacting those off-world. He'd already spoken to Security Guard Frnats's cohusbands on Bolarus, Engineer Orthak's egg-mates on Wadgira, Security Guard Loten Yovre's brothers and sister on Bajor, Engineer Alex Chhung's partner and adopted son on Canopus, Security Guard Andrea Lipinski's parents on Berengaria VII, and Chief Engineer Jil Barnak's sister on Atrea. Now he was waiting for the right time to contact Lieutenant Elleth Deo's parents on Betazed.

"I'm sorry, love, I was just thinking about Nate and Elaine."

Rachel came the rest of the way down the stairs. "That's all you've been doing—thinking. I thought the whole point of this time off was to not think for a while."

He chuckled bitterly. "That's like telling someone not to think about a pink elephant. The minute you're told that, you can't get pink elephants out of your head."

"I'd rather you were thinking about pink elephants. Maybe you could count them to help you sleep. In bed."

That's my wife, he thought, *subtle as a sledgehammer when she wants to be.* "I know," he said. She stood behind him and put a hand on his shoulder. He put his hand over it—it was warm and comforting. "But I owe it to them—to all of them—to be there. I think it helped them. For some of them, it helped me, too, to be honest. You'd like the Drews—they have an old stove and make a damn fine cup of tea. Hawkins was there, too, and—"

"David?"

"Yes?"

"Tell me in bed. You're pushing too hard. Take a rest.

You're no good to anyone if you exhaust yourself in an attempt to be the über-captain."

He looked up at those beautiful brown eyes. Over fifty years ago, he learned the hard way never to argue with this woman. Besides, she was right. How often did he come home? How often was he actually around to share his bed with her? *I'm so busy trying to do right by my crew I'm forgetting to do the same for the woman I love.*

Gold shut down the workstation and followed his wife to the bedroom.

Just one more trip to take tomorrow. . . .

CHAPTER 4

"I need to get out of here."

Sonya declared this to her parents and Belinda over breakfast one morning—the first meal she had eaten with them since her arrival.

"Is the food that bad?" her father asked with a wry smile.

"No, of course not, but—"

Her mother, wrinkles softening the same sharp cheekbones she had passed on to her daughters, gazed at her daughter with the family's hazel eyes. "What is it, *mija?*"

"I need to go to Portland. To see Kieran's mother—and his grave. I know he wanted to be buried next to his father, and—" She hesitated. "I don't know why, I just need to go."

José Esteban put a large hand over his daughter's small one. His hair, as jet-black as it was when he was a boy, a fact of which he was inordinately proud, fell down over his eyes, which Sonya had always thought made him look like a very dark sheepdog. "Then you need to go."

Her mother asked, "You want us to come with you?"

Sonya started to say no, then thought about it. "Let me ask Ms. Duffy tomorrow when I contact her. I don't want to drop in unannounced."

"Good thing," her mother said. "I raised you better than that."

Belinda smiled. "You did? I must've missed that part."

"Mostly, yes." Lupe Gomez fixed her daughter with a look.

Sonya wondered if she was missing something here. "Is everything okay?"

"Nothing you need to worry about, *mija,*" Belinda said with a glower at their mother.

"Okay." Sonya looked at her father, who had brushed the hair away from his eyes, so there was no mistaking what the message was behind the look he gave her: *Stay out of it.* The relationship between Lupe and Belinda was akin to an old roller coaster, and it looked like it was about to hit one of its downward cycles after years of steady upward climbing.

"It's not like there aren't other openings for soccer coaches," Belinda added, thus providing the reason for the latest difficulty. *Bee's gone and screwed up another career.*

Her mother raised an eyebrow in an almost Vulcan-like manner. "Really? Even ones who've been fired three times for violating school policy?"

"It's a dumb policy."

Lupe stood up. "Just once, would it be too much to ask, just *once,* for you to stick to something? To make a decision and actually abide by it for more than five minutes, like your sister?"

Sonya flinched.

"Lupe, please," her father said in the long-suffering tone that Sonya recognized from previous Belinda-*mami* fights, "don't drag Sonya into this."

"Why not, it's her favorite trump card to play,"

Belinda said, also standing up. "Sonya's the perfect daughter who does everything right. Except she doesn't always."

Shooting a look at Belinda, Sonya said, "Bee, what're you—?"

"Maybe if she'd actually told that guy yes when he proposed, he wouldn't have accepted a suicide mission."

Her voice barely a whisper, Sonya said, "That's not how it happened."

"That's how it looks to me, Ess. You didn't say yes, so he didn't have anything to live for. How's that for little Commander Perfect, huh? So don't go telling me that I'm the failure in this house."

With that, Belinda stormed out of the kitchen.

Sonya felt like she had been punched in the stomach. *My God, it is my fault.*

"I'm sorry, *mija,*" Lupe said. "You shouldn't have had to listen to that garbage."

Garbage, right. Then she thought for a moment. *Of course it's garbage. Kieran was crazy sometimes, but he wasn't stupid. He went only because Gold ordered him.*

"It's okay, *mami.* But—I think maybe I should go to Portland alone."

Her mother sat back down. "Don't let your sister—"

"It has nothing to do with her," Sonya lied. In fact, the knowledge that her mother had used Sonya's success as a weapon in her on-again, off-again war with Belinda was a major influence in her newfound desire to go alone. "I just need to do this myself."

José gave her a look, his hair once again falling in front of his eyes. *Kieran's hair used to do that all the time, too,* she thought sadly. "You're sure?" he asked.

She nodded. "I'm sure."

Gomez supposed she could have requisitioned a transporter to get her from Vieques to Portland, but she found that she preferred taking a shuttle service. Flying over the North American continent gave her a little bit of time alone to think.

What am I going to do now?

She couldn't go back to the *da Vinci.* Leaving aside the bad memories, there was simply no way she could serve under David Gold again. Being on the same ship with him would just be a constant reminder of Kieran's death. She knew that Starfleet had cleared him of any wrongdoing, and for the other twenty-two of her crew-mates, she agreed with the tribunal's decision. Gold didn't do a thing wrong—

—until the very end when he condemned the man she loved to die, knowing full well what that would mean, and concealing the information from her. That was something she simply could not forgive, even if Starfleet found they could.

At present, the other three *Saber*-class ships assigned to the S.C.E. had first officers/S.C.E. commanders, so a lateral move was out of the question. But there were plenty of ships out there, and one of them, she knew, had to have need of a chief engineer. She would miss the challenges of the S.C.E., not to mention the remaining *da Vinci* crew, but there was certainly a part of her that missed the thrill of running an engine room. *It might be nice to get back to that.* She made a mental note to compose a transfer request when she got back home.

The shuttle flew over the Rocky Mountains. For some reason, she was suddenly reminded of Kieran's love for flying around in gravity boots—a predilection that had been put to good use on Maeglin only a few months ago when they were trying to round up some strange creatures that had come to the planet through an interdimensional gateway. *I remember thinking I was going to kill him for being so reckless. Funny, how silly turns of phrase like that sound when the person actually dies.*

It wasn't long before the shuttle arrived in Portland. Gomez went the rest of the way on foot.

She had expected the house to be bigger, for some reason. *Kieran was always describing it as this huge place. Probably remembering it from a kid's-eye perspective,* she thought.

The woman who answered the door was, unlike the house, bigger than Gomez had been expecting. She had seen Christa Duffy only on a viewscreen, with nothing to really give her scale, so she hadn't been expecting someone so dauntingly tall. *Of course, Kieran wasn't exactly short, either, and he had to get it from somewhere.*

"Sonya! It's good to finally meet you!" She immediately drew Gomez into a hug that was, in its own way, as all-encompassing as one of Belinda's. "You're as beautiful as Kieran said."

Tears welled up in Gomez's eyes. "So are you." Christa had the same kind brown eyes, the same warm smile, and the same mousy brown hair as her son, though the latter was flecked with gray ("Less than you'd expect," Kieran had said once, "but more than she'd like").

After breaking the embrace, but still clutching to Gomez's arms, Christa said, "I'm so glad you came."

"I'm sorry I didn't come sooner, but I needed—"

Letting go of her arm with one hand that she held up in admonishment, Christa said, "I understand. Besides, plenty of people have been here. Kieran's sister Amy has been by so much she might as well move back in. Some of your crewmates have been by, and some of your old friends from the *Enterprise,* including that nice Mr. O'Brien and his family."

Gomez smiled. *Why does it not surprise me that the chief stopped by?*

"And I got a very nice letter from Fabian Stevens before he went off on a trip somewhere."

That made Gomez flinch. She hadn't even thought about Fabian. *He must be hurting in his own way as much as I am.* To her shame, she realized that she not only didn't know where he had gone for his trip, she didn't even realize he had gone on one in the first place. In fact, she didn't have the first clue as to where *any* of her surviving shipmates were. Vaguely she recalled P8 Blue saying something after the service about bringing her larvae home, but aside from that . . .

"And of course, Captain Gold is here now."

Were Christa not still holding her arm, Gomez might have stumbled. *That bastard is* here? *How dare he show his face in this house?*

"He brought the Federation Medal of Honor they gave Kieran, and— Oh, but where are my manners? Come in, please. Let me show you the house."

Christa tried to lead her in, but Gomez started to move backward. "Maybe it's best if I—"

Then the captain himself appeared behind Christa in the doorway. "Gomez. Good to see you. I was starting to get worried."

Just standing there, like nothing happened. "I don't have anything to say to you," she said coldly.

Gold flinched, as if he'd been slapped. *Good,* Gomez thought.

Christa looked back and forth between the two of them. "Am I missing something?"

"If you are, Ms. Duffy, so'm I. Gomez, what's the—"

As they had with Belinda in the attic, the words suddenly came pouring out of Gomez's mouth. "It's all your fault! You killed him, you son of a bitch, and then you have the *gall* to show your face here!"

"Gomez—"

"You *murdered* him! He wanted to marry me, and you killed him, and you wouldn't even *tell* me!"

"Marry you?"

Gomez had no idea whether it was Gold or Christa who had made the exclamation, nor did she care. "I will *not* stay here with you, so either get the hell out of this house, or *I'm* leaving."

"I'll decide who stays in my house, Sonya, if you don't mind," Christa said with a steely tone.

Realizing she'd overstepped herself, Gomez quickly said, "I'm sorry, Christa. I didn't mean—"

"To tell a woman who just lost her son how to run her own house? To insult a guest of that house?"

"You don't understand—"

"My son is *dead,* Sonya. It wasn't enough that I had to bury my husband, now I've buried my son. You don't know what that's like, nor how much you need family and friends who understand at a time like this."

I know now, Gomez thought, but wisely did not say aloud. "You weren't there, Christa, you don't know what he did."

"He didn't do anything Kieran didn't ask to do," Christa said.

That brought Gomez up short. "What?"

In as gentle a voice as Gomez had ever heard Gold use, the captain said, "Duffy volunteered to disarm the device. And he knew full well what that meant."

"No. You're lying. He wouldn't have done that. He *asked me to marry him.*"

"As God is my witness, I had no idea. He didn't tell me that."

Gomez turned and ran into the yard, screaming, "You're lying!"

She ran around to the back of the house, all the way to the big oak that was the centerpiece of the large lawn, collapsing onto the well-manicured grass and leaning against the massive tree. At waist-height, she could see some bark scarring—a remnant of a German shepherd named Alexander, the so-called "Houdini dog" of Kieran's youth. They could, of course, have repaired the bark, but Kieran had asked to leave it there as a memento of Alexander's many escapes from his tether to that tree.

To her lack of surprise, Gold had followed her. He was dressed, she noted, in civilian clothes that only served to add to the grandfatherly mien he usually carried. *All the better to fool you with,* she thought.

"I'm not lying, Sonya," he said.

She looked up at his blue eyes, which were, maddeningly, filled with sorrow and compassion. He had never called her by her first name before that she could remember.

"Even if he did volunteer, how could you—"

"Let him? It was his *job,* Gomez. Yes, you two were a couple—and more than that, apparently, if he actually popped the question—but that had nothing to do with my decision, or his volunteering. I took a helluva gamble even *letting* you two have that relationship. But I assumed that you were professionals and understood the risks of what might happen. If you did, then what the hell are you complaining to me for? And if you didn't, then I question whether you belong in Starfleet."

Gomez wanted to object, to ask how he dared to question her commitment to Starfleet—but she found she could not. *He's right,* she finally admitted to herself.

"He didn't tell you he proposed?"

Gold shook his head. "He came to me with his *farkakte* plan to stop Wildfire after you gave me your *farkakte* plan for getting the engines restarted. You came up precisely once in the conversation. You know what he said? 'Don't tell Sonya.' "

Tears now streaked from Gomez's eyes. "Why didn't he—"

"He said you had enough on your mind. Which, considering you were about to run the world's fastest warp-core installation and startup, was not an irrelevant concern."

"It still doesn't make sense," she muttered. "Why did he—"

Unbidden, Belinda's words came back to her: *"I don't think you ever met a decision you didn't like—and didn't stick with."* More words from the previous day: *"You didn't say yes, so he didn't have anything to live for."*

And something Geordi La Forge said on the *Enterprise* over a decade ago: *"You're awfully young to be so driven."*

"Oh, God."

Frowning, Gold asked, "What is it?"

"He thought I refused." Gomez felt like a black hole had opened in her stomach. Her breaths came shallowly. "It's my fault. I didn't give him an answer right away, and he assumed that meant no."

"That's ridiculous."

"No, sir, it isn't." Gomez clambered to an upright position. "I've always been—well, decisive. When I decided to go into Starfleet, I didn't rest until I qualified for the entrance exams. At the Academy, I was determined to be on the *Enterprise,* so I made sure I was the best. When I met Kieran, I was the one who made the first move, and when I got the promotion and the transfer to the *Oberth,* I was the one who broke it off. For that matter, us getting together again after Sarindar was my decision." She looked away. After spending the last several weeks hating this man for something that was, in fact, her own fault, she found herself unable to look him in the eye. "When Kieran proposed, I couldn't give him an answer. I was indecisive. He must've interpreted it as a negative answer, and—and he volunteered to die instead."

"Gomez, that's the dumbest thing I've ever heard in my life."

She looked up sharply at Gold, who was regarding her with an expression that reminded her frighteningly of the one her father used to have when she and Belinda got themselves into trouble as kids.

"Yes, Duffy volunteered for the suicide mission, but he was the only one who *could* perform it. He had started the deactivation sequence of the Wildfire device back on the *Orion;* if anybody else went, they'd have had to start from scratch. It's pretty damned unlikely that anyone else would have made it. Hell, the only other people who knew the codes were me and Corsi, and neither of us were in any shape to do so."

Involuntarily, Gomez looked down at Gold's left hand. The doctors on the *Mjolnir,* the ship that rescued the *da Vinci* after they escaped Galvan VI's atmosphere, had given him a perfect biosynthetic hand that looked just like the old one, but at the time of the mission, Gold had been literally crippled. As for Corsi, she had still been partially paralyzed.

"Besides," Gold said, "if Duffy hadn't done it, *he still would be dead.* And so would the rest of us. The engines didn't come online until *after* the point of Wildfire's detonation. You, me, Duffy, Stevens, Corsi, Blue, Ina, Wong, Lense, and the rest of us would be bits of protomatter making up whatever it is Galvan VI would get turned into by that damned thing—and so would the Ovanim."

Gold put his artificial left hand on Gomez's shoulder, and reduced his tone to a near whisper. "Sonya, Kieran didn't do what he did because he wanted to die. He did what he did because he wanted you—and everyone else on the ship, *and* the Ovanim—to live."

Now Gomez did look David Gold in the eyes. What she saw was a man in tremendous pain for the losses he suffered. She knew that he blamed himself as much as she blamed herself—maybe more so. But he also knew what a fool's game that ultimately was.

"It's easy to assign blame," he said. "It's hard to go on living. It's been my impression that Commander Sonya Gomez is the best there is at doing what everyone thinks is hard and making it look easy."

Do I want to do that? Do I want to go back to the da Vinci *without Kieran—and with constant reminders of his death around me? It would be easier to just go home and write up that transfer request. No one would think ill of me.*

In her mind, she heard Belinda's voice: *"Make a damn decision, already, Ess!"*

"I'll have to go on living, then," she said.

"Good. Now let's go back inside. There's an old woman in there who had to bury her son. Having done that myself all too recently, I know this isn't a good time for her to be alone."

Gomez saluted. "Yes, sir, Captain."

He smiled, apparently understanding what she meant by the anachronistic gesture.

"Apology accepted, Gomez. Let's go."

CHAPTER 5

The next several days were a whirlwind of activity for Gomez and Gold both. They had twenty-five vacancies to fill—in addition to those who died, Lieutenant Ina Mar had requested a transfer and Medtech John Copper opted to retire. *The surprise,* Gomez had thought upon reading Ina's transfer request, *is that she's the only one.* As for Copper, he'd been making noises about retiring for as long as Gomez had been on the *da Vinci,* so that wasn't much of a shock, either.

The last time a member of the command staff died in action, Gold had left it to Captain Scott to recommend a replacement—he suggested Gomez—and both captain and first officer were happy to solicit another recommendation from Scotty to replace Duffy.

Even with fobbing replacing Kieran off on someone else, Gomez found that Gold's prediction was holding true: It was hard. Every requisition, every upgrade, every crew replacement was a reminder of what they had lost—of what *she* had lost.

Is it going to be the same? She'd been on the *da Vinci* for almost a year, yet the place felt as much like a family as her own home. *More, sometimes,* she amended, thinking of Belinda and *mami*'s latest spat.

In fact, Gomez had spent most of her time leading up to the *da Vinci*'s relaunch at Gold's house in New York. They were able to do their jobs as efficiently from there as from Starfleet Headquarters, and it enabled them to do so away from the hustle and bustle. They both made regular trips to McKinley Station, particularly Gomez, making sure that the upgrades that she and Kieran had been talking about for months were being integrated. Gomez was especially glad to see that several modifications were based on Kieran's ideas for the *Roebling,* the ideal S.C.E. ship he'd been designing in his spare time. In addition, the computer was getting a massive upgrade courtesy Soloman's designs, which the Bynar—having returned from a mission to Vrinda with Carol Abramowitz and Bart Faulwell—was also overseeing personally.

Yes, it was hard, but it was made easier by doing much of the work from the Gold-Gilman residence. After weeks of barely eating, Gomez found that working proximate to Rachel Gilman's kitchen enabled her to make up for that, with interest. *I think I've gained a kilo a day since we came back from Portland.*

One afternoon, Scotty contacted them with his recommendation for a new second officer. *"Also, you'll be happy to know that the* da Vinci*'ll be ready two days ahead of schedule."*

"Good," Gold said.

Scotty shook his head. *"Good isn't the word for it, lad. In my day, it'd take six months to do a repair job like she needed, not a few weeks—and we probably woulda just scrapped the lot and started from scratch."*

Gold snorted. "'Your day,' hell. Five years ago."

Gomez smiled wryly. "Nothing like fighting a war against a technologically superior foe to motivate you to improve your repair efficiency."

"Aye, more's the pity. In any event, I think you'll like the lad I'm recommendin'. He's a Tellarite, name'a Mor glasch Tev. He's as good as they come."

"That's good enough for me," Gold said.

"I know that name." Gomez thought for a moment, then the memory came bubbling to the surface. "Isn't he the one who wrote that monograph on methods of penetrating cloaking shields last year?"

"Aye, and the one on miniaturizin' transporters."

"Sounds like a winner," Gold said.

They discussed some other business, then Scotty signed off. Rachel Gilman then came in from the hallway—they had been working in the study upstairs. "So how soon before you sally forth again?"

"In three days," Gold said.

"Perfect. I have an idea."

Gomez smiled. Rachel having an idea usually meant that said idea would be implemented, one way or the other.

When she gave her idea, Gomez's smile widened further.

The day before the *da Vinci* was to be released from McKinley Station, Gold tethered Freser to the dogwood in preparation for several arrivals. He and Gomez had sent out messages to the remaining fifteen Galvan VI survivors who were remaining aboard the *da Vinci,* and one by one, they all beamed or shuttled or walked up to the house in the Bronx.

Freser tried desperately to leap about, but the leash was intact. *Obviously,* Gomez thought with a pang of sadness, *he's not a Houdini dog like Alexander.*

Some were dressed in uniform—like Soloman, who had beamed down from McKinley after giving the new computer a final once-over. Others were in civilian garb—like Carol Abramowitz, who had come straight to the Bronx from her trip to Pacifica. Both she and Bart Faulwell were looking especially pleased with themselves as they listened to Fabian Stevens tell of his adventures doing a cargo run with Domenica Corsi and her father. *Wonder what Fabe's gonna say when he finds out the species of our new second officer,* Gomez thought, and wincing only a little at the thought of Kieran's replacement.

Very few were listening to Fabian, however, as they were either pestering Pattie Blue with questions about the rather historic rediscovery she'd made on the Nasat homeworld of a sentient, plant-based species living on the planet's surface, or pestering Robin Rusconi about her rather bizarre experience with an interdimensional portal on the moon.

Before long, though, Gold called the "meeting" to order. Which, in practical terms, meant that everybody stood on the lawn and faced Gold as he addressed them.

"We've been through hell and back—almost literally. A lot of good people gave their lives. Other ships have survived disasters like this only to see the remaining crew split up, sent to the nine winds. But that's not the way we do things around here. We're the S.C.E., after all, and if there's one thing I've learned is that when we see something that's broken, we not only fix it, we make it better. I have every faith that you'll do the same for the *da Vinci* tomorrow when we take her back out.

"But we're also a family—a big family, and believe me, I know from big families." Several people chuckled at that. "And I was reminded of something recently. In times like this, families come together. So I've brought you all here today, on the eve of our going back out into space, to reassure you of that, and to invite you all to join me in celebrating our lives. We've had time to mourn our losses—it's time we started moving forward. Now before we take this party inside, I want to deal with some business."

That was Gomez's cue to step forward with the large box that Starfleet Command had sent. "Promotion time came and went while we were in drydock," Gomez said, "so we've got a few to take care of." She reached into the box and pulled out a hollow rank pip. "First of all, to Nancy Conlon, I hereby promote you to the rank of lieutenant junior grade, and also officially give you the position of chief engineer of the *da Vinci.*"

Conlon had stepped forward to accept the pip, but stopped short at the second part. "What? You're making *me* chief? Sir, I'm flattered, but—"

Gomez attached the rank pin to Conlon's collar. "You earned it, Nancy. Hell, if helping install a warp core and starting it up in less than an hour doesn't qualify you for chief engineer, I don't know what does."

"I'm not sure what to say," Conlon said.

Gold grinned. "'Thank you' works."

"Yes, sir," she said quickly. "Thank you both, sirs. I hope I can live up to this."

"You will."

In turn, Gomez doled out promotions to Songmin Wong and Anthony Shabalala, both also to lieutenant junior grade. Shabalala was also taking over the alpha-shift tactical officer duties from the late David McAllan; Wong was remaining alpha-shift conn officer.

Then Corsi stepped forward. "The officers don't get all the fun here. Vance Hawkins, step forward."

Hawkins did so at full attention, which looked amusing to Gomez's eyes, since he was still wearing civilian clothing.

"I hereby promote you to the rank of chief petty officer, and appoint you deputy chief of security." She allowed a small smile. "You and Robins are going to be the only ones I can count on for a while, and I want you to help me beat the new recruits into shape."

"I won't disappoint you, sir."

"Damn straight you won't," Corsi said, meaning every word of it.

Still, Gomez thought, *Domenica sounds a bit more playful than usual. Maybe that trip with Fabian did her some good.*

"Now then," Gold said, "there's a fine old Jewish tradition: When major life events happen, we respond by gathering in a large group and eating copious amounts of food. Conveniently, I married the best cook on the planet to provide us with the latter. So, if you'll follow me . . ."

Gold led the other sixteen inside. As soon as he opened the front door, Gomez caught a whiff of the kitchen. Rachel had made some amazing dishes over the last several days that Gomez had been spending at the house, but this beat all of them into olfactory heaven: fish, chicken, beef, assorted sauces and soups, and fresh bread that Gomez knew would melt in her mouth.

It's going to be very hard to go back to replicated food after this, she thought.

Gold had set up the large wooden table in the dining room with eighteen chairs—including one specially modified for Pattie—and invited everyone to take a seat as Rachel brought in the matzo-ball soup.

After the third sip, Abramowitz turned to Gold. "Captain?"

"Yes, Abramowitz?"

"I was wrong."

Gold smiled. Gomez, for her part, frowned, and wondered what that was about.

Soon, people were telling stories. Hawkins talked about one of his and Drew's shore leave misadventures, which led to Stevens' telling a similar story about a bar crawl he and Duffy had engaged in during the war shortly after Stevens signed on to the *da Vinci.* (Gomez was torn between anger and gratitude that Kieran had never told her the full story.) Wetzel described the entertaining process of separating Robins's and Lipinski's hair after it was fused together, with Robins adding colorful commentary, and Conlon—the instigator of the practical joke—sinking deeper into her chair. Blue then told a tale of her, Barnak, Feliciano, Frnats, and Orthak on leave on Starbase 96, when some idiot had a problem with a group of five people from five different species sitting together, which almost led to a brawl, and did lead to the person in question's having five different drinks spilled on his head. Lense even told a story about her and Emmett.

Gold then asked Soloman, "Were you able to restore any of Emmett?"

"Not as such. I'm afraid that the EMH on the *da Vinci* will be akin to what he was when he was first installed." He turned to Lense. "I'm sorry, Doctor. I did attempt to retrieve the data, but the damage was too extensive."

"It's all right," Lense said. "I was hoping he might be restored, but I wasn't really counting on it. I don't think I want to call this one Emmett, though."

The stories continued through the fish course, the chicken course, the beef course, and dessert. As he was polishing off his baklava, Stevens decided to do something he'd never done before.

He told the Tellarite story.

Gomez forced herself to keep her composure, but she appreciated what Fabian was doing. Everyone here (except Rachel) had heard the Tellarite story—from Kieran. He loved recounting it, though it was hard to say which he enjoyed more: embarrassing Fabian by telling it behind his back or embarrassing Fabian by telling it in his presence.

By telling it now, Fabian assured everyone that none of the dead would be forgotten, but that the living were, as Gold had said, moving on.

Eventually, the party broke up, though some decided to stick around for coffee, tea, and fruit in the living room. More stories were exchanged, and some started talking about the modifications and improvements to the *da Vinci*—the addition of guest quarters, for example, as well as the expansion of the hololab, the more versatile tractor beams, and the industrial replicator.

Sonya Gomez wasn't sure if she was going to be able to face going back up there. It had been one thing to reconcile her own feelings of anger toward Gold and her ambivalence about Kieran. Even there, she still, weeks later, had no idea what answer she was going to give Kieran to his marriage proposal. All she knew for sure was that she missed him terribly.

Tomorrow, she'd find out if she could go on without him.

ABOUT THE AUTHORS

SCOTT CIENCIN is a *New York Times* best-selling author of adult and children's fiction. Praised by *Science Fiction Review* as "one of today's finest fantasy writers" and listed in the *Encyclopedia of Fantasy*, Scott has written over fifty novels and many short stories and comic books. He has written in many shared worlds, including *Star Wars*, *Dinotopia*, *Transformers*, *EverQuest*, *Charmed*, *Godzilla*, *Buffy the Vampire Slayer*, and *Angel*. He is the co-author with Dan Jolley of the *Star Trek: S.C.E.* adventure *Some Assembly Required*, and his original *Dinoverse* series has been optioned by Critical Hit Entertainment. Scott lives in Fort Myers, Florida, with his beloved wife, Denise.

KEITH R.A. DECANDIDO is the co-developer of the *Star Trek: S.C.E.* series, with John J. Ordover, and, in addition to *Breakdowns*, he has written or cowritten the stories *Fatal Error*, *Cold Fusion*, *Invincible*, *Here There Be Monsters*, and *War Stories*; his next *S.C.E.* tale will be *Security*, coming in July 2005 in eBook form. His other *Star Trek* work includes the novels *Diplomatic Implausibility*, *Demons of Air and Darkness*, *The Art of the Impossible*, and *A Time for War, A Time for Peace*; the cross-series duology *The Brave and the Bold*; the Ferenginar portion of *Worlds of Star Trek: Deep Space Nine*

Volume 3; short fiction in *What Lay Beyond, Prophecy and Change, No Limits,* and *Tales of the Dominion War* (which he also edited); the comic book miniseries *Perchance to Dream*; and the first three *I.K.S. Gorkon* books (*A Good Day to Die, Honor Bound,* and *Enemy Territory*), an ongoing series of novels taking place on board a Klingon ship. Forthcoming *Trek*s include *Articles of the Federation* (a look at the Federation's government) and *Tales from the Captain's Table* (an anthology of stories featuring various *Trek* captains), with others in development beyond that. Keith has also written novels, novelizations, short stories, and nonfiction books in the media universes of *Farscape, Gene Roddenberry's Andromeda,* Marvel Comics, *Resident Evil, Xena, Buffy the Vampire Slayer, Serenity,* and more. His original novel *Dragon Precinct* was published in 2004 and his award-nominated original SF anthology *Imaginings* was published in 2003. Find out more silly things about him at DeCandido.net.

After fifteen years as a newspaper reporter and editor, **KEVIN DILMORE** turned his full attention to his freelance writing career in 2003. Since 1997, he has been a contributing writer to *Star Trek Communicator,* writing news stories and personality profiles for the bimonthly publication of the Official *Star Trek* Fan Club. Look for Kevin's interviews with some of *Star Trek*'s most popular authors in volumes of the *Star Trek* Signature Editions. On the fictional side of things, his story "The Road to Edos" was published in the *Star Trek: New Frontier* anthology *No Limits*. With Dayton Ward, he has also written the novels *A Time to Sow* and *A Time to Harvest,* seven other *Star Trek: S.C.E.* eBooks, and a story for the anthology *Star Trek: Tales of the Dominion War*. A graduate of the University of Kansas, Kevin lives in Prairie Village, Kansas, with his wife, Michelle, and their three daughters.

HEATHER JARMAN grew up fantasizing about being a writer the way many little girls fantasize about being ballerinas and princesses; she had all the lyrics to the Beatles's "Paperback Writer" memorized by age six. But in her wildest childhood dreams, she had no idea how Saturday afternoons spent lazing in her beanbag chair watching *Star Trek* would dramatically impact her lifelong aspiration. Indeed, the *Star Trek* universe played host to her professional fiction debut, *This Gray Spirit*, the second novel in the critically acclaimed *Mission: Gamma* series of *Deep Space Nine* books set after the TV series. She's also written *Paradigm*, the Andor part of the *Worlds of Star Trek: Deep Space Nine* miniseries, and contributed "The Devil You Know" to *Prophecy and Change*, the *DS9* tenth anniversary anthology. With Jeffrey Lang, she collaborated on "Mirror Eyes" for *Tales of the Dominion War*. Forthcoming in 2005 are short stories in the *Tales from the Captain's Table* and *Distant Shores* anthologies, and co-authoring with Jeffrey Lang and Kirsten Beyer a *Voyager* trilogy written in honor of that show's tenth anniversary. She lives in Portland, Oregon, with her husband and four daughters. She rarely finds time to lounge about in beanbag chairs these days, much to her regret.

DAYTON WARD has been a fan of *Star Trek* since conception (his, not the show's). After serving for eleven years in the U.S. Marine Corps, he discovered the private sector and the piles of cash to be made there as a software engineer. He got his start in professional writing by having stories selected for each of Pocket Books's first three *Star Trek: Strange New Worlds* writing contests. In addition to his various writing projects with Kevin Dilmore (see Kevin's bio above), Dayton is the author of the *Star Trek* novel *In the Name of Honor* and the science fiction novels *The Last World War* and *The Genesis Protocol*. Though he currently lives in Kansas

City with his wife, Michi, Dayton is a Florida native and still maintains a torrid long-distance romance with his beloved Tampa Bay Buccaneers. Readers interested in contacting Dayton or learning more about his writing are encouraged to venture to his Internet cobweb collection at http://www.daytonward.com.